Reiko's Garden

Brenda Adcock

Regal Crest

Nederland, Texas

ISBN 978-1-932300-77-2

First Printing 2007

9 8 7 6 5 4 3 2 1

Cover design by Donna Pawlowski

Published by:

Regal Crest Enterprises, LLC
4700 Highway 365, Suite A
PMB 210
Port Arthur, Texas 77642

Find us on the World Wide Web at
http://www.regalcrest.biz

Printed in the United States of America

Acknowledgments

Two centuries of family history, kept alive through oral language, breathed life into this story, and although they live in my heart, there are too many to mention. The roots of Appalachia run deep and never let go.

Ten years in the writing and eight rewrites later, I would be remiss in not thanking those who guided me along the way. My special thanks to my colleagues Linda Bernardy, Becky Rose and Donna Davis for enduring the earliest drafts. My deepest gratitude, again, to my best friend, Ron Whiteis, whose keen insight and boundless enthusiasm made this the story I wanted it to be.

My loving thanks to Cheryl, who, for some reason, has always believed in me. The hard work and honest input of my amazing readers Kim Miller, Ruta Skujins, and Susan Fabian shaped the story into a better manuscript than I could have imagined and my editor, Q, added the final touches. The cover I envisioned was brought to life by the wonderfully talented Donna Pawlowski. Last, but never least, my sincerest gratitude goes to my publisher, Cathy LeNoir, who forged everything into the final product. I am so glad I have met you all. Together, as a team, we have created a work we can all be proud of. Thanks will never be enough.

Dedicated to

Charles Kenneth Denny

A son, a brother, a husband, a grandfather, and a friend –
my father.

I miss you.

Chapter
One

Thursday, April 1, 2004 – 1:30 P.M.

I WAS EXHAUSTED. The phone call came early Tuesday morning, and a short five hours later, after rescheduling appointments and throwing clothes into a suitcase, Jean and I drove south toward San Francisco International Airport. Our children were to meet us to fly back east to the valley I had once called home, even though they hadn't been there since they were in elementary school. It had somehow seemed important to me that we all returned as a family one last time, although no one there would ever accept us as one. We would barely make it in time, and I was more than a little aggravated that my sister Katie had waited so damn long to call.

It would have been the easiest thing in the world to say I was too busy, too tired, too anything not to make this trip. But I had to go, and Jean was probably the only person who understood why. I wasn't sure how I would react to returning to a place with so many memories, and even though I still didn't like to admit it, I knew that I might not be able to face my old fears without Jean beside me.

Over forty-five years had slipped by virtually unnoticed as I had busied myself with work and family. Now, after a long flight and a short nap, I slowed our rental car on the steep, twisting two-lane road that descended into the valley floor and felt my past rushing up to greet me. The road made speed impossible, as though deliberately trying to slow our progress in preparation for the pace of life that awaited us at the bottom of this final hill. The trees, a mix of pine, walnut, chestnut, spruce, and other varieties, formed the beginnings of a deep green canopy, allowing occasional filtered strips of light through to the road. Gray clouds scudded their way across the ridgeline, adding to the solemnity of the day.

As I glanced in the rear view mirror, I saw Rachel and Nolan looking out the side windows as if they had never seen trees before. I took my foot off the brake and let the car roll downhill and around curves until I saw the gray ribbon of the valley road disappear on the horizon. I looked at Jean and smiled slightly. She rested her arm along the back of the car seat and stroked my neck.

"Tired?" she asked softly.

We'd been together almost thirty-five years, and I wondered if she knew that her touch was as exciting to me now as it had been the first time. Age and long familiarity had failed to diminish the joy I felt when I looked at her.

"A little," I answered. "But we're almost there now."

"Do you still remember where to turn off? It's been a long time, Callie."

Looking around at the fields on either side, I said, "It's barely changed even after all the years I've been away."

Accelerating through low, rolling hills, freshly mowed and plowed, that stretched across the valley floor until eventually disappearing into the tree-lined ridge that sheltered the valley on both sides, I glanced around at familiar sights. Old, two-story houses, some already whitewashed for spring, dotted the wide, open fields. Occasionally, a newer brick home came into view, having all the signs of belonging to an outsider fleeing Knoxville. Perhaps newcomers had hoped to find what a presidential candidate had once euphemistically called "a kinder, gentler America." But even with its natural beauty, Frost Valley had never been a kind or gentle place. The peacefulness and serenity of its rural setting was never more than an illusion that constantly challenged anyone who lived there to tame it and survive. Everything about it seemed benign now, but I knew that anyone digging deeper into its past was sure to discover the dark secrets that scarred some of the valley's inhabitants forever, driving them away. I was one of those who had chosen to run away.

My foot involuntarily eased off the accelerator as we approached the house that had been my childhood home. Glancing past Jean out the passenger side window, I was saddened to see the once beautiful house, alive with love and laughter, had deteriorated badly over the years. The wide porch that encircled the house appeared to be on the verge of collapse. The fields surrounding the house were unplowed, and the yard in front of the house was littered with children's toys. I couldn't help but wonder whether everything eventually ended in such ugly decay. Then, taking in Jean's gentle and still beautiful profile with the deteriorating house in the background, I knew that wasn't true. No matter how old she became, Jean would never be anything but beautiful.

"Isn't that your old house?" Jean asked.

"I'm surprised you remember," I said, smiling at her.

"Looks like a dump," Rachel said from the back seat.

I looked over my shoulder toward my outspoken daughter. "It used to be a fine house. Just getting old like the rest of us."

"Your great-grandfather built it," Jean said as she looked back at Rachel and Nolan. "There are some beautiful hand-carved mantles in the main rooms. I always wished we had one of them for our house."

"You've been there, MJ?" Nolan asked. When the kids were little, they had called us Momma Jean and Momma Callie. But by the time they became teenagers, they had decided it was hipper and took less energy to shorten them to merely MJ and MC.

"A very long time ago," she said, gently squeezing my shoulder.

I slowed down even more and flipped on the left blinker. Nolan leaned into the front seat and grinned broadly.

"Afraid you'll get rear-ended by all that traffic behind you, MC?"

"Been living in the city too long, smart-ass," I said.

I turned onto an even narrower road, just wide enough for two pickups to get by one another and negotiated a series of three or four curves.

"Didn't the people who laid out this road ever hear that the shortest distance between two points was a straight line?" Rachel groused.

"If your butt wasn't so round, you wouldn't have a problem," Nolan kidded her.

"You try having two kids and see what happens to your butt."

Even though Rachel was thirty and Nolan was almost twenty-seven, their back seat banter hadn't improved much with adulthood. Their little barbs were interrupted by the abrupt appearance of a small white church as the rental car glided around yet another curve. There were only a couple of cars in the gravel parking area, and I quickly looked at my watch.

"Are we too late?" Jean asked.

"I don't think so," I said. "I've got one forty-five, and Katie told me the funeral was scheduled for two. They were probably late leaving town."

I pulled the car onto the grass between the simple church and its cemetery and turned the engine off while Jean flipped the visor down and checked her face in the mirror. I needed to stretch my legs, but as I opened the car door, I was greeted by an unexpected blast of cold air that made me catch my breath, suddenly grateful for the white turtleneck under my black suit.

"I hope you packed coats," I said, leaning down to look at Jean.

"It's April," Rachel said.

"There are coats in the trunk, sweetheart," Jean said.

I closed the car door behind me and walked to the back of the car, lighting a cigarette as I went. As I pulled our coats from the trunk, I scanned the horizon above me. The wind had picked up a little but was broken by the line of pine sentinels along the top of the nearby ridge. I didn't know how old the pines around the church were, but they were tall and slender. When a good breeze caught them, they swayed gently back and forth in unison, as my father used to say with a smile, "like the hips of a fine woman taking a lazy stroll on a warm summer evening." I closed the trunk and went to Jean's side of the car. She shivered as I opened the door and helped her put her coat on.

"Looks like it could snow," I said.

"A little late, isn't it?"

"Yeah, and those farmers planting their fields won't be happy about it," I said as I exhaled smoke that mixed with the frost from my breath.

She put her arm around me and said, "I thought you were going to give up smoking."

"I've been thinking about it. But since we're standing here in the middle of Tobacco Row, I thought I'd help out the local economy a while longer."

I reached down and brushed a few strands of black hair away from her face. When we first met, her hair had fallen to the middle of her back, but now she kept it a more manageable shoulder length. She had aged more gracefully than I had, and at sixty, there were few wrinkles on her delicate face and just a hint of gray in her hair. I kissed the top of her head and hugged her.

"Thanks for coming with me, baby," I said.

"I know how much she meant to you. I just wish Katie had called a little sooner."

"Some things never change."

"You mean some people never change," she frowned.

Out of the corner of my eye, I saw headlights slowly approaching and rapped on the top of the car. Nolan got out first and I tossed him a jacket and another one for Rachel. As they joined us, I wished Reiko could have seen them as adults and almost regretted my long absence from this serene place.

The gravel on the drive crunched beneath the tires of the hearse as it pulled in next to the church, followed by a black sedan. There were only five or six cars in the whole procession, and I was saddened that even death had not diminished her unacceptability in the community that had been her home for more than half a century. At least now she would rejoin her beloved Thomas again.

The doors of the black sedan immediately behind the hearse opened, and four people I didn't recognize got out. A man in his mid- or late-fifties helped the others out. A woman about his age took his hand as two young women joined them. I smiled to myself when I realized that it had to be Tad and his family. The last time Jean and I had seen him he was only in his early twenties. Was it possible that so many years had flown by unnoticed? They waited at the back of the hearse as a simple bronze-colored casket was removed and carried toward the church. As they followed the casket, the man looked around. He hadn't seen me in over thirty years, but as our eyes met momentarily, he paused slightly and nodded in my direction.

We waited until everyone else had gone into the church before we entered and took seats halfway down the aisle of the simple rustic sanctuary. Even though she had called to tell me of Reiko's death, I wasn't really surprised when I didn't see my sister Katie and her husband among the small group of mourners. A black pot-bellied stove near the front of the church had managed to warm the interior to a comfortable level. The service that followed seemed to be non-denominational and obviously intended more for the mourners than the deceased. I leaned over to Jean and whispered, "Guess they couldn't find a Buddhist monk."

She smiled and squeezed my arm.

In less than thirty minutes, we were back in our car waiting for the hearse to begin the final leg of its journey. As I watched Tad and his family settle back into the sedan, I didn't know what I would say to him if I had the chance. The little procession of cars followed the hearse as it made its way across the valley floor and turned up a narrow road toward Sanders Cemetery, which was situated on a level area about halfway up the ridge, overlooking the valley below. The hearse pulled onto a grassy drive and stopped near a site that had been reserved for her many years before. I parked my car just outside the entrance of the cemetery, and we walked up a small rise toward the site. Nolan stopped to read the sign at the entrance to the cemetery.

"Sanders Cemetery. Established 1839," he read.

"Most of my family is buried here," I said.

By the time we walked to the gravesite, the pallbearers were carrying the casket toward an area where folding chairs had been set up for the family. The wind was slightly colder than on the valley floor, and I wrapped an arm around Jean to keep her warm. We stopped several feet from the gravesite and waited for the final prayers to begin. The family had already been seated, and the minister seemed ready to finish and retreat to a warmer place when Tad got up and said something to him. The minister nodded, looking mildly irritated, as Tad walked toward me. As he got closer, I saw a strong, yet gentle, face that reminded me of his mother. His black hair was peppered at the temples with gray, and his distinctly Asian features had blended well with those of his Appalachian father.

"Aren't you Callie Owen?" he asked, bowing slightly toward me.

"I didn't think you'd remember me, Tad," I replied, acknowledging his greeting with a slight bow of my own.

"My mother never stopped talking about you." He looked at Jean and smiled warmly. "And if my memory serves me, you are Jean."

"I was so sorry to hear of your mother's death," she said.

"Please, sit with us. My mother regarded you as part of her family."

I hesitated for a moment but didn't want to delay the service any further. Jean and I sat behind Tad and his family, with a confused Rachel and Nolan seated next to Jean. I was preoccupied with my own thoughts and didn't notice for a few moments that it had begun to snow lightly. By the time the last prayer was over, the flakes had become larger. I felt them land on my cheeks briefly before they melted and turned into small droplets that ran down my face like tears.

Almost as soon as it began, the graveside service was over. I handed Nolan the keys to the car and asked him to get it warmed up while I spoke to Tad, who seemed engrossed in private thoughts. But as I reached him, he turned and smiled.

"Mother would have been happy that you came, Callie."

"I'm sorry I didn't get to see Reiko before she passed away."

"I hope you'll come back to the house with us. I'd like for you to meet my family. Mother told me you and Jean had adopted children. They are very handsome."

"Thank you. I'll try to swing by before we leave. I should stop and see my sister for a few minutes while I'm here."

"My wife has prepared enough food to feed the proverbial army. Please come by and help us get rid of it. I'd love to catch up, and Mother left something for me to give you."

That surprised me, but I promised to meet him at his mother's house later.

Now that the last real tie I had to Frost Valley was gone, I doubted that I would ever return again. I watched as people I didn't know or remember slowly left the little cemetery overlooking the valley. Who I was and the events that had shaped my childhood were all bound up in this place, and no matter how old I was or how much I thought I had changed, this valley was a part of me that would never truly go away. I had stood in this same cemetery at least three other times while still a child. Now I stood here once again as an adult approaching the end of my own life, surrounded by the ghosts of people who had each been important to me in their own unperceivable way.

The light dusting of the late snow had stopped as I looked around at the silent reminders of my past. Jean slid her arm into mine as we walked among the old headstones, now discolored with moss and darkened by years of assault by the elements. I read the names on each stone as we walked silently through my history until I found a family headstone simply engraved, "Owen." Six feet from the headstone I looked down at the dark footstones that marked the resting places of Preston and Elizabeth, and a more recent one for Woodrow Wilson. I had been a child when Mama and Papa died of illnesses that were barely more than the common cold today. I was an adult when Willie had died mysteriously, probably due to his own maladjusted lifestyle, but I could still see his sweet, laughing face as I gazed down at his name. Jean stood silently as I squatted to remove twigs and leaves that had broken away from nearby trees, touching the names lightly with my hand in what I knew was a last goodbye. Events in the valley from decades before had changed my life forever, and I knew that even though I had come to terms with most of my demons, I would never be able to forget them.

Finally standing, I wrapped my arm around Jean, and we turned to walk away. Squinting a little against the cold air, my eyes swept across the stand of trees behind the cemetery and stopped. They were all still here, and I saw them clearly standing in the shadows of the pines. Mama and Papa and Willie were watching us, and they were all smiling. Not far away I saw Thomas Sanders still in his military uniform and smiled to myself as I watched his hand reach out to greet Reiko as she joined him. Just as Reiko had promised, the souls of good people never died. They remained in our minds always. Almost as soon as the apparitions had appeared, they began fading away.

"What's wrong, Callie?" Jean asked.

Looking down at her, I shook my head and breathed in the cold air. "Just thought I saw something."

By the time we got to the car, the snow had stopped, and I braced myself for a visit to my sister's house. I knew Jean would take it all in stride as she always had but wished I didn't have to subject Rachel and Nolan to meeting their Aunt Katie again. Although we hadn't made many trips back home, Katie always made sure everyone we met knew they had been adopted, so they wouldn't be confused with "real" family members.

As I backed the car onto the narrow road leading down the hill and away from the cemetery, my exhaustion from the flight finally hit me. Now I wished I could simply get my family back to our hotel room, and get a good night's sleep before flying home the next afternoon. I almost suggested it to Jean, but as I glanced across the front seat at the woman who had shared my life for so many years I didn't say anything. Jean rode calmly looking out the window. For some reason, Jean, like Reiko, had come to appreciate the simple beauty that was Frost Valley, and took its idiosyncrasies in stride. She blamed the residents' attitudes toward strangers on basic ignorance rooted in a total absence of multiculturalism.

But Jean was not a stranger. She had been to Frost Valley on at least two other occasions that I could recall. When Nolan and Rachel had been grade school age, we had returned to the valley to allow them to visit Reiko. Already a woman in her sixties, she had lavished attention on our children, and they had thought that her home was a wonder. As she had with me, Reiko introduced them to the simple beauties of nature, taking them for long walks through the hollows and back valleys in search of things they had never seen before and that were unheard of in California. My life had been shaped by the strong, yet gentle woman of my youth, and I hoped I had passed on a tenth of the wisdom she had given me to them.

"If you don't want to go to Katie's, you don't have to, you know," Jean said softly, interrupting my thoughts.

"Thank you. I was hoping you would say that," I said.

"Of course, it could be the last chance you will have to see her. We're not getting any younger, my darling, and you might regret having had the chance to see her and not taking it."

Even though she had given me what I silently wished for, she had jerked the wish away from me almost as quickly as she had granted it.

"Well, shit," I muttered to myself. Nothing like a little guilt trip to make my day even more depressing.

"We can't stay long anyway," I said with a poor attempt at a smile. "I promised Tad we would stop at Reiko's to meet his family before we left the valley."

"We can leave whenever you're ready, sweetheart," Jean smiled back genuinely, her black eyes filled with the love I saw every time she looked at me. That never ceased to amaze me. We had had some bad times, but overall it had been the life I had always dreamed of. She had given me that dream. I took her hand in mine and held it as we drove down the road bisecting the valley.

Three miles later, I slowed to make the left turn onto the steep gravel drive leading to Katie's house. The house, which had been built by her husband before they married, had been modernized over the years. From across the valley, the stark white house stood out against the green backdrop of pine trees behind it. I had personally always thought it was a wonderful home, even though Katie never failed to complain about something every time we had visited.

Chapter
Two

I HADN'T SEEN Katie or her husband at the funeral, which hadn't surprised me very much, and although I could have called her on my cell phone to let her know we were coming, I hadn't. I think that secretly I was hoping they wouldn't be home when we arrived, but it just wasn't my day. As soon as I stopped the car on the edge of the grass, the side door of the house swung open, and Katie stepped onto the walkway connecting her house with the painted cinder block garage. She hadn't changed very much as far as I could tell. She was two years younger than I, and her hair remained as dark as it had always been. She smiled broadly as I walked around the car to open Jean's door. Nolan had already opened the back door for Rachel, and a moment later, we were all making our way toward my sister. She briefly hugged us before opening the side door and inviting us in. Before stepping inside, I glanced around and saw Edwin's truck parked near the garage. Entering the mudroom next to the kitchen, I helped Jean remove her coat and added it to mine on a hall tree near the back door.

"It smells wonderful in here, Katie," Jean said pleasantly.

"It's unusually chilly today, and I thought you and the children might like some warm lemon cake and coffee," Katie said as she opened the oven door and used an oven mitt to remove a Bundt pan.

"We won't be staying very long, Katie," I said as I cleared my throat. "We're all tired, and our flight home leaves a little after one tomorrow. We can use a good night's sleep."

"I'm sorry I called you so late, Callie, but I wasn't sure whether I should call at all," Katie said as she ran a knife around the edges of the cake pan.

"You should have known I would come, Kate."

"It's just that you haven't been home in so long, and I haven't heard from you. For all I knew you might have been too ill to make the trip," my sister shrugged.

"You still..."

"We still made it in plenty of time," Jean said as she touched my forearm. "Is Edwin home?"

"He's out in the barn." Turning to smile at Nolan and Rachel, she added, "We had twins last night, and Edwin has to bottle feed them. Why don't you children go see if he needs any help? They're hungry little critters. I know he would appreciate some advice from a veterinarian, Rachel. By the time you get back everything should be ready."

Rachel looked less than thrilled, but Nolan couldn't wait to head out the back door. I was tempted to go with him but didn't want to leave Jean alone to deal with my sister. We pulled out chairs around the dining room table and waited for Katie to join us.

"The place is looking good," I said as I swiveled and looked into the living room. "I see you finally got new furniture."

"I always said that as soon as the boys all moved out, I was going to burn everything in the house and start over."

"It's lovely," Jean observed. "Callie, have you noticed their garden?"

"I tried that thing with the marigolds you told me about, and so far, it seems to be working," Katie said.

"I told you it would keep some bugs off the rest of your plants. They look good, but their odor isn't very attractive to insects," I shrugged.

"Oh," Katie looked up suddenly, "you have to see the night bloomers we have next to the garage. You can watch them open every evening. It's amazing. They should wake up any time now."

"I'd love to see that," Jean smiled.

Following Katie out the side door, we were led to a small garden. Tall, green stalks lined the wall next to the garage, topped by a light yellow bloom tightly curled and looking like a bud not quite ready to open. "Just watch," Katie whispered as if the plants might hear her and be afraid to do what they were genetically programmed to do. Standing there waiting for the plants' internal clocks to start gave me a whole new appreciation for the term "watching the grass grow." Just about the time the unseasonable chill in the air was starting to get to me, Jean lightly touched my arm. The first bloom had finally awakened and began a slow twisting movement as it began uncurling itself. I had to smile as I watched one bud after another begin the same dance. The flower itself was a vibrant yellow and was actually quite beautiful once fully opened.

"Right after dawn they begin closing again," Katie said.

"That's really amazing all right, Katie," I said. I had seen plants like these before when I had been stationed in Japan during my twelve-year stint in the Navy, although these were a different variety. I was sure that if these grew wild anywhere in the valley, Reiko would have some at her home as well.

"Did you see Reiko much before she died?" I asked.

"Once or twice, but never for very long."

"Why was that?"

"Just never seemed to find the time."

"There's not that much to do out here, Katie," I fumed. "Edwin is basically retired. You should have made the time."

"I never knew her as well as you did, Callie. I was only ten when Pa died, and then Annie and I were shipped off to town to live. I didn't return to the valley until I married Edwin."

"Still, you could have been neighborly and checked on her. After Tad left, she was alone."

"There are a lot of widows out here, Callie. I can't check on all of them."

"I'm assuming that no one's attitude toward her changed over the years," I frowned.

"She could have sold that place and moved somewhere where she would have been more comfortable. Edwin told me she had been offered quite a bit for that old place, but she always turned it down."

"It was her home," I said flatly.

"I suppose. So how have you and the children been doing?" Katie asked, diverting our conversation to something less contentious.

"I'm semi-retired now. Just helping Nolan out a few times a year. Jean is still working though."

"What is it you do again, Jean?"

"I'm still teaching at the University of California in Berkeley," Jean said modestly.

"Jean's the Director of their Asian Studies Program," I added proudly.

Since Jean had been appointed as the program chairwoman five years earlier, it had tripled its enrollment and was considered one of the ten best cultural studies programs in the country. I admired her tenacity tempered with a judicious diplomacy I wouldn't have believed possible when we first met.

I saw Jean shiver slightly as she continued observing Katie's little miracles and instinctively wrapped my arm around her. Although I was sure Jean didn't see it, there was a frown of disapproval from Katie as Jean leaned closer into my arms for warmth. We were so accustomed to acting in what seemed like a natural manner to us that I had to remind myself that Frost Valley wasn't now, and never had been, the liberal atmosphere we were used to living in. No one at home considered us unusual, but that frown on my sister's face quickly reminded me that we were standing in the land that time had indeed forgotten. It was a simple place that abhorred change or any-one who might disturb their comfortable status quo. If I had really wanted to scandalize Katie, I would have taken Jean into my arms and kissed her passionately right there in front of God and everybody. The thought of her reaction brought a smile to my face.

I had no idea what my sister thought my relationship with Jean entailed but was pretty sure the idea of anything even remotely sexual between us had never crossed her closed, little mind. As I thought about it, I had a very difficult time envisioning my sister in the throes of passion with her husband. Other than the fact that she had popped out three strapping, healthy boys, which must have involved sexual relations of some type, I just couldn't picture Katie as a seductress nor Edwin as a Casanova. I almost laughed out loud at the thought of it.

I had often wondered what our parents would have thought about the way their children had all turned out. We had been a pathetic lot after Papa died unexpectedly. Cleve had been the first to leave to join the Army, always sending money back for our care. Grover Cleveland Owen couldn't wait to get away to see the world outside our small valley. I hadn't seen him in years. He had served two tours in Vietnam, but his luck ran out the second time over. The doctors hadn't been sure how he had survived his injuries after being trapped between two machine gun nests in the jungle. When he was flown to a Veteran's Hospital in California, he gave credit for his life to a medic who Superglued him together in the field. Once he was released from the hospital, I lost track of him for several years until I heard that he finally met and married a nice woman in Georgia and wound up farming. I guess you could take the man off the farm but couldn't get the farm out of the man. Cleve must be pushing seventy by now, and I really should try to contact him even though I wasn't sure how he would take my relationship with Jean.

Willie, our youngest brother, never seemed to be able to get his life together, especially after Cleve left. He had wandered aimlessly though life, occasionally dropping in unexpectedly to visit. He had visited me in California many years earlier, and he had seemed so unsettled even though he put on a pretty good act. He had some "deals" he said he was working on, but I knew all of his bragging was pure bullshit. He had been married for a while, long enough to father three little girls, but the marriage had disintegrated at least in part due to his drinking and gambling problems. I had loaned him some money the last time he visited me even though I knew I would never get it back and that he would run through it within a few weeks to support whatever his habit was at the time. Willie had grown into the handsomest man I had ever seen, with dark wavy hair and beautiful gray eyes. He could have had so much but had squandered his life.

When I was awakened in the middle of the night by a phone call from the State Police, I couldn't say I was surprised. Willie's body had washed ashore about a hundred miles north of San Francisco. The police said he had been in the water for a few days, but they found my laminated phone number in his wallet. He was only in his thirties at the time. There wasn't much I could do for my youngest brother other than make arrangements to have his remains cremated and shipped back home for burial next to our parents. Katie had agreed to take care of the burial once his ashes arrived. Willie's ex-wife and daughters still lived in California, and Jean and I had seen them many times over the years. The girls had all inherited their father's dark, swarthy features.

Like Katie, my sister Annie had remained near Frost Valley, still living in town. Her husband was a good man, and she lived a comfortable life, but the unhappiness I saw in her eyes after our parents died had never gone away, and I had felt sorry for her in many ways. She was about a year younger than me but looked a hundred years old. Of all my siblings, she never seemed to fit in anywhere and had not managed to inherit the same genes from our parents that the rest of us had. On the rare occasions I had seen her over the years, she had never smiled. Her hair had turned prematurely gray many years earlier, and although she managed to marry a man who was almost as plain looking as she was, she never wanted to have children of her own. The loss of our parents had left her a bitter, unhappy woman, and she swore she would never have children who might wind up abandoned like we had been. Even though I had always gotten along better with Annie than I had Katie when we were children, by the time we were teenagers she had become a hateful young woman I hadn't wanted to associate with.

My middle brother, William McKinley, seemed to be about the only one who had muddled through a fairly normal, uneventful life. Now in his early sixties, Mack was married and living peacefully in New Mexico. He had gotten my phone number from Katie, and we had spoken a few times but never made plans to get together.

My reminiscences were interrupted by the arrival of Nolan, accompanied by my brother-in-law. Edwin Morgan was a huge, gentle man. I had never seen him lose his temper even though I would have drowned one or all three of his sons when they were puppies. Compared to Nolan, who was always a quiet, sensitive child, Katie and Edwin's boys had been loud, rowdy, and overly rambunctious. Edwin smiled broadly as he greeted Jean and me. I found it interesting that he always firmly shook my hand while he would hug Jean, giving her a light kiss on the cheek. The last time we had visited I had commented on that to Jean, who had only chuckled. I didn't know what was so damned funny about Edwin's little quirk until Jean kissed me softly and told me that he shook my hand because, being the traditionalist that he was, he regarded me as the "man" of our household.

"That's ridiculous!" I said, flabbergasted that she could say such a thing.

"Well, think about it, darling," Jean smiled. "Edwin only knows how to relate to couples who are a man and a woman. Because you're taller and stronger, and probably because he's noticed that I do defer to you in some matters, he's simply assigned the male role in our relationship to you. Even Nolan and Rachel come to me when they're hurt or want to ask a question."

"But it's obvious that I'm not a man," I said, pointing to my chest.

"Has Edwin ever seen you in a dress?"

"Probably not," I frowned. "It's a farm, for God's sake!"

"What do you and Edwin talk about when you're together?"

"I don't know. It's usually just small talk."

"You talk about the farm, the animals, his new tractor, and this year's tobacco crop. He discusses those things with you but never talks to you about the kids or anything else remotely domestic. He accepts those things as our roles. Haven't you ever noticed that he *always* calls you Cal instead of Callie? It's the way he adapts to our relationship, sweetie."

"And here I thought he was just too lazy to say my whole name," I laughed.

I thought about what she had told me and started paying attention to the way my brother-in-law interacted with each of us. Damned if she wasn't right...as usual. Ever since that conversation, a knowing little smile would pass between us whenever we were engaged in a conversation with Edwin. It worried me that perhaps in some way I was placing Jean in what could be considered as an inferior position. However, every time I tried to explain that that was not my intention and to let her know how much I loved and respected her, when we were alone she would let me know in her own special way who was truly in control. She was indeed a strong, sexual woman who could make me feel totally inferior to her any time she chose to.

"Where's Rachel?" Jean asked, breaking into my private thoughts.

"Oh, she's still feeding one of the twins," Edwin laughed. "Pays to have a veterinarian in the family, eh? Hope she don't send me a bill."

Rubbing his hands together, Edwin looked at the clouds building up over the valley. "Looks like it just might pucker up and snow some more. What do you think, Cal?"

Jean squeezed my hand as I rolled my eyes.

"If it does, it won't help your tobacco crop," I finally laughed.

"That's for damn sure," he said as he slapped me on the back. "That cake about ready, Katie?"

Choosing not to delve into the complexities of Edwin's interpretation of my relationship with Jean, we all made our way back toward the warmth of Katie's kitchen. Before I could save her, Edwin wrapped a big arm around Jean and escorted her inside.

"Nolan, go see if Rachel's about finished. I'm sure she'd appreciate some cake and coffee about now," I said.

Nolan trotted off toward the barn as Katie and I started up the three steps into her house.

"You know, Callie, you can really be proud of Nolan and Rachel. They've turned out much better than anyone would have ever expected," Katie said, which stopped me in my tracks.

"What does that mean, Katie?"

"Well, it's just that, you know, considering their backgrounds and raised the way they were..."

"What do you mean 'the way they were?' And what about their backgrounds?"

Setting her jaw in a way that convinced me she would always remain ignorant, Katie looked at me and placed her hand on her hip. "You know very well what I mean, Callie."

The look of misplaced superiority on her face made me want to just reach out and slap the shit out of her. Jean would have been proud of my self-restraint.

"Yeah," I seethed, "I do know what you mean, and it's horseshit. What, you don't think we could raise them with enough love that they would turn out acceptable even to you and your narrow tight-assed little mind?"

"Well, it's just not a normal situation, and I'm sure they must have suffered because of it whether you want to admit it or not."

"Well, thank God the whole world isn't like this valley!"

Lowering her voice as if she were passing along some juicy piece of gossip, Katie said, "But they're still half Japanese even if they do look much less Oriental now than they did when they were little."

"Since we adopted each of them when they were infants, they have never known any parents other than Jean and me. They're successful and well adjusted because of the way we raised them, like human beings who are no different from anyone else," I said indignantly through clenched teeth.

"Don't get huffy with me, Callie Owen," Katie frowned. "Even you have to admit that your family isn't exactly normal, and any problems Rachel or Nolan might have had were brought on by the way you've chosen to live your life. It's always the children who suffer."

"No, I don't have to admit that. We are two people who love each other and have raised two children together as parents. I can't see that it's any different from what you and Edwin have done."

"Well, it is different, whether you want to admit it or not," Katie said looking over my shoulder. "The children are coming. Let's not argue in front of them."

I let Katie go into the house alone. I suddenly needed to smoke a pack of Marlboros and calm the hell down. She always did that shit. Everything would be going along just fine, and then bam, she just had to say something so incredibly ignorant that I was ashamed to admit I was related to her. And I knew she was ashamed she was related to me. Maybe, I thought, that was why she hadn't bothered to attend the funeral. Some of her tight-ass friends might have seen her there and would have known we were related.

"You coming in?" Rachel said as she hurried toward the warmth of the house.

"In a minute," I frowned.

"Is something wrong, MC?" she said as she stopped next to me.

I smiled at my beautiful daughter who could read me almost as well as her mother. "No, honey, everything is fine. Go on in and warm up. We'll be leaving very soon," I said as I reached out and stroked her long, silky black hair.

Chapter
Three

IT MAY HAVE been the shortest visit in history, and I was still fuming about Katie's remarks as I turned onto the long drive leading to the Sanders home. Jean had been quiet since we left Katie's but had noticed my bad mood. I glanced at her and saw her looking at me.

"Well, that was certainly entertaining," she said.

"I'm sorry, Jean. I hoped things would've improved after twenty goddamn years."

"My goodness, Nolan, aren't we lucky that our Oriental features are barely noticeable now that we're all growed up," Rachel said in a voice that sounded remarkably like Katie's.

Nolan laughed. "Yeah, if MJ hadn't been with us, no one would have ever known."

I slammed on the brakes and the car slid on the gravel road. Turning around in the seat, I glared at them.

"I don't want to hear that shit!"

"We're just kidding around, MC," Nolan said.

"You don't have to make apologies for who you are to anyone. In fact, maybe I should apologize to you for subjecting you to a family as ignorant as mine."

"Get a grip, MC. Nolan and I don't take any of that crap seriously," Rachel shrugged. "We've heard it plenty of times before and are perfectly capable of defending ourselves if we have to."

"Yeah," Nolan grinned. "Remember Eddie Trautman?"

"Who the hell is Eddie Trautman?" I demanded. "And what's he got to do with any of this?"

Nolan and Rachel glanced at each other and giggled.

"Eddie Trautman was a little dweeb who used to steal Nolan's lunch money in elementary school," Rachel said nonchalantly.

"What? You never told us that."

"I took care of it, MC," Rachel smiled.

"And just how did you do that?"

"I snagged him after school one day and beat the shit out of him, of course. And I didn't need to know kung fu to do it. Besides," she sneered toward Nolan, "you know how much I *love* my baby brother, even if he was a total wimp back then."

"You should have..."

"Callie," Jean said in her irritatingly calm voice as she patted my hand. No matter how angry or upset I had gotten, her touch reminded me gently to calm myself down.

"Shit like that at Katie's was one of the reasons I couldn't wait to get the hell away from here in the first place, Jean. The narrow-mindedness. Even at the funeral today. The war ended over fifty fucking years ago, and these fools haven't gotten over it yet."

Jean grinned at me. "Now there's the rabble-rouser I fell in love with. Striking another blow for justice and equality."

She always knew how to make me smile. "Hell, you know damn well that I was never a rabble-rouser. I just fell in love with one."

"Well, this one is getting hungry," Jean laughed, "and Tad said his wife had a ton of food. Breakfast wore off hours ago."

THE HOME OF Thomas and Reiko Sanders was situated at least a quarter mile from the main road and hidden by a row of slender evergreens that served as a windbreak. Once a visitor got past the trees, a wide field opened up in front of the house, broken only by a small bridge over the drainage culvert that ran along the front of the property. On either side of the house were enormous chestnut trees. They were twice as large as I remembered, symmetrical twins framing the front porch of the old two-story house. Thomas had added to the house after he bought it, but the central portion was constructed of bricks, handmade by the slaves of a much earlier owner. As we approached the house, I saw a small marker on the side of the drive that announced that the house had been designated an historical site by some group whose name I didn't catch. The front yard was well landscaped, and Reiko's personal touches were everywhere. Simple yet elegant gardens seemed to surround the house. I promised myself to examine them more closely before I left.

I parked near the house, and before we could all get out of the car, Tad was striding briskly toward us. He had changed from his suit and looked the picture of a country gentleman in his jeans and forest green sweater.

"I'm glad you could make it, Callie. Carolyn was afraid we'd be eating leftovers for a month. How is your sister?"

"Disgustingly unchanged," I said flatly. "Tad, these are our children, Rachel and Nolan." Looking at them, I completed the formal introductions. "And this is Thomas Sanders, Jr. Also known as Tad."

"Is that short for something?" Rachel asked.

Tad laughed, "Yes, and I'm afraid it's not very flattering. It's short for tadpole, something my father called me when I was a baby.

Well, let's go inside where it's warmer," he said rubbing his hands together. "Carolyn is anxious to finally meet you."

As we followed him to a side door, I wondered what Tad had already told his wife about us. My worries evaporated as soon as we entered the house. Carolyn walked up to me, soup ladle in hand and hugged me warmly, as if she had known me all her life. She hugged Jean as well and shook hands with Rachel and Nolan. Carolyn Sanders was a rather plain-looking woman with blonde hair, sparkling blue eyes, and an outgoing personality.

"Please, make yourselves comfortable while I finish heating a few things up. Tad, why don't you see if you can round up the girls and introduce everyone?"

"Do you need help?" Jean asked as I helped her out of her coat.

"No, no. Everything is under control in here. I imagine it's been a long time since you've seen the house. Why don't you look around, and I'll call you when dinner's ready."

We followed Tad through the dining room and into an octagon-shaped parlor. I remembered the room, but the furnishings had changed. The furniture was simple yet had an understated elegance one wouldn't have expected. The parlor was one of the original rooms and boasted a twelve-foot ceiling. The walls had been covered with muted wallpaper accented by a subtle Oriental pattern. A massive fireplace spanned one of the eight walls and made the room warm and inviting. Aside from the furniture, the only other new addition I noticed was a large portrait of Thomas and Reiko Sanders that now hung over the fireplace, having replaced the country landscape I remembered.

"What a lovely portrait," Jean said.

"Thank you," Tad said. "I had it done for mother two or three years ago as an anniversary present."

The portrait showed a pleasant-looking Thomas Sanders standing behind his wife in his military uniform, his hand resting easily on her shoulder. Reiko Sanders was seated in front of him and was dressed in a white and sapphire silk kimono. Her black hair was swept on top of her head by an ornate gold comb and decorated with flowers that resembled baby's breath.

"It was their wedding picture," Tad said, looking up at the portrait. "We didn't have many pictures of Dad, and I always liked that one."

"It's beautiful," I said. As I was thinking how exquisitely delicate looking Reiko had always been, my thoughts were interrupted by the entrance of the two young women I had seen at the funeral.

"Ah, the offspring arrive," Tad said with a warm smile. The girls stopped talking when they saw us while Tad motioned them toward us.

"I want you to meet a very good friend of your grandmother's,

Callie Owen and her partner, Jean. And these are their children, Rachel and Nolan. These are our daughters, Lauren and Monica," he said pointing to each of them with obvious pride.

We exchanged pleasantries for a few minutes, which I always found awkward, and was relieved when Carolyn Sanders stuck her head in the door to announce that dinner was on the table.

As Tad helped his wife carry platters and large bowls of food into the dining room, Jean leaned toward me and whispered, "Where's Nolan?"

"I thought he was right behind us," I shrugged. "I'll go find him."

Excusing myself, I retraced my steps toward the parlor. As I approached the entry to the room, I could hear Nolan's voice and wondered what he was up to now. Entering the parlor quietly, I saw him standing in his stocking feet on a wide brocade ottoman, closely examining the portrait of Reiko and Thomas Sanders.

"These brush strokes are amazingly complex," he observed as he delicately ran his fingertips over the brush ridges left in the oil paint used on the portrait. "How did you get them so fine?"

Lauren Sanders stepped up onto the ottoman beside him and ran her fingers over the brush strokes as well. "I used very small sable brushes, which was a different technique for me. I actually prefer wider, stiffer brushes or a palette knife to make the paint lines more pronounced to create the perception of depth. My grandmother inspired me. She was a very delicate woman with an unimaginable inner strength. I think it's the best portrait I've ever done. And she was so happy when she saw it the first time."

"I think you made the right decision. It reminds me of some of the paintings I've seen by Andrew Wyeth," Nolan commented, still looking at the picture. "There's a realism to it that you don't see very often."

A slow blush moved up Lauren's neck as she glanced shyly at Nolan. "Thank you, but I wouldn't compare it to Wyeth."

Looking down at the young woman, Nolan smiled at her. "You shouldn't be so modest. I'd like to see some of your other work sometime."

Lauren Sanders was a reserved young woman and obviously humble about her talents. I had to smile to myself as I watched my son. Nolan had always been the same way, shy and reserved. There was a gentleness about him that made him the opposite of my outspoken daughter. It was apparent to me that Nolan was taken with Lauren Sanders, and they made a handsome couple. Both were the offspring of Asian and Caucasian parents, and both had inherited the more dominant Asian black hair and dark eyes. Of Tad's two girls, Lauren had inherited more of her father's Asian genes than her younger sister had. Although I knew I was biased, I thought that Nolan had grown into an unusually handsome young man. With the right incentive, I knew he could blossom into an incredible human being. Finally, I cleared my throat to announce my presence.

"Dinner's on the table, Nolan," I said.

"Oh, sorry, MC. I was just admiring this portrait and had to have a closer look." He stepped down from the ottoman and offered his hand to assist Lauren as he slipped his shoes back on.

"I can understand that. It's very beautiful," I agreed as I glanced once again at Reiko's youthful face, captured forever on the canvas.

The table was set with china that I remembered. It seemed to have held up well over the years, and I suspected it had only been used for special occasions. As bowls of food made their way around the table, I noticed that Nolan had seated himself next to Lauren as they remained engrossed in conversation. Our generally shy son seemed to have suddenly overcome his shyness. Sometimes, all it took to make any young man more talkative was an attractive young woman.

The food was delicious, and I was hungrier than I had realized. We were more than halfway through the meal before the conversation resumed.

"What kind of work are you doing now, Tad?" I asked.

"Systems analyst for one of the labs at Oak Ridge."

"Top secret stuff, huh?"

"Ironic, isn't it? Considering Mom's background."

"You have a lovely family. Where did you and Carolyn meet?" Jean asked out of nowhere.

"At UT," Carolyn said. "A blind date, actually."

"You know how those are. Nice personality and all that," Tad added, "but it was love at first sight for me."

She reached over and put her hand on his.

"We were married right here six months later," he continued as he looked at her.

She blushed a little and looked around the table.

"My parents weren't happy when Tad and I decided to get married, so we asked Reiko if we could hold our ceremony here," Carolyn explained.

"We lived with Mom until I graduated, then left for a few years before I was offered a job at the lab, and we moved back. Oak Ridge is fairly diverse now as far as people are concerned. We haven't had many problems."

"Except with my parents," Carolyn sighed.

"We had a few problems with my parents, too," Jean said. "But thankfully they went away, for the most part, after we adopted Rachel and Nolan."

"They didn't like MC?" Rachel asked.

"It wasn't that they didn't like her. They just thought I could have done better," Jean said winking at me.

"And she could have," I said.

"Well, you're so different, personality-wise, that I don't know what you ever saw in each other anyway," Rachel said.

"Opposites attract," I shrugged.

"Besides, I see a side of Momma Callie that you children will never see," Jean added as she reached over and squeezed my hand. "The softer, more affectionate side."

I took a long drink from my glass in an attempt to conceal my own embarrassment. Jean's total lack of shyness and habit of saying precisely what she was thinking had never ceased to astound and, occasionally, embarrass me.

"Isn't that the reason you married Ron? Because he's affectionate," Jean asked, looking back at our daughter.

"It wasn't the only reason. Ron's a wonderful man," Rachel said.

"He's an idiot," I said bluntly.

"Don't be shy, MC," Rachel grinned as she stabbed another bite of her salad. "Tell us how you really feel."

Rachel's husband had been a source of contention between us for the last few years. It wasn't that I didn't like him; I just considered him lazy. He hadn't held down a decent-paying job in the seven years they had been married and hadn't decided what kind of work he was best suited for yet. He seemed to prefer living off the income Rachel earned from her veterinary practice.

"He hasn't found himself yet, MC, but he's not an idiot."

"I hope he's planning to find himself soon," I frowned.

"This sounds like a familiar conversation," Monica piped in. "Daddy doesn't approve of my boyfriend, either."

"Is he an idiot, too?" Rachel asked with a smile as she slid her eyes toward me.

"He's actually quite brilliant," Tad said. "Unfortunately, he knows it. If his head were any bigger, he'd have to turn sideways to get through the door."

"John has been recruited by every prestigious university in the United States," Monica defended.

"Has he selected one yet?" Jean asked.

"He'd really like to go to Stanford, but his father is pushing him toward Harvard."

"John's father, Dr. Surti, works with me at the lab. Not very friendly though."

"You just don't like him because he's Pakistani," Monica said matter-of-factly.

The thought struck me as more than a little humorous. Tad and Carolyn and Jean and I had fought the prejudices of both our families and the public most our lives, and now Monica was accusing her father of the same thing.

"That's not true, Monica," Carolyn said. "John certainly hasn't gone out of his way to win your father over."

"Where are you planning to go to college, Monica?" I asked, changing the subject.

"I've been accepted at the University of California at Berkeley, but haven't made a final decision yet."

"Really?" Jean smiled. "I teach at Cal Berkeley."

"It's so far from home," Carolyn groaned.

"At least if she goes, now she'll know someone there," Tad said.

"I'll give you our phone number and address before we leave. If you decide to enroll, call me. I'll be glad to help you out."

"Jean and I met at Cal Berkeley," I said.

"I didn't know you attended Cal," Tad said between bites.

"Jean did. I went to San Francisco State. She was majoring in student protests while I studied landscape architecture."

"Did you meet on a blind date, too?" Carolyn asked.

I glanced at Jean and shook my head.

"We met in jail," Jean said, rather nonchalantly.

"More accurately, I believe it was in the back of a paddy wagon," I said. "She was the most incredible-looking creature I had ever seen. Long black hair, lavender tinted granny glasses, all dressed in tie-dye and denim."

"You were protesting the war?" Tad asked, looking at me quizzically.

"I was an innocent bystander. Jean and her little group of fellow student radicals were protesting at a park in San Francisco. I was there drawing up a plan for renovating the park as a class assignment, and the police weren't very picky about whom they arrested."

"Do you remember the first thing you said to me?" Jean asked with a familiar twinkle in her black eyes.

"I love you?"

"More like 'shut the hell up,'" Jean laughed.

"There were a lot of student protesters in that van. I thought I'd go deaf from all the hollering they were doing, and I already had a splitting headache from getting clobbered by a nightstick."

"Doesn't sound like a very auspicious way to begin a relationship," Carolyn observed.

"I ran into her accidentally a month or so later when I was out with some friends. It was a little disappointing that she didn't remember who I was, so I must not have made much of an impression."

"I remembered, darling. I just didn't want you to think I was interested," Jean smiled. "I knew I'd see you again."

"Oh, really?" I smiled back

"You're a landscape architect then," Tad said.

"Mostly semi-retired, but I still love it. I primarily do special commission work out of my home. Nolan works with me."

"Really," Tad said looking at Nolan. "Are you in landscaping as well?"

"No, sir," Nolan answered.

"Nolan is a sculptor," I said. "And it's not just a parent bragging when I say that he is really quite gifted. Many of the people who hire my company want to incorporate some type of sculpture as part of the landscape, but he's done several independently commissioned pieces as well."

"You didn't tell me you were an artist," Lauren said softly as she gave Nolan a sideways glance.

"MC interrupted us before I got around to it. But I haven't done much painting. I prefer sculpture even though I admire artists who paint."

"I find sculpture fascinating. The ability to feel what's lying dormant within the stone, the tactile sense of it, and to draw that image from it is a special talent."

It could have been my imagination, but I would have sworn that Lauren was flirting with Nolan. I watched the top of his ears redden slightly as he listened to her soft voice. It seemed that he had also picked up on the signals she was sending him through their discussion of the various art forms.

"Wow!" Monica exclaimed suddenly, getting up from her chair and interrupting my thoughts. "Look at that!"

She went to a window in the dining room and looked outside. I turned in my chair and saw that it was snowing again. This time it wasn't a light anything. Snow was coming down in buckets, reminding me of those old movies I had seen where stagehands threw fake snow in front of a wind machine to simulate a blizzard. We all got up and went to the windows and doors. Tad and I went onto a side porch for a better look. My car was already covered with a blanket of white that was getting deeper by the minute.

"Looks like you won't be going anywhere tonight, Callie."

I had seen late storms like this one before and knew he was right. The roads over the ridge were probably already impassable and likely to stay that way for a day or two.

"I'll need to use your phone. We have reservations back home tomorrow."

"We better get your stuff out of the car while we can still find it," he said.

I broke the news to Jean, who didn't seem in the least upset about staying, and Nolan looked positively ecstatic. Rachel announced that she had to call Ron and check on her children. Tad and I waded through ankle deep snow to retrieve our luggage while Carolyn and Jean worked out the sleeping arrangements. I knew there were plenty of rooms for us in the old house and had learned a long time ago not to get overwrought by things beyond my control.

An hour later we sat around the parlor fireplace with Thomas and Reiko watching over us. As we chatted and drank hot chocolate and coffee, I could feel Reiko looking at me. In the portrait, she was still young and exotic, just as she had been the first time I saw her.

Chapter
Four

IT HAD BEEN cold in mid-March of 1949. The remnants of the last snowfall were still hanging on tenaciously in low areas and in the shadows beneath the pines. For people who never saw snow, it would have been picturesque. But for farmers anxious to get their spring crops in the ground, snow was a pain in the ass and only meant they couldn't plant. Even after the snow was gone there were still problems. The narrow roads over the ridge were never completely free of icy patches until early April, leaving many an old truck in the ditches waiting for a tractor to tow them out. Occasionally, a particularly unfortunate soul would slide over one of the steep embankments and be killed.

People in Frost Valley were from the same families who had settled it nearly a hundred and fifty years earlier. Only good sense and the good book had kept them from intermarrying closer than second cousins, but there were a few around we were all suspicious about. Statistically speaking, one family shouldn't have more than one or two idiots over the passage of two centuries. Everybody whispered about the Johnson family because it seemed that they were all idiots or morons, at least according to the census takers.

Like everyone we knew, we had endured the Depression and World War II and had survived it the best way we could. Because he was a farmer, my father hadn't been called to fight with the Army overseas, and my mother had been grateful for that. I wished my mother could have lived to see the end of the war, but I guess God had other plans for her. She died in the summer of 1944, leaving my father to care for six children alone. My brother, Cleve, and I were the oldest and became adults ahead of our time. By 1949, we were all old enough to pretty much take care of ourselves, or at least old enough to go to school every day. Papa had stopped farming and had been working two jobs since Mama died. Cleve and I tried to do the farm work but only managed to grow enough to keep our family fed and not much more.

It wasn't a bad life, but we all missed Mama. The day that

changed my life started out as just another school day. I got up, washed my face, and pulled on a wrinkled shirt and overalls before waking up the little ones. By the time I got downstairs, Cleve was frying something in an iron skillet.

"You get 'em up?" he asked.

"'Course," I mumbled.

"Then get some more firewood in before we leave."

Before I could get out the door, an arm wrapped itself around my leg. When I looked down, Willie was grinning up at me.

"Wanna help, Willie?"

He nodded vigorously and scampered for the back door. He never could carry more than one piece of wood at a time, but it kept him busy and out of the way. Soon enough, hauling firewood would become just another necessary chore with little or no adventure in it.

By the time we finished stacking the wood, Cleve came out the back door followed by Annie, Katie, and Mack. He looked like a mother duck being trailed by ducklings. He handed me a sausage and egg sandwich as he adjusted his cap on his head and had another one ready for Willie. It was a couple of miles from our house to the school, but we had plenty of time and walked at a leisurely pace. The air was crisp, but the sun was shining and felt good as it was absorbed into our coats. When we reached the main road, we saw three boys coming down the road and waited for them. Most of them were Cleve's age, around fourteen. Jake Sanders was the oldest one, and that morning he didn't look very happy. As they approached us, the other boys, Edmund Rutledge and Carter Talbot, were laughing and talking to Jake. Jake stopped and said something to the other two that we couldn't hear. He looked mad and didn't stop walking even when they reached us.

"What's with Jake?" Cleve asked.

"His brother, Thomas, got home last night," Edmund said.

We stood there looking at Edmund. Thomas had been away at the war and then working for the military government in Japan when the fighting ended.

"So?" Cleve shrugged as he turned toward the school.

"Well," Carter whispered conspiratorially, "when he come home, he didn't come alone."

"He brung a Jap wife home with him," Edmund snickered. "Got the whole family in an uproar from what Jake says."

"He married a Jap?" Cleve asked in disbelief.

"What's a Jap?" I asked.

Cleve shushed me with a wave of his hand and stopped to talk again to Edmund and Carter.

"What did old man Sanders say?"

"Jake said he couldn't repeat it, but I think he threw Thomas out of the house," Edmund said shaking his head.

"Don't forget the best part," Carter smiled, poking Edmund in the ribs.

"They got this half-Jap baby, too."

"What's a Jap?" I repeated.

Cleve snapped his head around. "The enemy, stupid! Now shut up."

I didn't have the slightest idea what they were talking about and went on to school, leaving the older boys to gossip like a bunch of girls.

All day long, small groups of kids stood around huddled together whispering and giggling amongst themselves. Occasionally, someone would spot Jake, and there would be some finger pointing, followed by more whispering and giggling. I still didn't know what a Jap was, but whatever it was seemed to be humiliating to Jake.

Jake's family was the oldest family in the valley, as well as the biggest landowners. Everyone said they were rich, but at ten years old, I didn't know how much money it took to be rich. Jake had always been one of the most popular boys in school. He was an okay-looking kid and pretty smart, even though we all knew his future would be as a farmer.

Chapter
Five

Thursday, March 17, 1949

THE NEXT DAY started out as a pretty average day until lunch. I noticed then that, for the first time I could ever remember, Jake was sitting alone while he ate his lunch. When he finished, he got up to throw away his trash. Before he got to the trash barrel, another boy, Harley Finlayson, got up and blocked his path. Jake tried to get around him but was blocked by Harley's friends. Any kid can tell when a fight is fixing to break out and is drawn to it like a magnet. I managed to get close enough to hear what was going on.

"Get out of my way, Harley. I don't want no trouble," Jake said.

"I'm surprised you can keep your lunch down, Jake. If I knew my brother was screwin' some nip bitch, I'd throw up."

"I'm not responsible for what Thomas does," Jake said, trying to push his way past Harley.

Harley grabbed Jake's shirt. "Is that what your folks teach you at home? To shack up with the enemy?"

"Leave my folks out of this, Harley."

Harley pulled Jake close to him. "My uncle was killed by Japs. Now Thomas has the balls to bring one of 'em here. Why don't he just spit on us?"

Jake jerked away from Harley and looked at the other students staring at him.

"Thomas says the war is over. It's time to move on," he tried unconvincingly.

"My uncle was a hero. He killed the enemy instead of sleepin' with 'em! Thomas is a coward. You a coward, too, Jake?"

We all knew there was no way Jake would escape without a fight. Someone had run to get the principal, but he didn't make it until after the fists had started flying.

"Break it up!" Mr. Duncan bellowed as he reached the circle we had formed around Harley and Jake and pushed us away. Jake had already taken a couple of pretty good hits and had a nasty cut above his right eye. He was on the verge of landing a punch of his own when Mr. Duncan grabbed his arm.

"I said break it up! Who started this?" he demanded.

Neither boy spoke, and then Mr. Duncan looked at the rest of us. No one said anything, and a few kids began wandering away. Someone who wasn't even there had started the fight, but I guess there wasn't any good way to explain that.

"No one's talking, huh?" Mr. Duncan finally said. "Harley, you go wait in my office until I get there."

Harley wiped his nose with the sleeve of his shirt and glared at Jake before lumbering away. Mr. Duncan stood with one hand on Jake's shoulder and waited until Harley was out of earshot before speaking.

"I understand Thomas is home, and I got a pretty good guess what this was about, Jake. I think you should go on home for today. In fact, maybe you should stay home until Monday."

Jake looked up at Mr. Duncan, and there were tears in his eyes.

"I'll come by and speak to your folks later today. This will blow over, son, but you gotta remember that more than one family around here suffered a loss in the war. You really can't blame them for bein' upset with Thomas right now."

I'd been taught not to eavesdrop on other people's conversations, but I was still trying to figure out what Thomas Sanders had done and what a Jap was. Harley had only made it worse because I didn't know what a nip was either.

That afternoon on our way home, I couldn't stand it any longer.

"What's a nip, Cleve?" I asked.

"A Jap."

"Well, what's..."

He stopped in the middle of the road and looked at me.

"Look, Callie, you remember the war, don't you?"

"Of course. I ain't stupid like you said."

"Well, Japs is who we was fighting. They are the enemy. The bad guys."

"But I thought Pa said the war was over a long time ago."

"It was, but Japs is still the enemy. They ain't like us. I heard folks say they wasn't even human."

Images of creatures with multiple arms and eyes flashed through my mind.

"How're they different? You ever seen one?"

"No, but I've heard what other folks said."

"Tell me, Cleve! What if I run into one? How will I know?"

"Well, they ain't white like you and me. They're yellow."

"Like butter?"

"Yeah, and they can't see too good, so they have to get real close to you. Something's wrong with their eyes."

He could tell from my expression that I didn't understand that part. He stopped and put his books down.

"Here. I'll show you," he said with a grin.

He took my head in his hands, with a thumb next to each of my eyes. Then he pulled the skin on the corner of my eyes back toward my ears. Everything went blurry, and I saw two of everything around me.

"No wonder they lost," I said.

We walked on a ways before Cleve said, "I heard they ain't got any hair on their bodies, but don't know if that's true or not."

"Thomas married a bald woman?"

Cleve laughed. "They might have hair on their heads."

He leaned down closer to me. "I heard their women ain't got hair, you know, on their private parts."

I didn't know anyone had hair there, but tried to act like I knew what the hell he was talking about anyway.

"Who told you that?"

"Lawrence said his daddy told him."

"How does his daddy know?"

"I don't know, Callie! Maybe he stood one on her head and looked. You ask too damn many questions."

Thomas Sanders and his wife became a continuous topic of conversation everywhere I went. Kids at school still shied away from Jake, but there weren't any more fights. Apparently, Thomas had decided to stay in Frost Valley no matter how much it upset the social balance. I don't know how he did it, but he bought an old house at the far end of the valley. Every now and then someone would spot him in town, but a month after he got home, no one had seen his wife yet.

Chapter
Six

Friday, April 29, 1949

BY LATE APRIL, my curiosity, fueled by speculation, had grown to a point where I thought I would burst. We had talked about the Sanderses some at home, and my father had forbidden any of us to go near their farm. I don't think there's anything more tempting than forbidden fruit. Pa might as well have dared me to go.

It was late afternoon near the end of April, and I was stuck with Willie, as usual, and tired of playing mumblety-peg and other games to entertain him. Pa wouldn't be home for three or four more hours. The weather was sunny and warm, and I figured there wouldn't be a better time.

"Hey, Willie, wanna take a walk?" I asked cheerfully.

"Where?"

"Maybe down the top of the ridge. Just to look around."

At nearly six, Willie was too young to understand any of the dinner conversations we'd had about the Sanderses. I'd make it look like an accident that we wound up at the Sanders place if anyone saw us.

Willie followed me into the tree line behind our house. It was cooler in the pines, and I thought we would be able to hide in the shadows once we got there. I could have covered the three or four miles twice as fast without Willie and began to wish I hadn't brought him along. Seemed like every few feet he had to stop to look at something or rest. Although he didn't talk too much, once he started you just about couldn't shut him up. A little over an hour later, we were on the ridge above the Sanders house. Looking around, I didn't see anyone, but an old pickup was parked near the front of the house. I let Willie forage around a while before deciding to get closer. Taking his hand, we walked toward the edge of the tree line. We were still in the shadows when the back door of the house opened, and Thomas Sanders stepped out. I grabbed Willie and pulled him down, signaling him not to talk. A few moments later, a woman carrying a baby came out of the house. From where I was squatting, I couldn't tell anything about her. She was wearing a simple dress and a wide brimmed straw hat that hid her face. At least she only had two arms and two legs. Willie started wiggling around.

"Be quiet, Willie," I whispered.

"I gotta pee," he whispered back.

"Can't you hold it?"

"No, Callie. I gotta go," he whined urgently, holding his hands against his crotch.

When we returned to the edge of the tree line a few minutes later, there wasn't anyone in sight. The truck was still there, so they couldn't have gone far.

Turning to Willie, I said, "You wait here. I'll be right back."

He nodded and sat down against a tree. I stood halfway up and picked my way down the slope leading to the back of their house, hiding behind or under whatever I could find. An old wagon sat near the barn, and I made a dash for it. I looked around and waited to catch my breath for a few moments before daring to get closer. I leaned over for a quick glance around and felt a hand on my shoulder. I jumped and looked behind me to see Willie smiling at me.

"What are you doin' here? Didn't I tell you to wait up there?" I whispered angrily.

"When're we goin' home? I'm tired, Callie," he whined.

"In a little bit. You stay right here. If you move, I'm gonna bust ya. Understand?"

He nodded and pouted, as he sat down and crossed his little arms across his chest.

The only thing between me and the back yard of the house was a short row of trees that served as a windbreak. I dropped to my knees and low-crawled through the knee-high grass toward the trees. My heart was still beating fast from Willie's surprise appearance, but I had already come that far. Once I got to the trees, I could only catch glimpses of what was on the other side. I pushed the low branches back with my hand and saw the woman at last. Her back was to me, and she couldn't have been more than fifty feet from me. She had a hoe in her hand and occasionally squatted down to pull grass and weeds from the furrow she was hoeing. Eventually she would have to turn around, and I settled down to wait. A few seconds later, I found myself face to face with a baby about a year old. I hadn't seen it before, but it must have been playing in the shady area just the other side of the trees. I had been so intent on seeing the woman that I had missed the baby.

I looked quickly back to where Willie was sitting and pulled my hand back from the tree. I could hear her speaking to the baby, and by then, she couldn't have been more than ten feet from where I was sitting. I was afraid she could hear me breathing, and panic began to set in. A tree branch in front of me moved, and I jumped up and began running toward Willie. He saw me and stood up.

"Run, Willie! Run quick!"

For once in his life, Willie minded me and took off like the devil himself was after him. I glanced over my shoulder in time to see her step through the windbreak, holding the baby in her arms. I still hadn't seen her face when I fell.

SOMEONE WAS PRESSING a cold cloth to my head, and I felt dizzy.

"Thomas!" a woman's voice called in an unfamiliar accent.

I reached up to touch my head and felt a warm hand holding the cloth. A sweet smell entered my nose, and I opened my eyes, almost afraid of what I would see. When I saw her, I was startled and pressed myself down on the couch, shielding my face with my hands. It was *her*, and I was alone with her! I hadn't heard any rumors about Japs eating children, but maybe they did just like everyone said the gypsies did.

"Sh-h-h," she said softly, brushing my hair back with her hand.

"She awake?" a man's voice asked.

"Do you know her, Thomas?"

"I've been away a long time, honey."

A firm hand gripped my shoulder and pulled me upright on the couch. I had been too scared to notice before, but the movement made my head throb.

"What's your name, girl?" the man said.

My eyes were clamped shut so tightly that I wasn't sure I could open them. I cracked them open and looked through my fingers. Thomas Sanders was kneeling in front of me holding the baby on his knee. Thomas had changed some, but I recognized him. His face was broad and gentle, and his brown hair was combed straight back.

"Get your hands down, and tell me your name," Thomas ordered.

I let my hands slide down to my lap and stared at the baby. It had the fattest cheeks I'd ever seen. The cheeks seemed to push his eyes into little slits. Thomas snapped his fingers in my face to get my attention.

"You're not one of those Johnson idiots, are you?"

"No, sir. I'm Callie Owen."

"Preston's girl?"

"Yes, sir," I said looking around the room. She had disappeared.

"I gotta get home," I said as I quickly stood up. A wave of nausea overcame me, and I quickly sat back down on the couch.

"You better rest a few more minutes, Callie. You got a nasty bump on your head."

I leaned forward and rested my head in my hands.

"What were you doing sneakin' around here anyway?"

"Nothin'," I lied.

"You came to stare at my wife, didn't you?" he accused.

"No, sir! I was just takin' my little brother for a walk."

"You must live three or four miles from here. That's a pretty long walk."

"Drink this. Then you feel better," she said.

I looked up and finally had a chance to look at her face. Her mouth curled shyly into a smile as she handed me a cup. Despite all the rumors, I hadn't known what to expect. But she was pretty, in a different sort of way. Maybe she was beautiful. I didn't know anyone to compare her to. Her black hair was pulled back away from her face except for wispy bangs. Her hands were slender and delicate as I took the cup.

"Thank you, ma'am," I said weakly.

"After she gets her bearings, I'll take her on home," Thomas said as he stood up again.

I tasted the light brown liquid in the cup. It was sweet and hot and felt good as it went down my throat.

"Her name is Callie Owen," Thomas told his wife. She nodded and smiled at me again. The baby started to wiggle, and she took it from Thomas while making those noises adults always make around babies. I watched as they both fussed over the baby.

"Is it a boy or a girl?" I found the courage to ask.

"Boy," she smiled.

"He looked like a tadpole when he was born, what with all that black hair, so we call him Tad," Thomas chuckled.

I noticed that she seemed to smile a lot, but her lips never parted when she did. It gave her face a gentle, benevolent look, and I knew there wasn't anything to fear from this stranger.

"How old is your baby?" I asked.

"Just over a year," Thomas said. "Getting into everything."

"You want to hold?" she asked.

I'd held plenty of babies before, and this one didn't look any different from the others. The baby looked at me and kicked his pudgy little feet as she lowered him onto my lap. I bounced him for a few seconds before he grabbed my fingers and pulled himself straight up, dancing around on stubby little legs. I guess I must have looked strange to him, too, because he released one of my hands and slapped at my face. I picked him up and set him on the floor between my legs. Hanging on to my fingers tightly, he waddled a few steps before he stopped and looked up at his mother.

"Walk to your mama," I whispered, as I pointed him in the right direction.

She squatted down and clapped her hands for him to see. In a shot, he let go of me and staggered toward her. When he reached her, she scooped him up in her arms and kissed his cheeks. I'd seen my mother do the same thing with my brothers and sisters. This woman wasn't any different from any other mother.

"Thank you for the drink, ma'am," I said. "I'm feelin' better and better get on home before my pa misses me."

"Reiko, please," she smiled as she held her hand out to me.

I wiped my hands on my overalls and pumped her hand once or twice.

Before I could get to the front door, I saw the headlights and heard the sound of a vehicle stopping in front of their house.

"Thomas! Thomas Sanders!" I heard my father's voice yell.

I knew I was in trouble from the sound of his voice, and Thomas knew it, too. I took a deep breath and exhaled before starting for the door. Thomas stopped me.

"You wait here with Reiko, Callie. Let me speak to your pa first."

I nodded, but already knew that all the talking in the world wasn't going to save me from a whipping. Willie had probably spilled his guts to save himself. Reiko stepped next to me and placed a hand lightly on my shoulder, almost as if she was trying to protect me, as Thomas went onto the front porch.

"Hello, Preston," he said. "It's good to see you again."

"I come for my girl. You got her in there?"

"She's here, but you won't be needing that shotgun."

"Send her out, Thomas. I don't want no trouble."

"Neither do we. Callie had a little accident, but she'll be okay."

"What kind of accident?"

"She was cutting across the field out back and tripped and hit her head."

"Her brother said your wife attacked them."

"She saw them, and they got scared. I reckon your boy made it home okay."

"He's scared to death."

"Why don't you come in a spell?"

"Just send Callie out, so I can get her on home."

When I walked onto the porch, she still had one hand on my shoulder and was holding her baby in her other arm. As soon as my father saw us, he raised the shotgun toward us.

"Stand away from my girl before I blast you back to where you belong!"

Thomas stepped between us and the shotgun and held his hand out.

"Put the shotgun down, Preston. There's no need for that."

I pushed past Thomas and ran down the steps toward my father. As soon as I reached him, I placed my hand on the barrel of the shotgun and pushed it down.

"I'm okay, Pa. Just a little bump," I said quickly as I looked back at the Sanders.

My father leaned down and looked at the knot on my forehead.

"Not as bad as the welts I'm gonna raise on your backside for disobeying me," he said in a low voice. "Now get in the truck."

He turned and walked around to the driver's side of the truck and got in. I stopped and nodded toward Thomas and his wife before climbing into the truck.

Chapter
Seven

Saturday, November 5, 1949

IT WAS WINTER before I saw Thomas and his family again. Whenever I was tempted to wander through the woods toward their place, I remembered the whipping I got after my first visit. Except for school, I wasn't allowed to go anywhere for a month. Cleve told the other kids I had seen the stranger, and they asked me nearly every day what she looked like. I would just shrug and not say much, figuring they wouldn't believe me anyway if I told them she was nice. Apparently, Thomas hadn't been able to change his family's opinion about his wife and baby, and they stayed pretty much at home. The only advantage to my prolonged punishment was that my school grades improved. The school library didn't have many books about Japan, and the ones they did have depicted the Japanese as nothing like the smiling young woman I had met.

The first weekend in November our school held its annual winter carnival. It was a big social event for the people in Frost Valley; a chance to see folks you hadn't seen in a while, and catch up on all the gossip. Games were set up in each room, and the teachers always had treats for all the kids. I had won a fresh apple pie once in a math contest, but most of the treats were little cookies or biscuits. Besides having fun, the parents got to see what their kids were doing in school, and talk to the teachers. Some of the men took the kids for hayrides on their tobacco sleds pulled by huge Belgian draft horses.

After all the games and rides, the grown-ups held a fundraiser in the school cafeteria. Each family donated items that were auctioned off, with all the money going into a fund for school supplies and books. Most of the items didn't bring much money, but it was fun watching. The auctioneer was always Burke Sanders, Thomas's father. Jake was his assistant, and his job was to walk around showing off each object up for bids and collecting money from the winners. That night I was sitting with my brothers and sisters at a table made of a long board resting on sawhorses, about halfway back in the long rows of homemade tables. Pa was standing with a few other men near the back of the room, smoking and talking.

"All right, folks," Burke announced loudly. "What am I bid for this first item? A one-pound sack of cornmeal donated by the Rutledges. I understand every ear of corn that went into this sack was hand picked by Mrs. Rutledge herself to make sure it was turned into the purest, whitest corn meal that went through the gristmill this year. In fact, it's so good, you might not want to eat it, just put it up on your mantle and admire it. Who'll start the bidding?"

"Ten cents!" a man yelled.

"That's an insult, brother," Burke yelled back.

"Fifteen cents," a second man hollered out.

Burke looked admiringly at the sack and said, "Hell, I'll bid fifty cents for it myself!"

"Sold!" someone else yelled, leading to a round of laughter.

The kidding around over the items was good-natured and provided a few laughs for everyone. I always thought Burke Sanders should have been a professional auctioneer. That night, he eventually got some fool to bid a dollar fifty for a sack of cornmeal that wasn't worth more than twenty-five cents. We all knew the money went for a good cause, and an occasional extravagance probably wasn't going to hurt any of us. In the midst of the laughter during the auction, I hadn't noticed Thomas and his family slip into the back of the cafeteria. Burke got a strange look on his face and paused for only a moment before going on to the next item. In the middle of the bidding, Thomas walked down one side of the cafeteria toward the front. When people saw him, they began whispering among themselves, and the bidding suddenly stopped. Heads turned to look toward the back of the cafeteria where Reiko and her son were standing. Burke tried to keep the bidding going, but it was clear that the item was finished.

Burke stepped down from the small stage and spoke with Thomas for a few moments. It seemed clear from their body language that it wasn't a pleasant discussion. Thomas had something in his hands and tried to get Burke to take it, but he refused. Finally, Burke walked away and left Thomas standing there. Thomas looked out at people he had known all his life and shook his head. Stepping onto the stage, he spoke in a strong voice.

"While my father takes a little break to rest his voice, how much am I bid for this delicious cherry pie? Still warm, just out of the oven."

"Who baked it?" someone asked.

"What's the difference, neighbor? It's a cherry pie, guaranteed to melt in your mouth."

"We ain't your neighbors no more," a woman said loudly.

"I've known most of you since I was born, but I didn't really know what kinds of folks you were until I came home. This is my home, and I'm not planning to leave it, so get used to seeing me and my family around."

Turning my head toward the back of the room, I saw Reiko stand-

ing passively against the wall. Tad was giggling and looking at the
men standing closest to him. One of the men made a face to show his
disgust, but it only served to make Tad laugh more. I reached into the
pocket of my overalls and pulled out the money I had been saving up
for a new pocketknife I had seen in town. My old knife was still good
even if it was a little beat up from a million games of mumblety-peg.
Thomas shook his head and headed for the steps.

"Two dollars!" I said loudly, jumping up.

Cleve looked back to where Pa was standing and tried to pull me
back down. I jerked my arm away from him and stepped into the aisle,
holding my money up. Thomas smiled at me.

"Sold!" he said as he pointed at me.

He came down the steps and strode toward me. I saw Jake out of
the corner of my eye and handed the money to him. He looked at me
and frowned. Glancing around the room, he wasn't sure whether to
take the money or not. Then he spit on my money and threw it on the
floor. As quick as that, the fight was on. Jake was three years older and
a head taller than me, but I guess there's something to be said for a
low center of gravity. There wasn't anything in my mind except rage
at that point, and I remembered everything Cleve had tried to teach
me about fighting dirty. Women quickly scattered, and men and boys
weren't sure how to handle their divided loyalties. Poor Cleve didn't
approve of what I did, but neither was he going to let Jake Sanders
beat up his sister. Mack grabbed one of Jake's legs and held on for
dear life, and Willie pummeled Jake with his little fists, which must
have felt like being hit with marshmallows. I would have laughed if
Jake hadn't gotten in a pretty good shove that sent me sprawling on
the floor. I jumped up and was ready to continue the fracas when
someone grabbed my overalls from behind. I whirled around, fist
drawn back, and saw Thomas holding my pie.

"Stop it!" he ordered, pointing a finger at Jake. "And pick up that
money for the school."

"Take your hands off my girl," I heard Pa say. He pushed his way
through the circle of people surrounding us. When he got to where I
was standing, he grabbed the back of my overalls, jerking me away
from Thomas and nearly knocking me down in the process. Holding
me with one hand, Pa got toe to toe with Thomas.

"This is your fault, Thomas. You show up here, embarrass yourself and your family, then get my girl dragged into a fight. Now that
you've disrupted everything, why don't you take your Jap wife and
that half-breed kid of yours and get on out of here."

A slow grin crossed Thomas's face, and there was a strange look
in his eyes. He thrust the pie toward me.

"Take this, Callie. You paid for it," he said.

Turning quickly back to my father, he spoke calmly, "Each man
picks his own fights, Preston."

With that, he hit my father and doubled him over. Pa released me and tried to catch his breath. While everyone was watching Pa and Thomas square off, I spun around and ran smack into Jake again.

"Nice lookin' pie," he said with a grin. Taking the pie from me, he smashed it into my face. "Hope you enjoy it."

I reached up and wiped the warm sticky filling from my eyes, as everyone around me started laughing. I ran my tongue around my mouth. It was a damn good pie. Jake was laughing at me, and as I blinked at him through cherry pie filling, I saw Cleve get down on the floor behind Jake and motion to me with his head. In the middle of his laughter, I pushed Jake backward hard enough to make him fall over Cleve. At that point I decided I'd had enough socializing for the night and ran as fast as my legs could carry me toward the back door. The door flew open as I rushed outside, trying to find a place to hide before Jake managed to pick himself up. The creek that ran the length of the valley floor was only a few yards away, and I ran toward it and jumped down the embankment to hide. It was dark outside, and the moon was hidden behind low winter clouds that held the promise of snow. Occasionally, I peeked over the embankment waiting for the coast to clear. It was freezing near the creek, but I was still running on adrenalin from what had happened. I felt my face. It was sticky and the pie filling was now mixed with pine needles and dirt. Scooting down to the edge of the creek, I dipped my hand in the freezing water and tried to wash the debris from my face.

I heard a sound behind me and spun around expecting to see Jake lumbering toward me. Instead, I saw Reiko and Tad Sanders standing above me. I jumped up and wiped my hands on my overalls. Puffs of my breath fogged the cold air in front of me.

"You hurt?" she asked softly.

"No, ma'am. I'm sorry about what happened tonight."

"I am sorry you had trouble."

I shrugged and stuck my freezing hands deep into my pockets as she turned to go back up the embankment.

"Your pie was delicious, ma'am. At least the part I got to taste," I smiled.

She nodded and disappeared. I needed to get home before I froze to death, but maybe freezing to death would be better than what would surely be waiting at home. Pa only whipped me the last time, but I could feel a real beating coming on now. I hadn't disobeyed him, and I hadn't started the fight. Maybe he wouldn't blame me.

I STAYED AWAY from our house as long as I could stand it. Sooner or later I would have to face my father's wrath. I opened the back door as quietly as I could and tiptoed through the kitchen and dining room. The glow from the fireplace flickered across the living room, and the house was quiet. Peeking around the doorframe into the living room, I saw Pa sitting in the dark, smoke from his cigarette curling around his head. He had a small bandage over his left eye, and I wondered whether Thomas had to have a bandage, too. Summoning up whatever courage I had left, I stepped into the doorway. Pa glanced up and saw me.

"Where you been, child?"

I shrugged. I hadn't been anywhere. As I looked down, I could see the remains of the cherry pie on the front of my overalls. My hands had turned damp, and I could feel that they were still sticky.

"Come over by the fire, and get yourself warmed up," he said as he got up. I braced myself for what was coming next. But Pa walked past me and went into the kitchen.

I held my hands out to warm them. I never could stand it if my hands or feet got cold. They would chill my whole body. A few minutes later, Pa reappeared carrying a bucket of water and a cloth.

"Strip outta them clothes, Callie," he said quietly.

Unfastening my overalls, I let them drop to the floor before peeling off my shirt. Pa wrung out the cloth and used it to wipe my face with warm water. Then he worked a while at getting the pie filling out of my hair.

"I'm sorry, Pa. Does your face hurt?"

"Not much. I've had worse."

"What about Thomas?"

"He's had worse, too. You know, Callie, that was a stupid thing you did tonight."

"I guess."

"But Thomas was right. You're practically an adult now. Or at least close enough. You can make your own decisions, just so long as you know you won't always like the consequences."

"Yes, sir."

"Here, you finish washing up," he said as he stood up and picked my clothes off the floor.

The warm water felt good as I washed off my neck and arms. The pie filling had left a faint red stain on my skin. By the time I finished washing, Pa returned with a quilt and placed it around my shoulders.

"Sit down. We need to talk," he said, lighting another cigarette with the glowing end of a small piece of kindling from the fireplace. He looked at me and said, "You want one? I know you and Cleve have tried 'em before."

I shook my head and tried to figure out how he knew that. I backed up until I found a chair and pulled it closer to the fireplace.

"You caused quite a little ruckus tonight, Callie. Can you tell me why you did it?"

"I don't know. I like cherry pie."

He smiled. "But you knew Thomas's wife probably baked it."

"Yes, sir."

"I can't understand this fascination you seem to have with her."

"I was just curious, I guess."

"Ain't you curious about gypsies, too?"

"Yeah."

"Then why don't you go sneakin' over to one of their camps and visit them?"

"'Cause gypsies steal kids," I said, my eyes wide with fear. "Everybody knows that."

"But I guess you didn't believe what you heard about Thomas's wife."

"Her name is Reiko, Pa. She's a nice lady."

"I've met some nice niggers, but I wouldn't get caught socializin' with 'em."

"That ain't the same thing. Thomas is one of us, and we always socialized with him."

"Until he betrayed us by bringing a stranger here. He should've lived somewhere else if he wanted to marry outside his own kind."

"I don't understand..."

"Would you marry a gypsy, Callie?"

"No, sir."

"How about a nigger?"

"No, sir."

"Do you think Thomas would have married a gypsy or a nigger?"

"No."

"Then why do you think he married this Jap woman? It's the same thing."

"I guess he loved her, like you loved Ma."

I knew Pa missed my mother, and he looked away for a moment. "Your Ma was white like me and you. Now that Thomas has a kid, it's that kid who's gonna suffer for his daddy sleeping with another race. What you think will happen once that half-breed kid starts school if they stay here?"

"Maybe they think folks will get used to him."

"Then they're not thinkin' straight. I'm tellin' you, Callie, it won't never happen. If that baby's own grandparents won't have nothin' to do with him, neither will anyone else. Just remember this, and I ain't saying this to be mean, it's wrong to marry outside your own kind. It's just the way it's always been and always will be."

I stared into the fire and thought about what my father was saying. Maybe he was right, but maybe the whole world wasn't like this valley.

"I want you to stay away from Thomas and his family, Callie. It's gonna be hard enough on you after tonight without you aggravatin' it even more. I want you to promise me that. You need to remember that whatever you do reflects back on me and your brothers and sisters. We could all be hurt by what you do."

I knew he was right about that part. Aside from me and Cleve, the others were too little to understand what was going on.

"I promise," I said softly, wishing I hadn't had to.

Chapter
Eight

Wednesday, March 28, 1951

THINGS IN THE valley were fairly peaceful in the spring of 1951. I had just turned twelve. I had kept my promise to my father and stayed away from the Sanders place. Cleve had started keeping company with Sally Wright, and she was taking up most of his spare time.

Right after Easter, I was walking to school with Cleve and Sally when we were nearly hit by an ambulance speeding down the valley road. There were a lot of elderly folks living in the valley, and after we regained our composure from the near miss, Sally speculated that one of the older folks must have taken sick.

Sally and Cleve had a special place where they stood and just looked at each other every morning before school started. They never did much except not-so-accidentally brush up against each other or hold hands. The older kids understood, but the younger ones always wanted to know what they were doing. About five minutes before the bell rang, I saw Burke Sanders's truck pull into the schoolyard. He looked around until he spotted Jake, who was standing with Edmund and Carter. Burke walked over to Jake and said something to him. Then Jake followed his father back to the truck. Edmund looked over at Cleve and motioned for Cleve to join him. The expression on Cleve's face told me something was wrong. I didn't think Burke's wife had been sick, but you never knew. I trotted over to Cleve.

"What's wrong?" I asked.

"Thomas is dead."

I felt like someone had knocked the wind out of me and didn't know what to say.

"Mr. Sanders said it was a tractor accident. Rolled over on him this morning."

"What about..."

"He didn't say. But I expect she won't be around much longer."

I only nodded. I didn't know the right thing to do or say. I still remembered when our mother had died, and the terrible feeling I had inside then. If Reiko Sanders felt half as bad as I had, she must be inconsolable.

The bell rang, and everyone began filing into school. Almost as soon as I entered the building, an impulse overtook me, and I left through a side door and sprinted into the trees behind the school. It was nearly six miles from the school to the Sanders farm. I would have made better time going down the main road, but someone might have seen me. Running as hard as I could, dodging branches and jumping over fallen trees, it took me well over an hour to reach the tree line overlooking the Sanders house. There was a sheriff's car parked in the drive near the front of the house, and the ambulance was backed into the field behind the house.

The tractor was on its side, and I saw two men with shovels digging under it. They stopped digging a few minutes later, and two other men pulled Thomas's body from beneath the tractor. Looking around, I didn't see Reiko or Tad anywhere in sight and hoped neither of them had been a witness to the accident. Even though Burke had picked Jake up, I didn't see his truck. Surely he would have come if his son had been killed. Thomas was covered with mud as they placed him on a stretcher and carried him to the ambulance. As they prepared to load his body into the vehicle, I finally saw Reiko and Tad. She had been standing on the other side of the ambulance and only came forward as the men approached with Thomas. She stopped them for a moment. She touched his face and leaned down to kiss him, picking Tad up to do the same before Thomas's body was taken away. I felt tears run down my cheek and quickly brushed them away. I wanted to go down and tell her how sorry I was but couldn't bring myself to move. As the ambulance pulled away, the sheriff came up to her with a pad in his hand. They were still talking as I began to retrace my steps away from their place.

Chapter
Nine

Friday, March 30, 1951

TWO DAYS LATER, I left school after lunch and walked through the woods to Sanders Cemetery. I stopped along the way to pick a handful of jonquils that had begun blooming at Easter. By the time I reached the cemetery, the service was nearly over, and I stood in the shadow of the pines as a silent, uninvited observer. There was a long line of cars parked along the road in front of the cemetery. Lots of folks paying their last respects to a man they wouldn't speak to when he was alive. Reiko and Tad sat alone facing the casket. She wore a calf-length plain black dress with a black veil that fell to her shoulders. She had dressed Tad in a suit, and the three year old looked uncomfortable although he didn't complain. Once he climbed into her lap and pointed at the flag-draped casket.

She whispered to him and held him in her lap. A military honor guard folded the flag that had covered the casket, and one of them knelt down and gave it to Reiko. The man stood, and in a gesture that made me feel good, saluted her. Tad stood on the chair next to her and saluted as well. It was a gesture that had to have broken the heart of anyone within viewing distance. Seven more men in uniforms fired their rifles in the air three times. The first shot startled me, and I thought I saw Reiko flinch as well. Somewhere I heard a trumpet playing softly and sadly but couldn't locate where the sound was coming from. When the final prayer was said, the well-wishers spent time consoling Thomas's parents and brother, but Reiko and Tad might as well have been invisible. The only person who spoke to her was the minister. She leaned over and said something to Tad, then got up, clutching the flag in one hand. She and Tad went to the coffin and bent down to kiss it.

When she stood up, she took Tad's hand and looked around. As she turned in my direction, she saw me and stared at me for a few moments, then nodded slightly before walking to the funeral home car and leaving. Gradually, the other mourners filtered out of the cemetery, and I waited until they were all gone before stepping out of the shadows. There were still a couple of men nearby who were preparing to fill the grave back in. I went to the casket and laid the jonquils on top of it, then turned and walked quickly away. I had promised my father I wouldn't go to the Sanders farm anymore, and I had kept my promise for nearly a year and a half. Now I knew I couldn't keep it any longer.

I saw the car from the funeral home pulling back onto the main road as I came out of the tree line and walked toward the back of the house. I still wasn't sure what to say but gathered myself together and knocked on the back door. When she opened the door, she was still in the black dress, but had removed the veil. Her face looked like porcelain, but I saw emptiness in her black eyes, and the sparkle I had seen the first time I saw her was gone.

"Ma'am," I said. "I just wanted to tell you how sorry I was about Thomas."

She nodded and pushed the screen door open for me to enter. As I stepped into the kitchen, I saw that there were no dishes of food like I had seen at other times when someone died.

"Would you like some tea?" she asked.

"Yes, ma'am. Where's Tad?"

"I put down for nap."

We didn't speak again until she poured the tea into two cups and sat down.

"Thank you for coming, Callie."

"Um, what are you plannin' to do now, ma'am? I mean are you goin' to stay here?"

"It is my husband's home," she said softly as she sipped her tea.

"If there's anything I can do to help, I'd be glad to do it."

"Thank you, but I don't want you to be in trouble."

"I'm almost grown. I can handle it," I said confidently.

She smiled at me. "I know."

"How about if I just check on you ever now and then? You might need somethin' from town or have some chores I can do for you."

"I cannot pay."

"I'm not lookin' for a job, ma'am," I said, looking insulted.

"Then I would like that. Thank you," she said again with a slight bow toward me.

Chapter
Ten

Tuesday, May 15, 1951

IT DIDN'T TAKE long for me to figure out that I might have bitten off more than I could chew. I still had school everyday, and Cleve and I had to work our own garden. As the daylight hours grew longer, I would finish my work at home and then head for the Sanders farm. I lied about where I was going, usually taking my rifle along on the pretext of squirrel hunting. When I did shoot something, I gave it to Reiko. Thomas had left some money, and I arranged to walk to town every other weekend to buy things she needed at the store.

There were days when I dozed off in school, and my grades suffered from my fatigue. In mid-May, as I was half-heartedly chewing on my sandwich and listening to Willie ramble on about something, I picked up parts of a conversation taking place at a table behind me.

"Well, it's about time. I wondered how long they would wait," a boy said in a low voice.

"They've just been waiting for folks to get over his death, I guess. But I heard my pa tell James that they were finally going to get rid of that bitch tonight," a second boy said.

"What are they gonna do?"

"I don't know. Maybe they'll burn her out. Then she'll have to go back where she come from."

"Man! I'd give anything to be there for that."

"I'll ask my pa. Maybe he'll let us go, if we promise to stay in the truck."

"When will we be old enough to join?"

"How old are you?"

"Sixteen."

"Then you gotta wait two more years. I can be official next year."

I knew what they were talking about, and the thought of it scared me. I knew I wouldn't be able to handle this alone.

"You ain't heard nothin' I said, Callie," Willie said.

"Yes, I did."

I picked up what was left of my sandwich and carried it to the trash, looking to see who the boys behind me were. I wasn't surprised to see Leo Harvey and Jeppie Leinart. I had heard my father call them white trash once. Both their daddies were drunk most of the time, and their houses were the disgrace of the valley.

When Cleve and I got home from school, I was relieved to see my father's truck parked next to the house. I ran ahead of Cleve and bounded in the back door.

"Pa!" I hollered.

"Up here!" he hollered back from upstairs.

I ran up the stairs and found him in his bedroom.

"You're home early," I said.

"Been working lots of overtime lately, so they give me the rest of the day off."

"What do you think about the Klan?" I blurted out.

He sat up on his bed and looked at me.

"Why?"

"I was just wonderin'," I shrugged.

"They ain't no good. I don't want you havin' nothin' to do with the likes of them. Buncha cowards runnin' around scarin' people. Hidin' behind them damn sheets like they was foolin' anybody."

"Are Mr. Harvey and Mr. Leinart in the Klan?"

"Probably. They're too lazy to do much else."

"If you knew they was plannin' to do somethin' real bad, what would you do?"

"I don't know. Might depend on what it was."

I frowned, no longer certain whether I should tell him what I overheard. Before I had a chance, Cleve joined us.

"We better jump on that garden, Callie, before the grass gets up to our knees," Cleve said.

"What are you tryin' to tell me, girl?" Pa asked as he stood up.

I'm a grown-up, I told myself. Pa had said so.

"I broke my promise, Pa. I been goin' over to the Sanders place and helpin' Mrs. Sanders with some chores around her place."

He frowned at me.

"You said I was an adult as long as I could handle the consequences of what I did."

"That's right."

"Well, the Klan is plannin' to burn her out tonight."

"Where did you hear that?" Cleve asked.

"At school. I heard Leo and Jeppie talkin' about it. I gotta help her out, Pa. If folks don't want to talk to her that's their business, and there ain't nothin' I can do about that. But this is different."

"You're right. It is. Do you know when this is supposed to happen?" Pa asked.

"All I heard was tonight. Should I call the sheriff?"

"What for?" he laughed. "He's one of 'em."

He looked at Cleve and said, "What do you think?"

"I could use a little exercise, so long as nobody saw me," Cleve said with a smile.

A LITTLE BEFORE dark, the three of us were making our way through the woods toward the Sanders farm. We didn't look like much of an army, but we knew we would be a surprise. When we reached the hill behind the house, my father stopped. There were lights on inside the house, and the only vehicle around was Thomas's truck.

"You go down and get her and the boy out of the house, Callie. Tell her what's goin' on if you have to. If this don't work out, they need to be outta there," Pa said.

As I started to go, he stopped me.

"You're doin' the right thing," he said with a wink.

I ran down the hill and knocked on the back door. When she opened it, she seemed surprised to see me there, panting for breath.

"You gotta get Tad and come with me, ma'am. Right now," I said as calmly as I could.

She looked at me and finally nodded. A few minutes later I led her and Tad back into the trees where Cleve and Pa were waiting. She stopped short when she saw them. I knew she trusted me, but her last experiences with my father hadn't been pleasant.

"It's okay," I said.

"Take her and the boy farther up," Pa said without acknowledging her. "And tell her to keep the boy quiet."

About a hundred yards farther up the ridge, I found an outcropping of rock and led them behind it.

"Stay here until I come for you," I said. "If I don't come, then you stay here until the sun comes up."

I rejoined Pa and Cleve, and we decided to spread out and take positions away from Reiko and Tad in case someone started shooting back at us. Just as we were getting ready to separate, Pa stopped us.

"Listen. This ain't gonna be no picnic. What we're gettin' ready to do is serious business. If we get caught, we won't be around to see the sun come up. But I don't want you two killin' no one. If shootin' around them don't drive 'em off, then try to just wound 'em. Understand?"

I don't think I had thought about shooting anyone until then and wasn't sure I could. There were serious consequences, indeed, when a grown-up made a decision. Pa picked a spot under the wagon next to the barn, and Cleve went to the far side of the house. The tractor that had killed Thomas was still on its side in the field behind the house, and I slid down into the depression where his body had been and shivered as I thought about it.

Nearly two hours passed, and I was beginning to think that Leo and Jeppie had made the whole thing up. I was getting tired and heard my stomach growling from hunger. Eventually, I laid my head down on my arm, and it was then that I felt the vibration. I didn't see it, but I heard it. Gravel being crushed under tires. I picked up my rifle and held it close to me. The lights inside the house were still on but only cast light a few feet. I couldn't see Pa or Cleve and hoped they were still there. Three vehicles came up the drive with their headlights off. A few minutes later, I saw a flash and suddenly the whole yard was lit up. One of the men had touched a torch to a large wooden cross and ignited it. More than a dozen men, dressed in white robes and hoods, encircled the house.

"Come out of the house!" one of them yelled.

I could see in the light from the cross and the torches they were carrying that at least half of them were armed with rifles and shotguns.

"Come out now or get burned out!" the same voice yelled.

I didn't know when or if I was supposed to start shooting, and I didn't know how this group operated, but I was afraid one of them was going to enter the house, or throw a torch inside.

"I reckon they can't hear too good neither," one of them laughed.

"Then let's drag the bitch out," another one yelled, taking a step toward the house.

I heard a rifle shot, and suddenly their attention was diverted from the house.

"She's shootin' at us," someone hollered. For a moment, they didn't seem to know what to do. One of them aimed a shotgun toward the back door. Before he could fire, I heard another rifle shot, and the man screamed.

"The bitch shot me!"

I figured I had waited long enough and fired my rifle, hitting the dirt at the feet of one of the men near the back of the house.

"She can't be the only one here," someone called out.

So far there had only been random fire from any of us. Suddenly a bullet ricocheted off the tractor, and I wasn't sure if it was a wild shot or not. Pa fired at the man who had shot in my direction and struck him in the leg. I was still scared, but anger at the whole situation was gradually taking over. I fired another shot and hit one of the men at the rear of the house in the leg. I felt good when I saw him fall.

As soon as the first man had been hit, they began to scatter, but their white robes made it easy to spot them. I was even thankful for the burning cross in the yard. It illuminated everything, and it occurred to me that it was a stupid thing to give your enemy enough light to see you. Of course, I was sure it worked much better when you were only dealing with women and children.

By that point, Cleve, Pa, and I were shooting at anything that moved. A few shots were returned, but they seemed confused more than anything else. In less than ten minutes, they were scurrying back

into their trucks, and hauling ass away from the house. When he was
sure they were all gone, Pa crawled out from under the wagon and
walked to the side of the house.

"Cleve?"

"Yeah, Pa."

"Callie?"

"Here, Pa."

"You can come out now. They're gone."

When we joined him, he was looking at the cross, still burning in
the yard.

"Sacrilege," he muttered. "Scarin' folks in God's name."

He stuck a foot against the cross and pushed it over.

"Now what?" Cleve asked.

"I don't think they'll be back tonight. That don't mean they won't
try again another night though," Pa said.

He turned to me and said, "We can't be runnin' over here ever
time, Callie."

"I know."

"How many you reckon we shot?" Cleve asked.

"Looked like about half," Pa said. Then he smiled. "Guess we'll
have to go into town tomorrow, and see who all's limpin' around."

We all started laughing, more from relief that it was over for the
moment than anything else.

"Go fetch the woman," he said to me. "But we can never talk to
anyone about what happened here tonight. Not even to each other.
And she can't either."

I nodded and ran up the hill. When I came around the outcropping, Reiko had Tad behind her to protect him and had found a tree
branch to use as a club. She almost hit me before she recognized me. I
helped her up and picked Tad up. We slowly made our way back to
the house.

Cleve was leaning against his rifle, and Pa was throwing water on
the cross.

"Ma'am," Cleve said as we passed him.

She nodded to him and stopped to look at Pa. He saw her but once
again refused to speak to her. She nodded toward him and took Tad
from me. I didn't understand how Pa could save her life and then
refuse to speak to her. He had always taught us to do the right thing,
and I suppose that's what he had done. It didn't mean he liked doing
it, and I knew he had taken no pleasure from shooting his neighbors.

"Thank you," she said softly.

"You'll be okay tonight, but it could happen again," I said.

"I will not leave my husband's home," she said flatly.

She carried Tad into the house, and I waited for Pa to rejoin us.
When he did, he looked around and squinted a little as he pulled his
tobacco and paper from his shirt pocket and neatly rolled a cigarette.

"You stayin' here tonight?" he asked me as he struck a match with his thumbnail and lit the cigarette.

"Yessir."

"Well," he said as he turned to walk away, "don't be late for school tomorrow." Cleve smiled at me as he ran to catch up with Pa.

Chapter
Eleven

THAT NIGHT I fell asleep between stacks of hay bales, waking periodically when I heard something. I don't know what time I finally fell asleep for the last time, but I was awakened by something hitting my leg. I grabbed my rifle and found myself pointing it at Tad.

"No!" I heard Reiko scream.

I was breathless as I lowered the rifle. He looked confused, looking first at me and then at his mother.

"It's okay," I said, trying to be calm and stop my arms from shaking.

Reiko rushed to where I was laying.

"I'm sorry," I said, scooting out from behind the hay bales.

"You sleep here all night?" she asked as Tad wrapped his arms around her leg.

"Yes, ma'am. I didn't mean to scare you."

"Come," she said as she picked Tad up and walked out of the barn.

I brushed hay out of my hair and off my overalls, stumbling as I followed her to the house. In the daylight, I saw the remains of the burned cross and saw that one of the chestnut trees near it had been scorched. The house didn't seem to be damaged, not even a bullet hole as far as I could tell. I stopped to stomp the dirt off my shoes before I opened the back door. When I got inside, she was setting a plate on the kitchen table and motioned for me to sit. There was an old icebox against the wall near the door, and I placed my rifle on top of it.

"What time is it?" I asked.

"Seven," she said as she moved gracefully about the kitchen.

"I gotta go. I'll be late for school."

"Sit first. Eat breakfast."

I was hungry and figured if I ate real fast, I could still make it. She poured coffee in a cup for me, and within minutes there were eggs on my plate. I ate quickly and wiped my mouth with my sleeve. Realizing my bad manners, I looked at her and smiled sheepishly.

"Sorry."

"Thank you for last night," she said softly. "Your father and brother, too."

"You can't never tell anyone who was here last night," I said as I got up from the table.

She nodded.

"I wish it was different, ma'am, but it ain't," I continued. "You got a rifle or shotgun here?"

"My husband had rifle," she answered.

"You know how to use it?"

She shook her head, and I took a deep breath.

"I'll be back later. I can teach you."

I picked up my rifle and saw Tad standing by the back door, looking at me. I smiled at him on my way out and tousled his hair, which made him giggle.

There was a lot of talk around school about what had happened at the Sanders farm the night before, and it didn't take a mental giant to figure out whose fathers had been involved. Cleve and I sympathized with the boys as they recounted what sounded like a Civil War battle. There was some speculation about who had helped her out, but no one had seen who it was. Someone even started a rumor that more Japs had sneaked into the valley after the war and were hiding out in the woods.

On our way home, Cleve and I laughed so hard that we could barely walk.

"Well, I have to admit it was fun," Cleve laughed. "Wished I knew which ones I got, though."

"Maybe they'll form one of them veterans' groups. Survivors of the Battle of Frost Valley."

"You goin' back over there?"

"I promised to teach her how to shoot Thomas's rifle. You're the best shot in the valley, maybe you should do it."

"I done all I could last night, Callie."

We climbed through a fence next to the road and started across the field leading to our house.

"You done the right thing," Cleve said. "Which makes you either the bravest kid I ever knew, or the stupidest. Sooner or later someone is gonna find out about your goin' over there."

I knew Pa was right about the Klan coming back. The next time I might not be lucky enough to overhear something that would tip it off. It was only a matter of time before they worked up enough courage to do something else.

BY THE TIME school ended for the year, Reiko was a fair shot with a rifle, but I didn't think there was any way she could defend herself if she was alone and more than one person showed up. And I couldn't spend the rest of my life sleeping in her barn or on the ridge behind her house.

I didn't know anyone except Pa who would know what to do, but I was reluctant to ask his advice. If it was true that the sheriff was a member of the Klan or ignored what they did, it would have been useless to contact him. I thought of everyone I knew and couldn't think of anyone who would be willing to help.

Her garden was better looking than any I had seen around. It was a huge garden for one person to tend, but she worked on it every day. She even got Tad to help out by pulling up the grass as she hoed. I would've asked her if she used some secret ingredient in the soil but didn't want her to think she knew more than I did about farming. There was still sporadic mischief around her place, probably done by kids with nothing else to do, although nothing as serious as the Klan. One night, someone turned a few goats loose in her garden, and by morning they had managed to destroy a pretty big chunk of it. She seemed to take it all in stride and simply replanted. I thought she was the most patient, persistent person I had ever met, man or woman. The thing that amazed me the most was how seldom she spoke. I knew she spoke good English, but we spent most of our time working in the garden or making repairs to equipment and outbuildings. She had decided to paint the barn, which seemed ridiculous to me. People in the valley never painted their barn. Just slapped them up and waited thirty or forty years for them to start leaning and fall down. Then they built a new one. She ordered red paint from a mail order catalog, and after a couple of weeks, we finally finished. Reiko had the stamina of two men and never seemed to get tired.

By mid-June, her garden was producing more than she would be able to eat or put up. I took some of it home, and nobody asked where I got it. She worried that most of her produce would rot.

Chapter
Twelve

Tuesday, June 19, 1951

"WHY'D YOU PLANT so much?" I asked her as I straightened up and leaned on my hoe, stretching the kinks out of my back.

"Nothing grow if seeds not sown," Reiko answered.

"Next time you might want to sow fewer seeds, ma'am."

"Thomas said to sell at market in town."

"The Farmer's Market?"

"Yes."

"You know they ain't gonna buy it from you," I said matter-of-factly.

"Yes, I know," she said sadly. "You could sell."

I laughed. "Nobody's gonna believe we grew this in our garden. Besides, we never sell anything at the market."

"You sell. I give you half the money."

There wasn't any question that we could use the extra money, but I didn't have a way to get the vegetables into town.

"Thomas's truck," she said.

The truck hadn't been moved since he died, and I doubted it would even start after sitting around for so long.

"Can you drive?" I asked.

She shook her head.

"Neither can I," I shrugged.

"I watch Thomas."

"You got the key?"

She went into the house and returned a few minutes later with a key ring. There must have been twenty keys on it. I looked at her.

"One of these," she said as she handed them to me.

We walked to the truck, and I pulled the driver's door open with a creak. Settling behind the wheel, I took one key at a time until I found one that would fit the ignition. There were three pedals on the floor, and I wasn't sure whether I had to push one of them to start the vehicle or not. Reiko was standing in front of the truck, and I motioned her to one side just to be safe. I turned the key, and the truck lurched forward a little. Every time I turned the key, the truck jumped. I had watched Pa drive our truck lots of times but hadn't paid much attention to what his feet were doing. Reiko came to the door and pointed to the gearshift.

"Thomas put on N," she said.

I found the clutch and shifted the gear to neutral and tried again. The truck started but died within a few seconds. One of the pedals on the floor had to be a gas pedal. The second time I started the truck I tapped on the pedals, finding the right one on the first try. The truck idled roughly, but it was running.

"Get in," I said with a broad smile.

She smiled and opened the passenger door, handing Tad up to me and climbed in. It took a little experimentation on my part to get the hang of changing the gears, but it was really easy. We traveled around the barn and across the bumpy field. Tad thought the bouncing was great fun, and she had to hang onto him to keep him from being thrown from the seat. I tried all the letters on the gearshift to get a feel for the truck. I finally stopped and turned off the ignition.

"You try," I said.

"Oh, no," she said shaking her head.

"You need to be able to get away from here if you have to. What if Tad gets sick, and I'm not around?"

She thought about it for a minute and got out of the truck. I slid across the seat and sat Tad on my lap as she got behind the wheel. I figured it couldn't hurt since there wasn't anything to run into in the field anyway. She listened intently as I gave her a few instructions. We lurched and stopped a dozen times, and I thought she was going to give up. Now, I think she was actually having fun. It was the first time I had seen her really laugh since Thomas died. She never got above ten miles an hour, but she was moving. Tad clapped his hands and was having a fine old time.

We practiced driving around the field for half an hour. I wished we could go onto the main road, but it was too dangerous. She stopped the truck next to the barn, and we got out.

"You use truck for market," she said.

"I can't, ma'am," I said. "I ain't got a license. But I know someone who does."

That night when we were alone, I explained my plan to Cleve. If we got up before daylight, he could drive me and Reiko's vegetables to the market in Thomas's truck. We would be there before anyone else, and he would be gone in case someone recognized the truck. After I sold everything, I would walk home.

"That's crazy, Callie. And Pa would have a stroke if he found out," Cleve said.

"I'll give you half of my half of the money, Cleve. I can't do it by myself, and if anyone caught her on the road, they'd run her off into a ditch for sure."

"And if they figure out them's her vegetables, they'll string you up in the nearest tree for sure."

"How'll anyone know? One damn tomato looks pretty much like another. It ain't like I'm gonna stick little labels on 'em sayin' 'Made in Japan.'"

"How you gonna explain how you got that stuff into town?"

"If anyone asks, I'll tell 'em Pa dropped me off on his way to work."

"You better hope nobody tells him how much they enjoy anything they buy."

He thought for a few minutes.

"I'll do it once, but no more. Understand?"

The next Friday evening we put the produce in baskets and loaded them on the back of the truck.

Chapter
Thirteen

Saturday, June 23, 1951

AT FOUR IN the morning Saturday, Cleve and I pulled out of the drive from the Sanders farm and headed for town. Cleve didn't turn on the headlights until we were on the main road in case anyone was up early. We unloaded the truck in record time, and Cleve left. I did the best I could at arranging the vegetables for sale, and since I was the first one there, I got a jump on everybody else. By one in the afternoon, everything was sold, and I had about ten dollars in my pocket. I was back in the valley by four and cut through the woods to reach the Sanders place. Setting the baskets down, I knocked on the back door. When she opened the door, I handed her the money.

"Ten bucks," I said with a smile.

She counted it out on the kitchen table and handed me half. I suddenly felt guilty about taking it but stuck it in my pocket anyway. I glanced at the clock on the kitchen wall.

"I better get on home. I still gotta work on our garden."

"Thank you, Callie."

"It's okay, ma'am."

She touched my arm as I turned to go.

"Reiko, please," she said.

I nodded and went out the back door and headed for the path I was creating in the tree line. Cleve was so impressed with his two-fifty for doing almost nothing that he agreed to drive the truck a few more times. Every Saturday morning, I set up in a corner of the Farmer's Market and never had a bit of trouble selling everything.

BY THE END of July, most of the gardens were about gone, and I was finishing up my last trip to the market. For two or three weeks, I had seen a group of boys watching me. Two of the boys were Leo and Jeppie, and I guessed the others were friends of theirs, but they didn't live in the valley. That last week it seemed that every time I turned around they were staring at me. Finally, Leo came over to where I was selling.

"Nice lookin' stuff, Callie. Where'd you get it?"

"We grew it."

"That's bullshit! I seen the garden at your place. You're barely growing enough to feed your own family."

"We got another garden. You musta missed it."

He leaned forward. "You're selling this for that Jap bitch, ain'tcha?"

"No," I answered flatly.

"Well, that was Thomas Sanders' truck that brung you here this morning. Your pa buy it?"

"No. My pa brung me here in his truck on his way to work."

"How stupid do you think I am? I saw you. Got up especially early just to see."

"Well, that's pretty stupid all right. Maybe your eyes wasn't working right, what with the dark and all."

"I know you're helpin' that bitch, Callie, and when I can prove it, your life won't be worth livin'."

"You don't know shit, Leo. So leave me alone."

He laughed and wandered off to rejoin his friends. Leo was Cleve's age and not much smarter than your average cucumber, but I was glad it was the last week I would be in town for a while.

At two-thirty, I stacked up my baskets and headed back home. Just outside of town, there was a shortcut through the woods that saved me nearly a mile of walking. It was cool in the shade of the trees, and there was a creek that cut across the side of the ridge. It was a good place to stop and rest, and sometimes I'd pull my shoes and socks off and wade a while. The water was very cold but always felt good in the summer. I dropped down on the ground, and let the water run over my feet. Pa said there was an underground river somewhere beneath the ridge, and that's why the water in the creek was cold year round. One day, I'd follow the creek to see if that was true. Not that I thought Pa was lying, I just wanted to see for myself. My thoughts were interrupted by the sound of leaves being crushed behind me. I looked around and saw Leo and Jeppie and their friends.

"I figured you'd take this shortcut," Leo said.

"Then maybe you ain't as stupid as I thought," I said.

Jeppie reached down and pulled me up by my overalls.

"Let's see the money you got today," he said.

"Why?" I asked, trying not to act afraid.

"'Cause you ain't takin' another dollar to that bitch," Leo said.

That was the third time he had called her that, and I was almost to the point where I wasn't going to be able to ignore it.

"It's mine, and I ain't gotta show you nothin'," I said.

"Hand it over, or we'll take it," Jeppie said.

"And I'll have the sheriff over to visit you tonight," I said trying to break Jeppie's hold on my overalls.

Leo laughed. "Sheriff ain't gonna believe you. I got all these witnesses who'll swear we never seen you today. Besides, he's a friend of my father's and don't like the bitch any more than we do."

That was one time too many. I swung my fist as hard as I could and was surprised that it actually hit Leo. The fact that Jeppie was holding onto the back of my overall kept me from losing my balance. Jeppie was surprised as well and released me as Leo got up rubbing his jaw.

"You learn that sneak attack shit from that Jap, Callie?" he asked.

"I don't need no one to teach me how to deal with white trash like you," I said while trying to keep an eye on all five of them.

Even though I managed to get in a couple of decent blows, there was no way I was going to win that fight. In the end, two of them grabbed me and held me down as Leo went through my pockets and took the twenty dollars I had gotten that day.

"Get her up," Leo said.

He counted the money in front of me and stuck it in his pocket.

"You know, Callie, it ain't the money I'm after," he said, standing in front of me.

"Then give it back."

"No, what I really want is for you to admit that you've been helpin' that bitch. To admit that you're a Jap lover just like Thomas was."

I didn't say anything but managed to wiggle around a little.

"How about it, Callie?" he asked leaning closer to me.

I didn't have anything else, so I spit in his face. A split second later, there were stars dancing across my eyes as the back of Leo's hand met the front of my face. The others released me, and I fell to my knees. Jeppie grabbed my hair and pulled my head up.

"We can beat it out of you if that's what you want," he said.

"Go to hell," I managed to croak, tasting the blood in my mouth.

What followed was a second strong hit to my face that split my lip and made my nose bleed. Leo's friends jerked me off the ground and had to support me.

"What about now?" Leo asked. "Had enough?"

I shook my head to clear my mind. "I had enough of you, asshole! Let me go!"

"A couple more like that, and she'll be ready to spill her guts," Leo said.

The boys holding me laughed.

"My turn," Jeppie said.

Jeppie grabbed the front of my shirt and seemed to be aiming his fist at me. I saw the fist coming and moved my head so that his blow deflected off the side of my face and hit the boy on my right.

"You stupid asshole!" the boy hollered as he released my arm to feel his face. "Jesus Christ, how can you miss a target that ain't even movin'?"

With only one of them holding me, I slumped to the ground and started laughing.

"You think this is funny?" Leo said as he kicked me. I thought I heard a rib crack and grabbed my side.

I felt hands grabbing me again when a shot rang out, scattering birds from the surrounding trees.

"Let her go!" I heard Cleve yell.

"This ain't none of your business, Cleve," Leo yelled back.

"The hell it ain't. That's my sister you're beatin' up."

"She's helpin' the Sanders bitch."

"No, she ain't. Now back off."

"And what if I don't? You gonna shoot me?"

"You know I'm the best squirrel hunter in the county, Leo. And you're a helluva lot bigger than a squirrel. But you know, I been havin' a little trouble with my eyes lately. I could mistake your furry pansy ass for a squirrel."

"You gonna mistake us for five squirrels?" Leo smirked as he looked at the other boys.

"Good point," Cleve said as he came down the hillside still pointing his rifle at Leo. "But now that I think about it, this little crick is an offshoot of an underground river near here. Been there once. I could drop you in a sinkhole near it, and in a week or so, folks over in Carolina would be wondering where the hell your bodies come from." Cleve took aim with his rifle. "That what you want, Leo?"

"No."

"Then back off!"

Leo motioned to the others, and they started to walk away.

"My money," I said hoarsely, trying to breathe without aggravating the stabbing pain in my side.

"Give her back her money," Cleve ordered.

Leo took the money from his pocket and threw it on the ground next to me.

"Oh, and Leo," Cleve smiled. "If I catch you so much as lookin' at me or anyone else in my family, you're gonna be one sorry squirrel."

Cleve watched them until they disappeared and then helped me up.

"How bad you hurt?" he asked as he squatted down next to me.

"I don't know. Might of broke a rib."

He helped me get my shoes back on, and leaving the baskets behind, he half carried me back to the valley. I was surprised when he cut through the woods above the Sanders farm and took me to Reiko's house. Still supporting me, he banged on the back door with the butt of his rifle.

"She's hurt," Cleve said as she opened the back door.

He handed her his rifle and picked me up in his arms and carried me into the house. She led him into the living room.

"Put her on couch," she said.

This was the second time I had been hurt when I was on that couch. Within minutes, she was wiping my face with a cool cloth. Only my left eye would open completely, and I looked at Cleve.

"I hope you learned your lesson today, Callie. Bein' around her is gonna get you killed someday."

She looked at him and then back at me. I reached into my pocket and handed the bills to her.

"What happen?" she asked.

"Some boys beat her up tryin' to get her to say she was helpin' you."

"This my fault. You go home and don't come back."

"It ain't your fault, Reiko," I said, feeling the swelling on my bottom lip.

"Yes, it is," Cleve said.

"Shut up, Cleve," I snapped, wincing at the sudden movement along the side of my chest.

"Brother right," Reiko frowned

"She thinks she's got a broke rib," Cleve said.

Before I could object, Reiko had unfastened my overalls and was unbuttoning my shirt. I grabbed her hand.

"What're you doin'?" I asked.

"Must wrap ribs," she said.

"That's okay. I'll be fine," I said rebuttoning my shirt.

"Let her wrap it, Callie. You afraid she's gonna see somethin' she don't already know about?"

"I said it's okay," I glared at my brother.

"You get something for a wrappin', ma'am. I'll take care of this," Cleve said. Kneeling down in front of me, he looked up at her and grinned. "She's just a little shy is all."

I gave up arguing with Cleve. Most of the fight was gone from my body, and I was suddenly sleepy. It had been the longest day of my life.

Chapter
Fourteen

Friday, October 19, 1951

THAT FALL SEEMED to pass slower than usual. Farmers were busy turning their fields over preparing for their winter planting. The tobacco crop had been decent, and by the end of summer, Pa had finally managed to feel a little more at ease about our financial situation. We all got new shoes for school in the first time I could remember, and Pa had begun to kid around with us more than he had since before Ma died. Cleve and I took on more of the work around the farm, and my brothers and sisters were getting big enough to take care of things Cleve and I didn't want to do, like cooking and cleaning and washing. We had spent almost the whole summer and early fall tending Pa's tobacco fields. There was good money in it, but I hated the tobacco worms. They were gross little critters that seemed intent on living in our fields. My fingers were stained dark brown from pinching the worms' heads off between my thumb and index fingers. No matter how much lye soap I used, nothing seemed to remove the stains.

Cleve was a good tobacco man, and when we picked the last leaves and laid them out to dry in the barn, he smiled."In a month or two, I'll get Pa to haul these over to Knoxville. You done good, Callie."

Praise from my oldest brother meant as much to me as anything else I could think of. Somehow, it made me feel as if I had contributed to our family and helped keep it together. Ma always said that family was everything, and as long as we had that we would always be rich. I felt rich as I stripped off my work overalls and slipped into the tub to soak, hoping that the stains on my fingers would eventually fade and return to normal before the next year. I'd seen old men at the market before whose hands would always be the color of tobacco. Bringing my hands out of the water, I stared at them and turned them over to take in their lines. My fingers were long, just like Pa's, but my palms were calloused from working in the fields with Cleve. Rubbing the palm of my right hand with my fingertips, I kind of liked the feel of the calluses, which were proof of hard work. No matter what I did, I always had cuts on my hands. Most of them were healed now, but I could see the faint lines left by the cuts from plants and tools carelessly used. Working in the fields had caused my hands to crack some, allowing the dirt to work its way into the wounds, the soil becoming a permanent part of my body that would never go away. Running my thumb lightly over the tips of my other fingers as they soaked, I was amazed at how sensitive my fingertips were. They hurt a little, but this was a different kind of feeling. It seemed silly at the time, but I discovered that I liked the feeling my sense of touch gave me on the inside.

On a Friday near the middle of the month, Pa helped Annie and Katie clear the table that evening before going out on the porch and lighting his usual after-dinner cigarette. Cleve and I joined him a few minutes later after making sure the last of our chores were completed. I watched as Pa sat easily on the railing around the porch, squinting as smoke from the cigarette curled lazily around his head. I loved the smell of tobacco burning and wished I could share a cigarette with Pa. I knew he knew that Cleve and I were smoking, but so far neither one of us could bring ourselves to smoke in front of Pa. I saw the tip of his homemade cigarette glow in the dusky evening as he filled his lungs with smoke from the tobacco we had grown. He saw me looking longingly at his cigarette and smiled.

"Good crop this year. Ya'll tried it yet?" he asked.

Clearing his throat and glancing at me, Cleve shoved his hands in his pockets and said, "Some."

"Well, don't get carried away," Pa said, a blue cloud leaving his lips along with the words. Looking at Cleve and then at me, he smiled broadly, "Beats the hell outta cornsilk though, don't it?"

We laughed and chatted for a few minutes until Pa finished his cigarette.

"I'm...uh...goin' to town for a little while. You two be okay here with the little ones?" he asked as he slid off the railing and hiked his trousers up.

"Yes, sir," we nodded.

Striding across the porch, he kissed us both on the forehead as he headed back into the house where he hugged and kissed the others, reminding them to mind us. Not long after Pa drove our old truck down the dirt and gravel road, my sisters and I cleaned up the dining room and washed all the dishes from dinner. Cleve took Willie and Mack out to carry in coal for the potbelly stove in the kitchen. Our house, which had been built by my grandfather and great-grandfather from trees cut and milled right there in Frost Valley, sat back into the trees far enough that the house remained in the shade until nearly noon every day. Although it felt good, the early mornings were always slightly nippy, and just about every morning Pa started a small coal fire in the old stove.

Since Cleve and I were in charge of our younger brothers and sisters, we decided that it would be a good night for storytelling. Cleve got a small fire going in the parlor fireplace as we all huddled near it. After turning off the remaining lights in the house, Cleve sat on the floor in front of the fire. As usual, Willie insisted on sitting on my lap.

"Did you know that someone killed themselves in this old house?" Cleve smiled.

I remembered hearing something about that when I was about Willie's age, five or six, but didn't remember the details.

"They did not," Mack laughed.

"Yeah, they sure did, Mack," Cleve frowned, looking serious. "It was a lady who was some relation to us, named Lena Robbins. I think she was one of Grandma's cousins or something."

"What happened to her?" Willie asked as his eyes began to grow wide, and he scooted closer into me.

"Well, let's see," Cleve thought, scratching his head. "Mama told me the story, so I hope I can get it right. It seems that Lena was only about twenty, and she had this sweetheart, Gratz Pemberton."

"He related to those Pembertons at the other end of the valley?" Katie asked.

"Could be," Cleve said. "But anyway, it turns out that Gratz was keeping time with Miss Lena, and they was supposed to get married. Only problem was that Gratz was keeping time with a few other ladies in town as well."

"He was cheating on her?" Annie frowned.

"Sure was. I reckon he hadn't sowed all of his wild oats yet."

"What's wild oats?" Willie piped up.

"That just means he wasn't ready to settle down and get married right then," I explained, hoping Willie wouldn't ask any more questions.

"Anyhow," Cleve said taking a deep breath as he winked at me, "Miss Lena found out what Gratz was doing behind her back. And she was so heartbroken that she up and drank a bottle of poison Grandma kept for baitin' field mice and killed herself."

"What did Gratz do?" Katie chimed in.

"I don't know, Katie. He just disappeared and nobody ever saw him again."

Just as the mumbling started about the anti-climatic end of the story, Cleve said in a low voice, "But Miss Lena is still out there huntin' for him."

Willie grabbed my leg and squeezed it hard. "But you said she was dead."

"Oh, she is, Willie," Cleve said, leaning closer to Willie. "But her spirit didn't die. And every night Miss Lena is out there, walking through the woods, carrying a lantern, and searching for her faithless lover."

"You're lyin'," Mack said bravely.

"You ever been to the barn or gettin' firewood at night and seen a light across the valley movin' through the woods?" Cleve asked, his face a mask of seriousness.

"Of course I have, but that's just some hunter out runnin' his hounds," Mack grinned. "I asked Pa."

"Did you hear the hounds bayin'?"

Mack had to think about that one for a minute.

"Well, did ya'?" Cleve prodded.

"I don't remember."

"You couldn't miss the sound of coon hounds around here, Mack. Some hunter goes out, and he takes at least a dozen hounds with him. They're loud enough to wake...well...the dead."

I could feel Willie's fingers digging into my leg. "It's just a story, Willie," I said, frowning at Cleve. "You don't believe in ghosts, now do you?"

"You're scaring Mack and Willie," Annie said. "Now, they'll have nightmares for sure."

"They'll be okay," Cleve laughed. Then he stopped and looked menacingly at our youngest brothers. "But I'd keep my window shut at night if I was you, just in case Miss Lena decides to come floatin' in to see her old house."

After that night, it was nearly a month before we were able to convince them that, even though the story about Miss Lena and how she died was true, there were no ghosts in the woods at night or in the house.

It was nine by the time I herded everyone upstairs to begin their bedtime ritual of tooth brushing and bathing while Cleve checked around the house inside and out to make sure everything was the way it was supposed to be. By ten, Cleve and I were sound asleep, looking forward to a weekend that would be free of work. I was exhausted even though I loved working in the fields. The soil would need the winter to recuperate before the spring planting began again in a few months.

I didn't know what time it was, but a strange sound shook me out of a dreamless sleep. Propping myself up on my elbows, I closed my eyes and listened in the darkness. There it was again, a moaning sound like someone was hurt. Maybe Willie or one of the others was having a nightmare from the ghost stories we had told them earlier. I threw the quilt back and swung my bare feet to the floor, glancing across the small room at Cleve who was still sound asleep. I tiptoed to the bedroom door and cracked it open a hair before going out into the hall. I checked Katie and Annie's room, which was quiet except for the sounds of their soft snoring. Willie and Mack were in the room across the hall from the girls, and my hand just reached their doorknob when I heard the moaning sound again, only louder than before. It was coming from Pa's room, and it didn't even sound like him.

I went to the door of his bedroom and listened. I heard him wrestling around in the covers and moaning. He said he was going to town earlier, but maybe he'd got hold of some bad moonshine. Returning to my room, I knelt down next to Cleve and shook him. He rolled away from me and smacked his lips together loudly as he readjusted his body, still asleep. I could hear the sounds from Pa's room even more clearly now and was getting scared. I shook Cleve harder.

"Cleve!" I whispered as loud as I dared. "Cleve, wake up. Somethin's wrong with Pa. He's sick."

Blinking and rubbing his eyes, Cleve turned his head toward me. "What?"

"Pa's sick. He's in his room, moanin' real bad. You better go check him," I whispered.

The night had turned cool, but Cleve was wearing only his boxers as his feet quickly hit the floor and went out our bedroom door. I wasn't far behind him, nearly tripping over Ma's old nightgown that was still too big for my twelve-year-old body. Pa let out a loud moan as we approached his door.

"See, I told you," I whispered, grabbing hold of Cleve's arm.

Cleve stopped outside our father's bedroom door and leaned closer to listen. A moment later, he stood up straight and spun around, grabbing me by the shoulders and spinning me away from Pa's room. "Go on back to bed," he whispered as he pushed me down the hall.

"But Pa's...," I started as I planted my bare feet firmly on the wood floor.

"Pa's fine, Callie," he insisted with the hint of a grin. "Trust me, he's just fine."

"But..."

"Just go," he said, looking back at the door, "before he hears us and comes out to see what's goin' on."

Cleve closed our bedroom door and flopped on his bed. I lay down, still feeling uneasy about Pa. He was all we had. A few minutes later the house was quiet again, but as I rolled over to try to go back to sleep, I heard Cleve chuckle slightly. It hadn't been funny, dammit, I thought. If anything ever happened to Pa I didn't know what would become of us.

WITHOUT FIELDWORK TO do for the first weekend in months, I slept longer than I should have. Cleve was already gone from our room by the time I pulled on clean overalls and bounded downstairs. I would check on Pa later and make sure he had gotten over whatever had made him sick the night before. As I turned a corner leading into our kitchen, I stopped in my tracks. I looked around before backing slowly away and going quickly to the closet inside the front door where Pa kept his rifle. I pulled it out and checked to see that it was loaded as I made my way carefully back toward the kitchen. Standing just inside the door, I raised Pa's rifle to my shoulder and said as calmly as I could, "Don't move, or I'll blow your head clean off."

The woman stood still for a moment before she finally spoke. "I'm not here to harm you, girl. Preston invited me."

"Turn around real slow," I ordered. "Who are you?"

The woman turned to look at me and a slow smile crossed her bright red lips. "My name is Lil. Which one are you?"

She was wearing a solid red dress with matching high heels, and her hair was a mass of curls the color of corn silk. Her eyes were a bright blue that stood out against the dress and light hair.

"Can I put my hands down now?" she asked softly.

I nodded as I glanced around the kitchen. "Where's Pa?"

"He took your brother to get some firewood. They should be back any time now, I hope. Are you hungry?"

While I was trying to decide what I should do next, I heard the back door open. Pa and Cleve walked in with their arms loaded with wood and stopped and stared at me.

"Callie," Pa said calmly, "it's okay. Lower that rifle before your finger gets a twitch."

Looking at him, I slowly lowered the rifle and saw the woman lower her hands and take a relieved breath. "Thank God!" she said.

Pa dropped the wood into a box near the kitchen door and walked over to me, carefully taking the rifle from my hands as he looked over his shoulder at the woman. "I'm sorry about this, Lil."

"It's okay, sugar. Not the first time a female's got the drop on me, but they're usually older," she smiled. "I'll rustle up some breakfast."

"Cleve, you and Callie go on and get the others up," Pa said.

As I followed Cleve out of the room, I turned and saw Pa walk up behind the woman. Slipping a big hand around her waist, he pulled her closer to whisper something in her ear that made her laugh.

"Who is that?" I asked Cleve as we climbed the stairs.

"She was with Pa last night. I seen her around town a few times," he answered over his shoulder.

"She was here last night?"

"Yeah, I reckon she took care of Pa last night...when he was sick," Cleve smiled.

"She made him feel better?"

"Looks like she sure did better than that 'cause he's in a real good mood this morning."

It was a few more years before I figured out what Lil did to make Pa feel good and to learn that moaning didn't necessarily mean you were sick.

Chapter
Fifteen

Wednesday, February 20, 1952

THE WINTER OF late 1951 and early 1952 was the worst one anyone could remember. The snow was so deep we could barely get out
the doors of our house. Wind blew the snow into drifts that covered a
whole side of the house. Pa hadn't been able to get out to go to work,
but when he tried to call in, there wasn't anyone there. Every road in
the county was covered with record depth snow over a thick layer of
ice, and nothing could move. The snow around our house was too
deep for the younger kids to get out into, and it took an enormous
effort for Pa, Cleve, or me to make it to the woodpile for more wood.
At one time, some of the folks in Frost Valley had sleighs, but by 1952
most had quit using them.

The second day we were housebound, I thought Pa looked funny
as we were eating dinner.

"You okay, Pa?" I asked.

"Yeah," he said. "Just a touch of indigestion or somethin'."

After dinner, my sister Katie helped me clean up the kitchen
before going to the living room to listen to the radio. *Green Lantern* was
my favorite program, and it was nearly time for it to come on. Pa was
lying on the couch with his arm over his eyes. Periodically, I would
see him place a hand on his lower abdomen and shift his weight on the
couch searching unsuccessfully for a more comfortable position. After
Green Lantern, I played a card game with Willie and Mack, while Cleve
cleaned his rifle for the second time that day. It had only been two
days, but we were all beginning to suffer from cabin fever. By nine
o'clock, we trooped up the stairs to get ready for bed. Maybe the next
day the sun would break through the clouds and start melting the
snow.

When my eyes opened the next morning, Willie was staring down
at me.

"What do you want?" I rasped as I rolled over in my bed to keep
warm.

"Pa's sick," he said in a small voice.

"His stomach still botherin' him?" I said, sitting up.

"Cleve said for you to come down for breakfast."

"What about Pa?"

"Cleve took breakfast up to him already."

Willie ran out of the room, and I heard his footsteps as he went down the stairs. I swung my legs out of the bed and stepped into my overalls. The floor beneath my feet was cold, and I took a pair of clean socks from the dresser I shared with Cleve. Combing my hair with my fingers, I went down the hall to Pa's room. The door was partially ajar already, and I pushed it open far enough to look in. It was cold in his room, but I could see from a distance that his face was flushed, with little beads of sweat on his forehead. He saw me as I looked in.

"Mornin', Callie," he said with a weak smile.

"Willie says you're not feelin' any better."

"Might be the flu or somethin'. Can't seem to get rid of this damn bellyache, either."

I went to his bedside and touched his forehead.

"You got a fever," I said. "Did you take somethin' for it?"

"Yeah, a little while ago. Go on down and get your breakfast. I just need to rest up."

Over breakfast, I worried about Pa and hoped he was right about just needing rest. Cleve and I spent the rest of the morning cleaning up a few rooms we had been putting off for months and carrying in more wood for the fireplaces. We weren't worried about food. Katie and Annie had put up everything we had grown over the summer in addition to the extra vegetables I carried home from Reiko's. I brought soup up to Pa for lunch and set it down next to his bed. He was sleeping with his back to the door of his room, and I didn't want to disturb him but wondered if his fever was better. When I touched his forehead, it was dry, but he felt like he was burning up.

"Pa?" I said when he didn't respond to my touch.

I walked to the other side of the bed hoping he would at least look at me. As I looked down at him, there was a large greenish mass that ran down his pillow and onto the sheet under him, leaving a dried trail along the side of his face.

"Pa!" I said loudly, shaking his shoulder.

Again there was no response. I ran from his room and flew down the stairs.

"Cleve!"

Cleve stepped out of one of the rooms.

"What?"

"It's Pa," I said going to the phone and tapping the holder for the receiver as Cleve quickly took the stairs two at a time.

"Operator," a woman's voice said a minute later.

"Get me Doc Ayers. Fast," I said, scarcely able to breathe through my panic. I could hear the phone on the other end ringing, and it seemed like it was forever before someone picked it up.

"Dr. Ayers," a man's voice said.

"This is Callie Owen in Frost Valley. My Pa's real sick. We need you to come look at him," I said quickly.

"Do you know what's wrong with him?"

"No, sir. He was complaining some about his stomach last night. Today, he's burning up with fever. When I checked him just a while ago, he wouldn't wake up and had thrown up on his bed."

"I'll be there as soon as I can, but it could take a while in this weather."

"What should we do?"

"Try to make him comfortable and use cool wet cloths for his fever."

"Hurry!" I pleaded as I hung up the phone.

I stopped long enough to tell Katie to keep the others away from Pa's room and to holler when the doctor arrived, before running back up the stairs. As I ran into Pa's room, Cleve was pulling the bed sheet over Pa's head and looked up at me with tears flowing down his face.

"No!" I screamed as I started for the bed.

Cleve stopped me before I could reach Pa. He held me tightly as I fought to get away from him.

"He's gone, Callie. There ain't nothin' you can do," he said.

"But the doctor's on his way."

"There ain't nothin' he can do neither. Better call him back and save him the trip."

He put his arm around me and led me from the room, quietly pulling the door closed on our way out.

"What're we gonna do now, Cleve," I asked, trying to choke back my fear, and the tears that were rolling down my cheeks.

Cleve stopped and stood in front of me with his hands on my shoulders.

"You and me are the oldest, Callie. We gotta do what Pa would think best. Right now, we both gotta be strong for the younger ones. I'm gonna call Uncle Ethan 'cause he's the closest one. Then I reckon it's out of our hands."

Chapter
Sixteen

Monday, February 25, 1952

JUST A FEW days earlier, we had been a family, laughing and having a good time together. Now, we were six orphans burying our Pa. The weather had forced us to wait four days before we could hold a proper funeral, and our home had been filled with well-wishers and relatives. Every time the door opened, I expected to look up and see Pa coming through the door. My aunts spent most of their time in the kitchen cooking, and even later, as an adult, whenever I caught a whiff of certain foods cooking, it reminded me of death.

As I stood next to Cleve, oblivious to the cold, I wondered what would happen to the six of us. Even Cleve, who was nearly seventeen, wasn't old enough to take care of us. The sun was shining brightly the day of the funeral, and I had to squint my eyes from the glare of sunlight off the snow around us. I barely heard anything the minister said, and it wouldn't have mattered anyway. Pa had never been a religious man and wasn't a member of any church. I doubted the minister had even met Pa. Looking around, I saw that the cemetery was filled with people, but I felt alone. When the last prayer ended, we were hugged or patted by more folks than I could count. I finally managed to get a little ways away from the crowd and wandered around looking at the headstones in Sanders Cemetery. Not far from where we were burying Pa next to our mother, I saw Thomas Sanders' gravesite. I stood near the footstone that someone had cleared off and read it quickly. When I looked up again, I thought I saw someone standing among the pines and shielded my eyes with my hand. Reiko, dressed in black, and holding Tad's hand, was standing in the shadows of the trees, a silent, invisible attendee. She bowed solemnly toward me, and I wanted desperately to go to her, and let her comfort me. I took a step in their direction, but a hand stopped me. Looking around, I saw Cleve behind me.

"I was just...," I started.

"I seen 'em. They been there the whole time."

"She's just payin' her respects, Cleve."

"I know, so don't make things worse for her now. Let's go."

"Where?"

"I reckon we're fixin' to find out after we get back to the house."

I turned to walk away, looking back in time to see Cleve throw a small wave of his hand in Reiko and Tad's direction.

MY FATHER HAD three sisters who had all married decent men. Two of them lived in Frost Valley. I always thought they didn't approve of the way Pa did things, and we had seldom visited their homes except maybe at Christmas. One of them, Aunt Clara and her husband, Uncle Ethan, didn't have any kids of their own and lived in a log cabin a couple of miles from us. Uncle Horace and Aunt Daisy had a son about my age and lived at the far end of Frost Valley. Pa's youngest sister, Lizzie, and her husband, Clarence, lived in town. They had two girls of their own and were the family I knew the least about except that I had heard Pa say that Clarence had a lot of money.

The six of us sat on one side of the parlor in our house, while our aunts and uncles sat on the other side. Everyone seemed uncomfortable, and it felt like an eternity before Uncle Clarence finally cleared his throat and stood up.

"We've been talking it over, all your aunts and uncles, and we've made a decision. None of us can take all of you."

"But...," Cleve started.

"But," Clarence said as he held up his hand, "we can each take two of you. The way we have it worked out, you'll still see each other, and none of us will be, well, financially strained by trying to keep you all together."

Cleve and I looked at each other and didn't know what to say.

"Cleve," Clarence continued, "you and Willie will live with Horace and Daisy."

He continued through our names like he was counting an inventory.

"Callie and Mack will go with Ethan and Clara, and Lizzie and I will take the girls with us."

"But you and Aunt Lizzie live in town," I said.

"We'll bring the girls back out here every so often, so you can all visit," Clarence said.

"What about our house?" Cleve asked.

"I'm afraid it will have to be sold."

"You can't sell it," I objected. "Great-grandpa built it."

"I know you'll miss it, Callie. We all will, but it can't just sit here empty. The money from it will belong to you children and help defray your expenses."

"You plannin' on sellin' the stuff in the house, too?" Cleve asked.

"You can keep whatever you want from the furnishings, Cleve. And, of course, your personal belongings. After that, I'm afraid everything else will have to be sold."

"There ain't no other way?" I asked.

"None of us can think of anything else that makes sense," Clarence said.

It took about an hour for us to pack up enough clothes to last a few days. Uncle Ethan promised to drive me back to the house in a day or two, saying that he and Clara would help us go through Pa's things. Although I hated being forced to leave the only home I'd ever known, I knew that Pa had thought Ethan was an honest man, and Clara had been his favorite sister. We carried our bags out of the house and closed the door. I knew Mack and I would see Cleve and Willie every day at school but was worried about my sisters who would now be going to the school in town. Not that I thought Clarence wouldn't take good care of them. I hoped we wouldn't be separated emotionally as well as physically. As I got ready to climb into Uncle Ethan's truck, I turned to wave goodbye to the others, but they were already gone.

Chapter
Seventeen

Wednesday, February 27, 1952

TWO DAYS LATER, I longed to see our house again and decided not to go straight back to Uncle Ethan's after school. Instead, I turned in the opposite direction and crossed the open field leading to the house. It seemed oddly quiet as I approached the back door and opened it. The house had been so alive with voices and laughter not long before. Now it felt as if no one had lived there in years. There weren't any lights, and dust floated through the air and sparkled in the late afternoon rays of sunlight coming through the front windows. It was so quiet that I tiptoed across the wooden floor. Every sound seemed to be magnified by the silence, and I felt like a trespasser. I let my hands run over the carved opening of the fireplace.

"Callie," I heard Reiko say.

I looked over my shoulder at her, and a well of tears came to my eyes. I had held them back for the sake of my younger brothers and sisters, but now I couldn't stop them. I dropped to my knees in front of the fireplace, sobbing as I held my head in my hands. Almost as quickly, I felt myself gathered in by Reiko's arms. Clinging to her tightly, I cried until I couldn't any longer, as she stroked my hair and told me everything was going to be all right.

"I miss him so much," I sniffed, finally looking up at her.

"Your father was good man," she said softly, wiping my face with her hand.

"He tried to be."

"No. He was good man. Help me when he didn't want to."

"He said it was the right thing to do."

"If a man does right when everyone say it is wrong, then he is good man. In Japan there is saying. Bad deeds that hurt others easy to do. To do good deed, that is very difficult thing. Father good man."

"I wish you could have known him."

"Me, too. You come."

"I gotta get back to my aunt's house, Reiko."

"First, we show respect to father."

We left the house and walked into the tree line. Tad was waiting for us there and raised his arms to me. I picked him up and hugged him close to me. Reiko picked up a piece of wood about a foot square and handed it to me. Mounted on the wood was a colorful piece of thin paper that looked like a little chimney with some kind of writing on it. Inside the paper enclosure was a small candle. I set Tad down, and she handed him a piece of wood identical to mine. A third piece of wood was hers. We walked through the pines until we reached a stream along the upper ridge that ran the length of the valley but was hidden among the trees. Striking a match, she lit the three candles.

"In my country, we have ceremony for the dead," she said. "Little boats carry soul of person to Heaven. Lantern light way. Writing says this was good person. For man who act with pure heart, happiness follow him, like shadow that never go away."

The sun had fallen over the ridgeline casting deep shadows along the edge of the stream. She squatted down and pushed her boat into the stream. It bobbed around for a few seconds before the soft current of the water caught it and floated the boat away from us. As Tad placed his boat in the water, the two lanterns cast a shimmering glow that sparkled on the water and lit up the darkness as they passed through the trees.

"Mine for memory of husband Thomas. Tad for memory of father. This one," she said touching my boat, "your father. Two very good men."

I smiled at her and pushed my boat away from the edge of the stream. We stood there silently watching until the last one bobbed its way out of sight. There wasn't much more to say as Reiko picked Tad up and carried him piggyback through the forest toward her home.

Chapter
Eighteen

Thursday, April 1, 2004 – 9 P.M.

"WOULD YOU LIKE a refill?" Carolyn asked, snapping me back to reality.

"I'm sorry," I said as I looked up at her.

"More coffee?"

"Please," I said, handing her my cup.

Jean got up and came to where I was sitting. Kneeling down in front of me, she rested her hands on my knees and looked up at the portrait.

"Thinking about Reiko?" she asked.

"Yeah," I said, reaching out and touching her face.

She got up and sat down next to me, drawing her legs up under her the way she always did.

"What are you going to do with the house now, Tad?" she asked.

"Carolyn and I have talked about moving out here and selling our place in Oak Ridge but haven't made a decision yet. Monica will be leaving in a few months and there won't be anyone left at home but the two of us," he answered.

He must have seen the look of disbelief on my face.

"It's not as bad as it used to be, Callie. Most of the people who gave mother trouble are dead now. Their kids are too busy trying to keep their farms going to worry about us. Besides, a few of them actually became my friends before I left."

"How many black eyes did that take?" I asked.

"Enough for a lifetime," he laughed. "But I can be just as stubborn as mother."

"Remember all those nature walks she used to take us on?"

"Just that we spent most of our time looking at a billion plants that all looked the same to me. I was pretty young, so you probably remember it better than I do."

"I still use what she taught me in my work."

"Callie has designed some beautiful gardens back home," Jean said as she looked at me warmly. "Not really Japanese, but Asian inspired. Very delicate and restful."

"I hope you'll send me some pictures. I'd love to see them," Tad said. "The snow probably won't clear enough for you to see much, but mother created some gardens in the woods behind the barn."

"Really?"

"She hiked all over the valley and brought back one or two of just about everything and replanted them here. Sort of a wildflower Noah's Ark, I guess."

"When did she do that?" I asked.

"Started right after you left, I think."

"She never said anything to me about them when I came home."

"You only came back three times and then only for a couple of days. Then she was too busy meeting Jean or playing with your kids to show you."

"She was always very gracious when we came," Jean said.

Tad smiled as he looked at Jean. "She thought you were...what was the word she used, unusual?"

Jean and I both laughed. I was attending college when I met Jean, and she could have been the poster girl for student radicals in the early seventies, not at all what I would have pictured as the person I would spend the remainder of my life with.

That night, Jean and I slept in the upstairs bedroom of Reiko's house that I had slept in many times until I graduated from high school. I was almost too tired to sleep, and memories of the difficult life Reiko had lived in Frost Valley kept repeating in my mind. Gradually, over the years, people simply ignored her presence, and she seldom felt physically threatened. She and Tad became almost like that ugly wart you have on your face but never have removed. You just get used to it being there.

Living with my aunt and uncle hadn't been a picnic for me, although I worked hard on their farm and made good grades in school. I missed seeing my brothers and sisters every day. Cleve graduated and left the valley to see the world. Occasionally, I would receive a letter from him telling me he hadn't found the world very exciting. He finally decided to join the Army and began sending me a little money each month. I found out later that he sent each of us whatever money he could spare. He would forever be our father figure.

Every time I had the chance, I would stay with Reiko and Tad, helping her around the farm, which eventually became every Saturday after I finished the chores Uncle Ethan and Aunt Clara had for me. Her home became my haven, and the only school that ever mattered to me.

Chapter
Nineteen

Late March, 1952

WHEN THE SPRING weather finally began to warm the earth, Reiko led Tad and me every weekend into the deep woods and the back valleys to point out different plants and woodland flowers, patiently explaining their differences. Living alone with Tad, and occasionally with me visiting, she taught herself everything she could about the ecology of Eastern Tennessee. I checked books out of the school and public libraries for her, and within a few years, she knew more about the plants, birds and animals of the region than anyone I knew.

The sun was barely up when Reiko shook my shoulder to wake me. As I rubbed my eyes and rolled halfway over toward her, I thought maybe something was wrong.

"What?" I mumbled, still trying to get my eyes to focus and adjust to the dim light in the bedroom she kept ready for me every weekend.

"Must hurry," she said as she turned to leave the room.

"Is Tad sick?" I asked, propping myself up on my elbows.

"Butterflies come," she called over her shoulder as she disappeared out the door.

I collapsed back on my pillow, and threw my arm across my eyes, wishing I could get just ten more minutes of sleep. Reiko never seemed tired, and the idea that she was now all worked up over butterflies didn't make much sense to my thirteen-year-old mind.

Ten minutes later, I trudged my way into her kitchen, still unsuccessfully trying to get the straps on my overalls twisted in the right direction. The inside of the house was chilly as I padded in barefoot, carrying my socks and shoes, yawning widely. As soon as I sat down, a plate filled with sausage and toast and a pile of steaming scrambled eggs appeared in front of me. Glancing across the table, I saw that Tad looked about as excited as I did with the announcement that there were butterflies in the valley. There were butterflies every spring, and I couldn't imagine why this year would be any different. They were just pretty little insects that ended up stuck to the front grill of every vehicle in the valley for a few weeks this time of year.

Although Reiko had always been amazingly calm, that day it seemed like she couldn't sit still and was periodically examining my plate, hovering nearby like a vulture waiting to swoop down and grab it away the second it was empty.

"What's the hurry, Reiko?" I finally asked, taking a drink of hot coffee.

"Must prepare homes for butterflies. Weather still too cool," she answered as she scooped up Tad's plate and deposited it in the sink.

"It's just some butterflies," I complained. "There'll be plenty more later on."

A frown, something I hadn't seen very often, crossed her face. Holding a jacket for Tad, she opened the back door and left me sitting in the kitchen pulling on my socks and shoes. When I finally left the kitchen, I had to run to catch up with Reiko and Tad.

"I'm sorry, Reiko."

Handing me three slender wooden boxes, she led us up the gently rising slope behind her barn until we reached the edge of the tree line. One by one, she began attaching the boxes to the trunks of the largest trees.

"What are these for?" I asked.

"Home for butterflies. Very long journey and must have safe place to rest," she said.

"But these won't be enough."

Looking down at me, the corners of her mouth turned up slightly.

"Small step better than no step, Callie."

I already knew that every year Monarch butterflies passed through Frost Valley during their annual migration from Mexico, but I had never paid much attention to the large, bright orange and black insects before. Reiko described the long journey the butterflies took each winter and then again the following spring.

Two weeks after we had placed the butterfly habitats, I arrived at Reiko's just after noon on a Saturday. She seemed to be in a particularly good mood.

"Come, come," she motioned to me with a smile before I had barely had a chance to walk in the house.

"Are the Monarchs okay?"

"Come, you see," she beamed.

As we moved around the barn, she stopped me. "Must walk carefully and quietly. No talk."

Her enthusiasm was infectious, and I couldn't wait to see what she wanted to show me. I had visions of baby butterflies as we walked slowly toward the trees. We were only a few feet away when she stopped. I looked back over my shoulder, but she waved me on. I moved toward the habitats hanging on the trees and hadn't taken more than three or four steps when I saw what looked like clusters of tree fungus clinging to the branches of the trees. As I continued for-

ward, my next step was met with a sudden, unexpected burst of movement that nearly caused me to stumble backward. Within seconds, I
was encased in a whirlwind of black and yellow and orange as the
Monarchs took flight from the branches. The beating of hundreds of
wings around me sounded like water tumbling over rocks in a fast
moving stream. Butterflies flew around me, a few landing on my
jacket and head as I laughed out loud, causing them to disperse into
the trees, seeking a new temporary resting place.

Looking back at Reiko, she had her hands over her mouth for a
moment before bringing them together in a delighted clapping motion.
Each year after that she added a few new habitats, and we would
always find clusters resting in the trees, waiting to rise as one into the
clear blue sky to continue their journey northward. The whole butterfly march through Frost Valley only lasted three or four weeks each
spring, but it was amazing to behold. Eventually, Reiko saved enough
money to order a good camera and began to document what she saw,
and I never again questioned the work she wanted done in the woods
behind her home.

While the work I helped her with was exhausting, it was peaceful,
honest work. The feel of the soil in my hands held some kind of magic
for me, giving me time to contemplate life and nature and the complexities of both. Everything in nature was a struggle. It wasn't until
years later that I learned that each of our lives was an even greater
struggle.

Without even knowing it at the time, Reiko was preparing me for
what would become my life's work, and I incorporated what she
taught me in all of my landscaping designs. My life became a series of
small adventures and unnoticed wonders through her eyes. She taught
me patience and respect for nature, which, as she told me many times,
could never be controlled. All nature was beautiful in its own way,
and all humans could hope to do was allow it to display its inherent
beauty in a pleasing way.

As I lay in bed, holding Jean and thinking about Reiko, so many
memories of my life in the valley flooded my mind that I couldn't
sleep. Jean slept peacefully with her arm across my abdomen. Looking
down at her, I marveled at how much I loved her and how much she
had given me. Reiko had taught me how to find joy in even the smallest things in life, but it had been Jean who had taught me what love
was. She hadn't been the first woman in my life, but she would surely
be the last.

Chapter
Twenty

Saturday, September 28, 1957

BY MY SENIOR year in high school, I was eighteen years old and had grown into a tall young woman. That last year I became friends with an attractive new girl in school who had moved there when her father, a circuit rider preacher, took a job working in Oak Ridge to support his family. For some reason I couldn't explain, I enjoyed watching her walk, and there was something playful about her that made me smile. Her name was Jennie Patterson. I didn't know why, but suddenly I began finding reasons to spend time with Jennie. It was as if I couldn't take my eyes off her. My aunt had told me that one day I would find a nice man like Uncle Ethan and settle down. When I found the man I wanted I would feel differently. I didn't know how I was supposed to feel, but I knew I felt differently around Jennie. I loved the way she swung her long blonde hair over her shoulder when we walked, and the way she made me laugh when we talked.

It was early fall, and the weather was crisp but pleasant. After my chores on Saturday morning, Uncle Ethan drove me to town. I had saved my money from Cleve, and once a month, I was allowed to take it into town and buy things I needed. It would also give me a chance to visit my sisters who lived in town with Uncle Clarence and Aunt Lizzie. It was the only Saturday each month that I didn't visit Reiko. I had begun to notice that since Annie and Katie had moved in with Uncle Clarence and Aunt Lizzie they had changed and, in my opinion, not for the better. They never approved of the way I dressed, and I felt like I didn't really know them any more. We had been close until Pa died. In my senior year, Annie was a sophomore, and Katie was a freshman. Even though I saw them nearly every day at school, I still tried to spend one Saturday a month with them.

Uncle Clarence lived in a new housing development just outside of town where most of the wealthier families lived. I soon found that I couldn't spend more than an hour at their house before my sisters began to drive me crazy with their endless chatter about boys, and make-up, and the latest fashions. That Saturday in early fall I walked away from our uncle's house and swore I wouldn't go back again the next month. It was nearly a mile into town, but I was used to walking everywhere. As I turned the corner onto the next street, I heard someone call my name. When I looked around I saw Jennie waving her arm and trotting toward me.

"Hey, Callie," she said when she reached me. "What're you doing?"

"Just visited my sisters. They live the next street over with our aunt and uncle," I said.

"Want to go for a walk with me?"

"I have to meet my uncle in town."

"What time do you have to meet him?"

I looked up at the sun and squinted. "About four. Must be around noon now."

"Then you have some time," she said as she looked at me and smiled. "I thought we might spend a little time together. I found this really great place and wanted to show it to you. A secret place for getting away from parents."

"Okay," I smiled. "Lead on."

"I just had to get out of my house for a while. My mother is driving me crazy today."

"You're lucky to have a mother," I said quietly.

"Oh, Callie, I'm sorry. You told me your folks had died."

"It's okay. I just miss them sometimes."

We walked and talked for a couple of miles until we were well outside town. I knew the road wasn't traveled very much and wasn't worried about cars. The only places that I knew further down the road were a couple of taverns, but it was still too early to dodge drunks. We left the road and strolled down a path that would eventually lead to a stream that flowed into one of the TVA lakes the government had built during the Depression to provide electricity to the whole area. As soon as we left the main road, I was surprised when she reached out and took my hand in hers. Her hand felt soft and warm, and we walked without talking for a little while before we reached her secret place. It was beautiful. It was a shady clearing near an abandoned railroad maintenance shed. I couldn't hear anything except the stream tumbling over rocks, and the sound of birds in the trees.

"It's pretty here," I smiled.

"I come here all the time. Wait here."

Jennie let go of my hand, and it grew cold from the loss of her touch. She entered the old shed and returned a minute or two later carrying a quilt.

"Where'd you get that?" I asked.

"I've been bringing a few things out here for a while," she said as she handed me an edge of the quilt, so we could spread it out on the ground in a shady spot overlooking the stream. Jennie stretched out on the quilt and ran her hands through her long hair. I hesitated before finally sitting down next to her and pulling my legs up to my chest, wrapping my arms around them and resting my chin on my knees. The sound of water falling over smooth rocks along the stream was soothing, and I closed my eyes as I let the sound obliterate everything around me. My eyes were jolted open by a light touch on my back.

"Let's go in and get wet," Jennie said lazily.

"I...I don't have anything to wear," I blushed as I looked at her.

"There's no one around," she smiled, rolling toward me, stroking slowly up and down my spine. Licking her lips, she said, "I'd really like to see you naked, Callie. I bet you're beautiful."

I opened my mouth, but no words came out. I wasn't sure what I should say or what I wanted to say. I turned my head back toward the stream.

"I'm sorry," Jennie sighed as she sat up. "Maybe we should start back, so you can meet your uncle."

Placing my hand on her arm as she stood, I rasped, "No. I...I would like...to see you, too." I couldn't describe what I was feeling inside any more than I understood what it was. I just knew that whenever I looked at Jennie my stomach clenched and did little flips. Taking my hands, Jennie pulled me up, and I found myself standing with my mouth less than an inch from hers. I watched as the corners of her mouth twitched into a slow smile and felt her hands slide seductively down my hips, drawing them closer to her body. I was afraid to breathe and felt dizzy from being so close to her, inhaling the new and exotic scent of her.

"Do you...do you still want to get wet?" I managed.

"I already am," she said softly, pulling my lips to hers as she guided my hand inside the waistband of her pants. As my fingertips felt the warm moistness between her thighs, my hand stopped, unsure what I was feeling.

"Don't stop, Callie, please," she breathed heavily against my mouth. "Please...touch me."

"I want to...so much," I panted, my heart beating wildly against my chest. "I...I don't know what to do."

"I want to feel you inside me," Jennie groaned.

Covering my mouth hard with hers, she pushed my fingers through the wetness between her thighs until they were buried inside her. She gasped, clutching my shoulders while her hips moved insistently against my hand; her muscles squeezing my fingers until moments later I felt liquid heat flowing over them. Jennie collapsed against me, and I held her even though my own legs were shaking badly and barely holding up my own weight.

"Thank you, Callie," Jennie breathed contentedly.

Late that night, I couldn't sleep, trying to sort through the myriad of confused feelings my mind and body were feeling. I could still feel Jennie's body against mine as I held my hand up and looked at it in the moonlight from my window, remembering what it had brought forth from her body, and I felt strangely powerful as I smiled.

Chapter
Twenty-one

Friday, May 2, 1958

OVER THE MONTHS since our first intimate, heady time together, Jennie and I made love at every opportunity. I enjoyed and marveled at the things I could make her body feel and do. By the time the school year was beginning to wind down, I was spending more time with Jennie than I probably should have, even seeking excuses not to spend most of my Saturdays with Reiko and Tad. I had gotten a part-time job at the local dry goods store in October, and Uncle Ethan would pick me up when the weather was cold. Once the days lengthened and the weather became warmer, my aunt and uncle agreed that I could walk home from work on the weekends.

My graduation was only four or five weeks away, and I had already decided that when I graduated I would leave Frost Valley just as Cleve had. The first Friday in May I hadn't bothered to tell my aunt and uncle that I wouldn't be working that day, and as soon as school was out, I almost ran to meet Jennie. The abandoned railroad maintenance shed Jennie had discovered not far from town had become our secret hideaway. It had a solid roof, and Jennie had scrounged up some material from her mother that we used to cover the small windows.

As I left the road near the stream where we had first kissed and cut down the overgrown path leading to the shed and the pleasure waiting for me inside, I thought I heard something, but I shook it off as a squirrel or groundhog rooting around in the underbrush. Reaching the small building a few minutes later, I glanced quickly around and took a deep breath before opening the door. As I entered, Jennie turned and smiled at me. God, she was so beautiful. She walked slowly toward me, resting her hand in the center of my chest as she stood in front of me. Leaning down, I met her lips softly, my hands anxious to feel her smooth softness. Kissing her more urgently than I meant to, I was overcome with a wave of desire for her that grew stronger every time we secretly met. Pushing me away slightly, she turned and pulled her long silky hair up, revealing the whiteness of her neck. My mouth took in her neck as I unzipped her dress and pushed it down her arms. She smiled up at me as she turned to face me again and stepped out of the dress. My knees were threatening not to hold me up as I bent down and took her mouth eagerly, wrapping my arms tightly around her to pull her against me.

My mind was drowning in my desire and anticipation when the air was shattered by the sound of splintering wood. As we broke apart, hands grabbed my arms before I could respond and pulled me roughly away from Jennie, leaving her standing exposed in her slip and underwear. A large man stepped between us and raised his hand to hit Jennie's beautiful face.

"No!" I cried out as I struggled against the hands holding me. I saw Jennie's head snap to the side as the blow struck her, knocking her to the floor. The man turned back toward me, his face florid with rage. Pointing a shaking finger at me, he screamed, "Sodomite!"

"Please, Daddy, don't," Jennie pleaded through her tears.

"You promised, Jennie! But you still defile yourself in God's eyes!" With his hand still pointing at me, he looked at her. "Now you will see what your sick perversion has wrought."

"Jennie," I said, trying to be calm for her. My head flew back as Reverend Patterson's hand swung around viciously, carrying the full force of his rage with it. My legs collapsed under the force of the blow, but strong arms still held me as I shook my head, trying to clear my eyes. Grabbing Jennie, her father jerked her to her feet and led her, stumbling and half naked, out the shattered door. The hands holding me dragged me outside behind them as Reverend Patterson led us further into the coolness of the trees.

Stopping, he pulled Jennie's head up by her long hair, forcing her to look at me as he seethed. "I warned you what would happen to Sodomites."

I saw the terror in Jennie's eyes as tears ran down her face. I cried out in blinding pain as my arms were pressed behind my back until my elbows nearly touched, threatening to wrench my shoulders from their sockets. A young man I had never seen before stepped in front of me and drove his fist into my abdomen, knocking the wind out of my body. The arms holding me prevented me from doubling over with pain as I struggled to regain my breath. I had barely begun drawing air again when a second blow struck me, and I was finally released to sink to the ground as my knees buckled. My head was pulled up, and I saw stars dancing in the late evening shadows as the back of a hand knocked me onto my back, the unmistakable taste of blood in my mouth as I desperately tried to fill my lungs with air.

"Stop!" I heard Jennie scream as I struggled to clear my head.

As my eyes found her, Reverend Patterson ordered, "Do it!"

I heard a faint clicking sound and managed to open one eye enough to see the man kneeling over me with a knife in his hand. Terror coursed through my body as I tried to back away, only to be stopped by the second man who wrapped an arm around my neck and covered my mouth with his huge hand. My eyes wide with horror, I breathed rapidly through my nose as the man with the knife straddled my body and ripped my shirt open. I felt the knife cut through my bra as I fought to breathe through my strangling sobs.

Pain shot through me as I felt the tip of the knife cut into the skin of my upper abdomen below my breasts, and I felt warm blood slip down my sides. I grew lightheaded and was on the verge of vomiting when the hand and arm holding me finally released me. Reaching down next to him, the man straddling me wiped the knife blade on his pant leg. Taking a handful of soil, he pressed it into the wound before rising. Writhing on the ground in agony, choking on the air I breathed in through my mouth, my hands went to my upper abdomen, feeling blood ooze onto my fingers.

As I took in deep ragged breaths through my mouth, all I could hear was the sound of Jennie's crying mixed with the fast pulse of blood pounding past my eardrums, matching the sound of water rushing down the mountain creek near us.

Fingers dug into my arms again, dragging me, still gasping for breath as I was pulled up and shoved roughly against a nearby tree, my wrists held tightly around the trunk. I wanted to struggle against the hands holding me, but my legs felt like rubber, and the bark from the tree bit into the raw wound on my abdomen. A body pressed against mine from behind as my arms ached from being held.

"And God shall smite the wicked from our midst and drive the evil from within them," a low contained voice spoke into my ear. My head was jerked to the side, and I saw Jennie's tear-stained face, and I knew I was going to die because I loved her.

Before I could comprehend what was happening, I heard the faint clicking sound of the knife opening again and vainly tried to struggle as I felt the knife cut through the remains of my shirt and bra while I fought to breathe through my terror. A moment later my jeans and underwear were jerked down my hips, stopping mid-calf. In the time it took me to draw two rapid breaths, a searing pain shot across my back unlike anything I had known before. As I felt the skin on my back and buttocks shred, I threw my head back and begged him to stop, pleading for the pain to stop. But it didn't until I stopped struggling and couldn't hear Jennie's anguished cries any more.

LYING ON MY side, I groaned as I tried to open my eyes. It was dark, and I didn't know where I was, or how long I had been there. I tried to sit up, but I couldn't move my legs, and sharp searing pain riddled my back and abdomen with every movement of my muscles. I shivered involuntarily, which only brought new waves of pain. Everything around me was black, but I managed to turn my head far enough to make out stars twinkling overhead through the trees. I couldn't see anything else. My head pounded, and I tried to raise my right arm to feel my head. Something was wrong. My arms delayed in responding to the commands my brain was giving them. My hand moved jerkily as I tried to touch my body, and when I pressed my fingers gingerly along my upper abdomen, I winced in pain. I tried to sit up, only to be knocked back down by pain shooting through me like an electrical jolt. In a flash of memory, I knew where I was. Gathering every ounce of strength my body had left, I forced myself to roll onto my stomach. Stabbing pain through my chest made it almost impossible to breathe. My thighs and ass throbbed. Through the pain, I realized that my jeans were still holding my legs captive. I tried to calm myself, knowing I needed to find help, and although I knew I was hurt, I didn't know how badly. I managed to pull my right arm in front of me, feeling my fingers dig into dirt. Biting down hard on my lower lip, I forced my body upright as much as possible and eventually managed to push the jeans past my ankles and off my body. Moving forward, one small step at a time, I felt a new pain with each small exertion. My legs weren't working well as I stumbled forward. Finally, my leg muscles gave way to fatigue and I fell, my hip hitting something beneath me that was sharp and unforgiving. Grabbing my hip, I felt wet stickiness on my hand. My hand found a small sapling, and I dragged myself slowly upright again, but the sapling wasn't strong enough to hold my weight. When it snapped, I fell and began rolling downhill through the brush and rocks. I screamed as branches and debris bit into my already tattered back.

When I awakened again, my head was splitting with a headache that hampered my vision, and as I tried to look around, I didn't see anything. Wait! A light? How far away? I couldn't tell, but I knew I had to follow that light. I had to keep moving, if I could just stop shaking long enough. My teeth were chattering, and my body jerked involuntarily as it shivered in the cool, damp night air. It was so quiet. All I could do was move toward that light a few inches at a time.

I didn't know how long it had been. It seemed like hours, and I had to keep blinking to see the light. Sometimes it seemed to be moving farther away from me, and at other times, it appeared to pause and wait for me. Dirt and leaves scraped against my skin like sandpaper as I inched forward. Small pebbles felt like knives under my bruised feet. I wanted to sleep, and it was all I could do to stay awake. My body wasn't shivering as much now. Was that a good thing?

The sky began to turn to a dark gray. Maybe the sun was coming up. I could hear a bird somewhere. I began to panic when I could no longer see the light I had been following. Where did the light go? I couldn't see it any more. I was lying in a depression of some kind and tried to lift my head. It hurt too much, and tears from the pain began to fill my eyes. Mustering nearly the last of my strength, I threw my arms forward again. My hand hit something hard. Where was the dirt? When I looked at my hand, it was on a flat surface. No more grass. Pulling my legs up under me, I pushed my body as high as I could. The valley road! As my eyes moved up and down the road, I knew where I was. Reiko. The light was gone, but somehow I had followed it out of the forest. Exhaustion overtook every part of my body, and I was so tired. Maybe the light had been a hallucination. Maybe Lena's spirit had found me during her nightly wanderings. Resting my forehead on my arms, I took as deep a breath as I could. I had to make it to Reiko's before it became much lighter. Clenching my teeth against the pain that now ceaselessly racked my body, I forced myself to stand again and stumbled toward safety.

I collapsed at the bottom of the steps leading to Reiko's back door but couldn't force my body another foot. Pink streaks appeared over the top of the trees along the ridge and pushed their way into the gray sky. My body was shaking almost uncontrollably as I closed my eyes and curled into a tight ball for warmth. I wanted to call out for Reiko, but nothing came out of my mouth. I hurt so badly, and what I remembered brought the sting of new tears to my eyes.

My mother's voice, calling my name in a dream, woke me. I jerked away as a hand touched my shoulder and squeezed my eyes tightly, trying to move away from another assault. I didn't think I could survive more pain.

"Sh-h-h," a soft voice from my childhood said as I felt something warm fall around my body. I clutched at the object as a gentle hand stroked my hair. "I call doctor."

"No," I forced my throat to rasp out.

"No argue, Callie."

I was surprised as deceptively strong arms helped me to my feet. I opened my eyes enough to see Reiko's frowning, worried face as she wrapped an arm carefully around me to help me up the three steps into her kitchen. It seemed like Mount Everest. Looking down at my bare, bleeding feet, I fought to lift either one onto the first step.

"Lean on me," she encouraged. "Tad, hold door."

The thought of the nine-year-old boy whom I loved as a brother having to see me like this was overwhelming, and tears ran down my humiliated face. I sobbed uncontrollably. An eternity later we took the final step up.

"Call doctor," Reiko said calmly to Tad, and I heard his quick footsteps moving away.

I was never sure how such a small woman managed to get me into a downstairs bedroom, but by the time Doc Ayers arrived, Reiko had bathed me gently with warm water to remove the dirt and leaves from my body while trying not to hurt me. I was embarrassed when the doctor checked my body to assess my injuries and clung to Reiko's hand. Even though my arms were covered with bruises from being

held, the only position I could lay in without the burning pain was on
my side. Covering me with a light sheet at last, he stepped away and
shook his head.

"You should call her aunt, Mrs. Sanders," I heard him say gently.
"She should be taken to a hospital."

"No," I choked out, opening my eyes.

"Who cut and whipped you, girl?" Ayers asked, kneeling down
next to me again.

"Don't know," I lied. "Don't tell Aunt Clara...please."

"She stay here," Reiko said. "I speak to aunt."

"Keep the scrapes and cuts on her legs and feet clean, and put this
ointment on them," Ayers said as he handed Reiko a small jar from his
black medical bag. "But the wounds on her back and buttocks are
deep. Whatever she was beaten with had thorns, and I'm gonna have
to dig them out before I can stitch up her wounds. You and the boy
will have to hold her down, Mrs. Sanders."

"Wait," Reiko said. "I get something for pain."

Pulling a chair over next to the bed, Doc Ayers, who had known
me since before my mama died, ran his hand over my head. "I don't
have much with me to give you for the pain, Callie. I'm sorry, but I
have to clean out and close some of these cuts before a serious infection sets in."

Tears leaked out of my eyes as I nodded as much as I could. A
moment later, Reiko was beside me, thrusting a glass of clear liquid in
front of me. "Drink quick. No sip."

She covered my hand with hers to steady my shaking hand as I
brought the glass to my cracked lips, her other hand supporting my
head. The liquid stung the cuts on my lips and burned my mouth and
throat when I swallowed, nearly gagging me as she forced me to drink
it all. Within minutes my head was spinning with dizziness, and I
couldn't get my eyes to focus correctly.

"Give me that bottle," Dr. Ayers said. "I can use it to sterilize the
wounds and instruments. You'll have to lie as still as you can, Callie."

I locked my eyes onto Reiko's as we gripped one another's arms. I
felt the liquid flow over my back and into my raw flesh like scalding
water. A scream died in my mouth as I passed out from the burning
pain.

It was dark in the room when I finally managed to pry my eyelids
open. My back still felt like it was burning, and I groaned as I tried to
move my arms. Almost immediately, a cool hand stroked my hair. "Be
still," Reiko's voice spoke softly. "I fix soup for you. Tad watch."

I moved my eyes around and caught the worried look on Tad's
face and tried to force a smile for him. He was scared and so was I. I
wiggled my index finger, and he reached over and took it in his warm
little hand. "Don't worry, Taddie," I managed.

His eyes darted around as if he wanted to say something but

didn't know what to say. "Just hold my hand," I said. We sat like that, making the smallest of connections, until Reiko returned. Placing a small hand towel under my chin, she slowly brought spoonfuls of warm broth to my mouth, without speaking. There was nothing we could say. It was enough to know that she cared about me.

Chapter
Twenty-two

Tuesday, May 20, 1958

FOR A WEEK I barely moved, refusing to leave the bedroom even for meals. The longer I lay there, the madder I became. My injuries were healing, and Doc Ayers had decided to remove the stitches after ten days. I was worried that I would be jeopardizing my graduation from high school by missing so many days, but Reiko had gone into town and paid a visit to the principal of the high school, returning with the work I had missed and might miss during the time I was recovering. We made up a story that I had fallen on the ridge after dark and gotten tangled up in some barbed wire.

Although I still didn't want to discuss what had happened to me or why, I thought about it obsessively. The more I thought about it, the more bitter I became. My mother and grandmother had always told me that God was kind and forgiving. Yet He had allowed this to happen to me through one of His own messengers. Kind and forgiving my ass! My mother and grandmother had obviously lied to me. He had taken my mother away, allowed her to die before it should have been her time. Three years later, He snatched away my only other lifeline to a normal life by taking my father as well. What could I have done that would lead to such heartache and vengeance by a supposedly kind and benevolent God? The more I thought about it, the more I knew it had all been pure bullshit. I hated God for what He had done to me and my family.

The second week of my recuperation I was still wallowing in my bitterness and self-pity. On Tuesday morning, I was awakened by bedcovers being pulled off my body.

"Time get up, Callie," Reiko said.

"What's wrong? Is Tad sick?" I said through a sleep-clogged mind.

"No. Tad go to school. Need fresh air."

Holding my hand across my still sore abdomen, I pushed myself up and slowly swung my legs off the bed. Reiko held out a pair of jeans and a shirt.

"I can't wear those, Reiko," I frowned. "It still hurts to have clothes against my skin."

"These belong Thomas. Very loose. Stand up and I help," she nodded, shoving the clothing toward me.

"No. I'll do it by myself," I said uncomfortably, looking away from her.

Taking my chin in her hand, she turned my face up to meet hers. "I see wounds already."

I didn't want her to see my body but was sure I couldn't get dressed alone. Carefully, she placed soft bandages over my wounds and taped them in place before slowly slipping Thomas's old jeans up my legs. As I held onto the nightstand for support, she rolled up the legs, so they didn't drag the ground when I walked. Nearly half an hour later, I followed her out the back door. I hadn't breathed fresh air or seen the sunshine in over two weeks. It was going to be a hot day, and the early morning sun hurt my eyes. I hadn't walked very far when I felt the sun's heat penetrating the shirt, stinging the still healing cuts on my back. I hurried as quickly as I could into the woods behind the barn, praying the shade would end the burning sensation.

My legs and ass screamed against the pain caused by the jeans rubbing slightly against them as we climbed slowly up the side of the hill.

"Where the hell are we going?" I said shortly, grabbing a sapling to lean against for a moment. I couldn't remember ever feeling so weak and defeated.

"Creek. No curse," Reiko said over her shoulder.

"What about the creek?"

"Must clear to make pools for fish."

"There ain't no fish in these creeks, Reiko," I said, shaking my head.

"Yes, you see. Come."

When we reached the narrow creek that ran across the ridge, Reiko stepped into the water and reached her hand back to me. I was sure the woman had finally lost her mind from living in isolation for so long. Standing in the water, she looked around for a few minutes.

"We move this stone to make pool," she said leaning over what amounted to a small boulder protruding out of the water near one bank of the mountain creek.

I waded over next to her, bending over to feel along the bottom of the boulder, hoping there weren't any snakes around. The weather was plenty warm enough for them to have begun slithering out seeking heat. The movement of my arms pulled the skin across my back, and I bit back the pain.

"I can't, Reiko. It hurts too much," I shook my head.

"Is good. Skin must learn again how to move before wounds heal."

"Did you read that in another book or something?" I snapped.

"Doctor tell. No move, scars become stiff. Doctor say to stretch."

For the remainder of the week during the day, Reiko forced me, kicking and screaming, to retrain the skin and muscles of my back and thighs to move the way they had before my beating. At night, she heated my back with warm, wet cloths and forced me to do the assignments the school had sent home for me.

Math had always been a difficult subject for me to grasp, and it seemed that my math teacher was determined to make my life even more miserable by assigning page after page of problems that I was certain I would never use. I was supposed to return to school the following Monday and needed help figuring out a few math problems. It was almost ten o'clock on Saturday night when I carried my math book into the small room just off the parlor of Reiko's home. Reiko was kneeling on the floor in front of a small statue, her hands together under her bowed head. A small flame from a candle sent a dark stream of smoke toward the ceiling in front of the statue. I had never thought much about Reiko's religion and had never before observed her in prayer. I backed away from the room and waited in the parlor until she came out of the room, quietly closing the door behind her. A surprised look crossed her face when she saw me.

"I'm sorry to disturb you, Reiko, but do you know anything about algebra?"

She nodded slightly and walked toward the dining room. I settled myself into a chair beside her and showed her the problems I was having trouble with. She glanced through the textbook for a few minutes, following her index finger as she read. It took her about fifteen minutes to explain what my math teacher had been trying to get through to me all year long. When we finally snapped the book shut forty minutes later, I looked at her and smiled.

"Thanks, Reiko. You've saved my life again."

"Father teach me and sister."

"Is your father still in Japan?" I asked. It occurred to me that I had never asked about her family in all the time I had known her.

"Father and mother dead," she said flatly.

"I'm sorry, Reiko. I didn't know."

"They in better place now. Like Thomas."

"Are you a Baptist?"

"No," she chuckled. "Buddhist."

"Is that a religion?"

"Yes. Not like religions here."

"Do you worship that statue in the other room?"

"No. I pray to statue for guidance. Are you Bap...Baptist?"

"I'm not much of anything, I guess. My mother went to church, but Pa never did. Do you think he still went to Heaven?"

"Buddhists believe there is place where soul...spirit go. Buddha teach all life is suffering. Suffering caused by what we want. Must overcome to end suffering. If body die, spirit still live on. Then spirit born again."

"Everybody wants things."

"Things cannot bring us happiness. Must help others. Be happy. Forgive."

"My mother and father lived good lives and didn't hurt anyone, but they still died for no reason."

"All things happen for reason, Callie."

"I can't see a reason for their deaths, for me and my brothers and sisters being made burdens on other people."

"Your struggle just begin. Death of parents make you grow stronger...here," she said quietly, tapping her finger against my chest. "You need strength inside to face struggle."

"Is that why Thomas died, to make you stronger inside?"

"Yes. Thomas live good life. He good man. Be good man in next life, too. Thomas never leave, only reborn somewhere else. Maybe as butterfly," she smiled.

I had to smile at the idea of Thomas Sanders's soul returning to Frost Valley in the form of a Monarch butterfly.

"I...I guess I'm not that strong, Reiko. I hate the men who did this to me. Sometimes I wish I could find them, for just a few minutes."

"What you do then?"

"An eye for an eye, I reckon," I shrugged.

"Is that good thing?"

"I would feel good. Gettin' even."

"Would your life be better? Would scars disappear?"

"I don't know! I just want to do something," I said.

"Forgive," she said.

"You mean like turn the other cheek?" I snorted. "I have to live with this every day, and you expect me to just go on like it never happened!"

"Buddha say person can fight a thousand men in a thousand battles, but person who conquer himself is greatest of conquerors. You must find strength to conquer anger before you find happiness. Future is only important thing."

Reiko's religion was so foreign to me that it almost seemed like a fairy tale, something made up to explain the difficulties of life to children.

By the time I returned to school in time to take my final exams, Jennie was no longer there, and I never found out what had happened to her. I think I always knew what happened between us wasn't really love, merely lust and desire.

Gradually, over the summer months, my physical wounds healed completely, but I would always carry scars on my body as a reminder of what had happened. It took a lot longer for my emotional scars to heal.

Chapter
Twenty-three

Monday, July 12, 1971

I COMPLETED MY naval enlistment in June 1971 at Alameda Naval Air Station in California. During my last three months of service, I had been placed on limited duty, allowing me plenty of extra time. I decided to take advantage of my G.I. Bill, and go to college. During my separation period, I made trips to various colleges and universities in the San Francisco area and spent hours looking over the courses of study each had to offer. I knew I wouldn't feel comfortable at a large school and concentrated on small liberal arts schools. I didn't have a clue what I would be interested in studying until I took a summer job with the San Francisco Parks Department. I loved being outdoors and remembered what Reiko had told me about plants and balancing the environment.

During my last duty assignment near Osaka, Japan, I had spent almost all my free time visiting Japanese gardens throughout the country and found something intangibly soothing about them. They had incorporated everything Reiko had taught me and were so calm and peaceful that whatever troubles I had seemed to disappear. Some of the parks in San Francisco had attempted to recreate Japanese gardens, but there had always been something lacking that prevented them from having the same sense of serenity, and I knew I could make them better.

By mid-July, I found a small, fledgling department called environmental design at San Francisco State College. The listing of courses all sounded like Greek to me and had official sounding course names, which eventually turned out to be basically math and science with a little drafting and environmental safety thrown in for good measure.

I was granted a tour of their facilities, which were primarily a few classrooms and a complex of greenhouses and laboratories, but was drawn to the idea that half the coursework was hands on and outdoors. Unlike other majors, this one combined the actual field specific coursework with the prerequisites, which would allow me to begin immediately working on environmental design projects while slogging through the preliminary classes. In order to begin fall classes, I had to get my ass in gear and complete a mountain of paperwork pertaining to admittance and financial assistance. I had been fortunate to find a furnished apartment within a mile of the college as well as a used truck that looked like shit and had a cranky transmission but it did have a new engine and four new tires.

My landlady turned out to be a nice old lady who had divided up her older two-story home into four separate apartments when she bought a newer house nearly twenty years ago. The apartment was clean and neat, and I was surprised when I had to schedule an interview to become a tenant. One phone call provided me with a time and date to see the apartment, and I was told to bring references.

A little before my appointment time, I pulled my old truck to the curb in front of the building and walked to the front door of apartment two. Before I could knock, the door swung open and a wrinkled face looked me over from head to toe.

Removing my sunglasses, I smiled my most winning smile. "Mrs. Carothers? I'm Callie Owen."

"You bring references?" she asked without returning my smile.

"Uh, yes, ma'am," I said sliding the sunglasses onto the top of my head and holding up three pieces of paper. "I have three."

Mrs. Carothers pushed open the screen door and finally allowed me to enter the apartment. As I looked around, I could tell that it had been well cared for. It was furnished with antiques as well as a few more modern pieces. The front room was large and included a lovely secretary desk, couch, two rockers and a solid-looking coffee table. The carpeting was worn in a few places but was otherwise clean. She glanced over my references as she guided me through the remainder of the apartment. The kitchen was microscopic but complete. After all, I would be the only one living there, and I didn't need a big kitchen. The tub in the bathroom reminded me of our bathroom back home with its claw foot tub. The single bedroom was almost as large as the living area and came with two twin beds with a nightstand between them, and a generous walk-in closet.

"Let's go back into the front and have a chat," Mrs. Carothers said, although it sounded almost like an order.

As soon as she had positioned herself in one of the rockers, she began giving me a list of her rules. "I don't countenance any hanky-panky from my tenants. I expect them to obey my rules. I don't allow any loud music. I don't care if you drink as long as you're moderate about it. Do you smoke?"

"Yes, ma'am."

"Don't care if you smoke cigarettes, but no cigars. Never get the stink out from those. No animals, and that includes goldfish. All the furniture is mine. There is a separate water and electric meter for each apartment, and you would have to establish those accounts in your own name. I reserve the right to inspect the apartment any time I

receive a complaint from my other tenants or the neighbors. Otherwise, you will never see me except when I collect the rent on the first
of each month promptly. There is a parking carport in the rear, and the
spaces are numbered. No parties, which I define as more than two
other persons here at any one time. Any questions so far?"

"No, ma'am."

"Are you a religious woman?"

"Not very."

"Are you a liberal?"

"Excuse me, ma'am?"

"One of those people we have so many of around here who protest every little thing that comes along?"

"No, ma'am. I'm a student at San Francisco State."

"How old are you? Little old for that, aren't you?"

"I'm thirty-two, ma'am. I recently separated from the Navy,
ma'am, and decided to go to college."

"My husband was a Navy man. Anyway, I am very picky about
who lives here. Don't allow Jews or Catholics, Hispanics or Blacks or
Japs. Is that a problem?"

Although I still bristled inside at the word Jap, I shook my head in
the negative.

"Where you from?"

"Tennessee, ma'am."

She eyed me for a few uncomfortable minutes before the first
smile crossed her lips. "I'm a fair landlady, Ms. Owen, but I'm too old
to be chasing around after slacker tenants. The rent on this apartment
is eighty-five a month. If that's agreeable to you I have the rental
agreement in my car."

"That's more than reasonable, Mrs. Carothers. How soon can I
move in?" The rent was a third of what I had been led to believe the
average rent would be for anything comparable.

"As soon as the agreement is signed you can consider yourself
moved in," she said as she pushed herself out of the rocker.

That same day, I made arrangements to have the utilities turned
on and a telephone installed. I had never lived anywhere on my own
and spent the first two nights in my new apartment adjusting to the
sounds of the city at night. The weather was cool enough at night to
allow me to open the windows and enjoy a comfortable breeze as I
slept. By the time classes began for the fall semester, I had settled
down to a peaceful, uncomplicated life. The first person I called once
the telephone was installed was Reiko. It was wonderful to hear her
soft voice, and we talked for nearly an hour about my studies and my
work with the parks department. I promised that as soon as I could
afford it I would make a trip back to Frost Valley.

Chapter
Twenty-four

IN NOVEMBER, ONE of my professors handed each of the students in his introductory environmental design class an assignment to write a detailed study of one of the many parks within the environs of San Francisco: its purpose, foliage, actual usage by the public, and how well the integrity of the environment was being maintained. Through my job with the parks department, I was able to reference data concerning the maintenance and public usage of the park I was assigned but had developed a few ideas that I thought would make the park a more inviting place for people to go. What I had envisioned was something peaceful and serene incorporating pieces of sculpture with an Asian influence.

On a bright Saturday morning, I packed a small lunch and drinks in a cooler and set out for the park. I had a small sketchpad, a tape measure, and my list of indigenous plants found within the park. I also had a list of exotic plants the parks department had placed on the grounds as an experiment on how well they adapted. I stopped by the parks department offices and picked up a topographical map of the park on the way and spent a little time dividing the park into grids. Two hours later, I leaned back against a large California spruce and sketched each grid on my sketchpad, including the various plants and their locations. Although it didn't bother my work, I had noticed that by noon the park seemed much busier than normal even for a pleasant weekend. I was halfway through my lunch when I began to hear what sounded like chanting from the pavilion area of the park. Packing away my things in a homemade portfolio, I dusted myself off and began the trek across the park to the side street where my truck was parked. After I stowed everything in the passenger seat, my curiosity got the best of me, and I made my way back toward the pavilion to see what was going on. When I topped a small rise leading into the park, I saw what I estimated to be at least a hundred people milling around near a speaker's platform. I had heard the same rhetoric dozens of times and found it as misguided as usual. From the looks of the people in the crowd they were all young, probably college students, and a number of them were lying around, undoubtedly stoned. There was some type of anti-war, free love protest almost every weekend, and for the most part, average citizens chose to ignore them as nothing more than a nuisance. I leaned against a tree and watched for a few minutes. There were a few bored-looking police officers keeping an eye on the protesters to make sure the situation didn't get out of hand. As soon as one speaker finished his speech, another took up the microphone and harangued the crowd with inflammatory suggestions. I frowned as I heard American servicemen and women being referred to as warmongers by a bunch of student radicals who had no clue what they were talking about; their passion fueled by the pictures they had seen on television rather than first-hand experience. If I could have dropped any one of them into the jungle and turned them loose, I doubted that any of them could have survived twenty-four hours.

Deciding that I had had enough of fantasyland for the day, I turned to find my way back to the truck. I never was quite sure what started the fracas, but suddenly there was shouting, shoving, and screaming. Three or four mounted police officers waded into the crowd in an attempt to separate the protesters from another group. As I watched, I saw a little boy wandering around the edge of the fight, crying and in some danger of being tromped by either adults who couldn't see him or horses that wouldn't notice him until it was too late. I heard sirens in the distance and figured that the cops in the park had called for backup to manage the sizeable mass of people. Keeping an eye on the kid, I ran down the slope toward him. Out of the corner of my eye, I saw a mounted police officer reining his horse back as protesters surged toward him. He was swinging his nightstick at two men near him as they tried to grab the reins from him. The kid just stood there, scared and crying, as the adults around him seemed either to be ignoring him or totally unaware of his presence. Where the hell were his parents? As the horse reared up on its hind legs, I scooped the boy up with one arm and barely managed to get out of the way as the officer fell from his mount.

Looking quickly around, I was preparing to carry the crying toddler away from the crowd when I was grabbed by the shoulder. Spinning around, I came face to face with the furious fallen officer. Jerking loose from his grip, I took off away from the crowd of people to get the kid to a safer location. I hadn't gotten more than a few feet when I saw a dozen officers converging on my position. I stopped and set the kid down behind a bush, hoping that it would be enough to get him out of harm's way and that he had the good sense to stay put. I had no sooner set him down than I was struck on the back of the head and went down like a box of rocks. I reached up to feel the back of my head. When I brought my hand down to look at it, there was blood on it. Pushing myself up to one knee, I found myself shoved down again, my arm being twisted behind me. I felt dizzy and a little nauseated as a police officer handcuffed me and left me lying on the ground while he went to assist in quelling the riot that had broken out.

I must have lain there a half hour before anyone returned to check on me. Two officers finally took my arms and pulled me to my feet.

"You...you've made a mistake," I attempted. "I was just..."

"Tell it to the judge, lady."

I looked back over my shoulder. The kid was still cowering behind the bush.

"The boy. You need to find his mother."

"Someone will take care of him," an officer said as we reached a large van. "Step up."

My head was throbbing, and I wasn't sure how badly I had been hurt as I was forced into a seat. I watched as police officers loaded the van to its maximum capacity with protesters. As soon as the doors at the rear of the van closed, it lurched away from the park, and the protesters began chanting loudly, which made my headache even worse. A slim woman standing in front of me seemed to be leading the chanting, but I couldn't get her attention. She had long black hair that fell to the middle of her back and had a tie-dyed headband around her forehead. Finally my head couldn't stand the yelling any longer, and I kicked her with my work boot.

"Ow!" she hollered as she turned toward me. "What the fuck was that for?"

"Please shut the fuck up!" I said as loudly as I could.

"What?" she yelled as she leaned down toward me. If my head hadn't hurt so much, I would have smiled. Her round, distinctly Asian face was highlighted by lavender-tinted granny glasses that had slid halfway down her tiny nose, and she had to look over them to see me.

"I said shut the hell up! I have a headache!"

"Tough shit! Who are you?"

"I was arrested by mistake."

"Well, we all have our problems, don't we?" she said with a smirk.

"Jean!" a man shouted.

"Yeah!" she called back as she stood up.

"How long you figure we'll be locked up this time?" he asked with a laugh.

"An hour, max!" she said as she leaned her face against the shoulder of the woman next to her and pushed her glasses back up.

"Jesus Christ," I muttered to myself as I leaned back and rested my head against the van wall. I hoped Mrs. Carothers never found out that I had been arrested, or I would find my ass out on the street. I closed my eyes and tried to concentrate on anything besides the throbbing in my head. When I opened them a few minutes later, I saw the woman someone had called Jean looking down at me. When our eyes met she gave me a lop-sided smile that reminded me of the pictures I had seen of Yoko Ono.

Not soon enough, the van came to a stop, and the back doors were opened. I waited while the standing arrestees were assisted out the back. When I finally stood, my dizziness was overwhelming, and I sat back down while other prisoners went past me. I was the only one left as an officer jumped up into the van.

"What's your problem? Get up!" he ordered.

"I'm hurt," I said. "My head."

"Hey, Anderson," he called out. "Get the doc out here to check this one."

I leaned back and closed my eyes again. I was startled by someone lifting my left eyelid, shining a bright light into my eye and I shook my head away.

"Just let me check your pupils. You might have a concussion," a calm voice said.

"I have a headache. I got hit on the back of the head," I said as he checked my pupil reaction.

Bending my head forward slightly, he shined the light on my head. "Man, I bet that hurts. Probably gonna need a few stitches." Placing a hand on my upper arm, he helped me up and steadied me when the dizziness made walking a chore. Unlocking my handcuffs, he assisted me in climbing out of the van and took me to an infirmary. An hour later, a doctor had placed a neat row of six stitches down the back of my head, and I had managed to explain what had happened.

"LeMoyne," the jail doctor said to the police officer that had helped me. "I think you've made a mistake with this one. Why don't you take her back to her vehicle, so she can go home and get some rest?"

"I don't know, Doc."

"Well, I do. Look at her. Does she look like the rest of that load you brought in?"

"What will happen to the others?" I asked.

"They'll all be out on bail before the sun sets. Just another happy day in hippie land," the doctor said. "Better get your own doctor to check this out as soon as possible. I don't think you have a concussion, but let him check the stitches to make sure you don't get an infection. Should be okay in a week or so, and he can remove them."

"Thanks," I said as I slid off the exam table.

I was still a little shaky as I followed Officer LeMoyne down the hallway toward the back exit of the police station. We passed a small group of female prisoners on the way out, and I saw the Asian woman with lavender glasses waiting to be processed. It was hard to believe she was a protester. She was so delicate looking and couldn't have been more than five four and a hundred pounds dripping wet. Hardly someone I would have expected to see at a student protest.

Chapter
Twenty-five

Friday, November 19, 1971

TWO WEEKS PASSED after the park incident, and I was looking forward to the Thanksgiving break from school, projects, and tests. I was used to physical labor, but the mental fatigue was starting to get to me, and I needed to find something mindless to do during the week-long break. I was slumped over my drafting table, scanning the last touches I had added to my blueprints when my thoughts were interrupted by a tap on my shoulder, followed by the smiling face of Vickie Landry. Vic had become my friend not long after I enrolled. She was a career counselor for the university and had shepherded me through the mound of paperwork and miles of red tape necessary for me to begin the fall semester on short notice. We had spent hours filling out forms, mostly at the home she shared with her long-time partner, Janine DeBose.

"What's up?" I smiled.

"Got any plans for tonight?" Vic asked innocently as she looked at my blueprints.

"I don't make plans," I said as I stretched.

"Janine is forcing me to go to a gallery showing with her tonight. The woman is positively adamant about cultivating my taste in the arts for some reason. At forty, I doubt she'll ever be very successful."

I laughed. "Better you than me."

"Truthfully, I was hoping you might show up with some financial assistance forms for the spring semester that couldn't wait until tomorrow, and rescue me from an unwanted cultural experience."

"Not likely, sister!"

"Please, Callie," Vic begged, using her best pathetic look.

"Just tell Janine you don't want to go, for God's sake. What's she going to do? Ban you from the bedroom?"

"Probably not, but the silent treatment could last way too long. Just this one time, Callie."

"Where?" I finally sighed.

"The Griffith Gallery about eight."

"I'll think about it. That's the best I can do right now."

"You're my savior," she smiled. "I'll be looking for you."

IT WAS EIGHT-THIRTY by the time I found a parking place in a high-rise parking garage two blocks from the Griffith Gallery. The weather had been nice all week, but there was a slight chill in the air. I had taken time to go home and change into the only semi-dressy clothing I owned before setting out on my rescue mission. Tan chinos with a brown shirt under a camel-colored tweed jacket. As I entered the reception area of the gallery, I ran my hand through my short hair and brushed it back into place the best I could. A man appeared out of nowhere and handed me a brochure featuring the artist on display. Slipping it into my jacket pocket without looking at it, I glanced around for Vic and Janine.

The artist's works took up four rooms of the gallery, and the works seemed to be an eclectic assortment of mediums. The first room was primarily paintings, and I paused to look at a few of them. I assumed they were portraits, but none of the subjects had faces. However, everything else in the paintings was extremely detailed. The more I looked at the pictures, the more it seemed that the bodies of the people in them were semi-transparent, revealing items behind them that would have ordinarily been hidden.

"Do you like them?" a voice asked from behind me.

Glancing over my shoulder I saw a very attractive young woman with shaggy, streaked blonde hair.

"I haven't decided yet," I replied as I surveyed her from head to toe.

She was dressed in low riding black bell-bottom jeans that drew my eyes to her hips, and an unbuttoned denim work shirt over a white tank top that showed off a well-tanned abdomen and fully rounded breasts. "Neither have I," the woman said. "I guess everyone could see something different in them."

"Well, most things are never what they appear to be at first glance," I said.

"What do you see?"

"The transparency part is interesting," I shrugged. "I wonder why they don't have faces."

"Maybe the models were too ugly to be painted," the woman laughed.

"Perhaps," I smiled. "You'll have to excuse me. I'm meeting some friends here somewhere."

Reluctantly leaving the attractive blonde, I wandered into the next gallery room and spotted Vic, sipping a glass of something that I hoped was alcoholic. She smiled broadly when she saw me coming toward her.

"Where the hell have you been?" she asked under her breath.

"Sorry. Couldn't find a parking place. Where's Janine?"

"Trying to generate a conversation with the artist du jour, I guess. Seen anything you liked?"

"Yeah, I did. But it wasn't artwork," I grinned.

"Behave yourself, girlfriend. This isn't a pickup gallery. Check out the sculpture in room three. Janine saw a piece she thought would be simply *magnifique* in our garden," Vic said, giving her best imitation of Janine's French accent.

Nearly two hours later, Vic helped Janine slip into her jacket.

"Well, I am starving," Vic stated. "We're going to catch a very late dinner, Callie. Why don't you join us, and we'll go over those financial aid forms."

"It can wait, Vic," I said.

"Oh, come with us, Callie," Janine said. "I know Victoria asked you to save her this evening. The least she can do is buy you dinner to pay for your time."

I laughed, "How the hell did you know that?"

"Because I know my Victoria like no one else," Janine smiled coyly as she stroked Vic's blushing cheek. "Meet us at Francois's."

At least at Francois's, I didn't have to search for a parking place. Francois's was a beautifully decorated restaurant, and it was Janine's favorite since it offered authentic French cuisine. My shoes sank into the plush red carpeting as I was escorted to Vic and Janine's table.

"Janine has already ordered for everyone," Vic said as I sat down. The waiter was already pouring wine into a glass as I adjusted my chair.

"It is late, so dinner will be light," Janine said. "Otherwise, sleep will be difficult. And we must wait for our other guest."

"Janine also invited the artist to join us." Vic said as she rolled her eyes.

"Ah, the artist," I smiled.

"Be nice, Callie," Janine admonished.

"Actually, I found some of the work very interesting, Janine."

"And which pieces did you find less interesting?" a voice came from behind me.

I turned to look into the bluest eyes I had ever seen, dark blue with an ice blue starburst surrounding the pupil. I stood and turned toward the young blonde I had encountered earlier at the exhibition.

"Ah, *mai oui*," Janine said. "The artist arrives."

"Katherine Thomas," the woman said as she extended her hand to me.

"Callie Owen," I said as I took the proffered hand.

I held a chair for her before reseating myself. I cleared my throat softly and looked at Vic as I took a sip of wine.

"A toast," Janine said holding her glass high. "A magnificent and hopefully successful showing this evening."

"Thank you," Katherine smiled as she, too, lifted her glass. "I apologize for being late, but I had to wait for my girlfriend."

"No problem," Vic said. "We've already taken the liberty of ordering, and it should be here very soon."

Turning to me, I hoped she didn't see the disappointment concerning her unavailability on my face, as she said, "I found your comments about my girlfriend's work very insightful."

"What comments?" another voice contributed as I saw a slender hand slide over Katherine's shoulder.

"Finally found a parking place?" Katherine smiled as she turned her head up toward the newest arrival.

Long, thick black hair tumbled past the new arrival's face as Katherine's girlfriend leaned down to kiss her lightly.

As her girlfriend moved to a chair next to the artist, Katherine smiled at her and said, "This is Jean Nagouri, my girlfriend and occasional artist." When I looked over at the woman, she ran her hands through her hair and dropped it over her shoulders, revealing lavender-tinted granny glasses. She smiled pleasantly through the introductions and without the slightest hint of recognition as I shook her hand.

"Callie was just saying that she found your paintings interesting," Katherine explained.

"That's always nice to hear," Jean said as she picked up her wine glass without looking at me. "Are you an artist?"

Before I could reply, Janine laughed. "Callie is most definitely not an artist."

Setting my glass down, I looked across the table toward Jean and said, "I know what I like when I see it."

"And did you see anything in particular that you liked this evening?" Jean asked in a husky voice, her black eyes sliding seductively up to meet mine. I felt as if my heart had stopped beating.

"I saw something that interested me very much," I said as I recovered, hoping no one else had noticed when I resumed breathing.

"She seemed to be quite taken with the portraits," Katherine said as Jean's eyes continued to bore into mine. The intensity of her stare made me slightly uncomfortable, but I couldn't tear my eyes away from hers.

"And what message did you find in them?" Jean asked, finally releasing me as her index finger lightly traced the rim of her wine glass. Everything she did, each small movement seemed designed to tease. I had never experienced anything like it before and felt my mouth go dry, wishing I were the rim of that fragile glass.

For a moment, I considered the pictures I had been drawn to earlier before leaning forward and answering. "That people are too easily influenced by exterior trappings, such as beauty, and fail to see what lies beneath."

"That's very deep," Jean smiled warmly without looking at me again.

"Or maybe that people have things about them they wish they could conceal from others, but can't. Sometimes the truth within can be ugly. But then again," I said as I leaned back in my chair and picked up my wine glass, "I'm no art critic."

"You must have been hurt very badly to be so cynical," Jean frowned.

"Life happens," I said.

"Perhaps you will have the opportunity to explore your new-found interest in the arts then."

"I try never to let an opportunity pass me by," I said as my eyes took in the delicate beauty of her face.

Our verbal repartee and flirtation were interrupted by the appearance of our waiter who set elegantly appointed dishes in front of us and refilled our wine glasses. As Janine had promised, dinner was light but filling. I found that I was actually enjoying myself and felt relaxation flow through my body. At the end of the meal, Janine ordered a cognac for everyone, which she insisted would be better than a rich dessert that could sit too heavily on the meal just completed.

"We didn't see you at the gallery this evening, Jean," Janine noted casually.

"I had another project I needed to complete and couldn't get away," Jean explained as she covered Katherine's hand with hers. "I knew I could trust Katherine to act on my behalf."

"Jean is a professor and has been busy putting together some Asian exhibit at the university," Katherine shrugged.

Jean's eyes flashed with a hint of anger as she half smiled at Katherine. "It's not just 'some Asian exhibit,' Katherine."

Sensing the tension between the two women, I asked, "What's the subject of your exhibit?"

Still looking at Katherine, Jean answered. "It's a photographic exhibit chronicling the history of Hiroshima and Nagasaki before and after the atomic attacks on them."

"It's too depressing for me," Katherine said softly.

"I've been to Nagasaki," I said. "I'd like to see the display sometime. Is it open to the public?"

"You've been to Nagasaki?" Jean asked, her eyes shifting quickly toward me.

"When I was stationed in Japan a few years ago," I answered over the top of my glass before downing the remaining contents.

"I'd be interested in your opinion."

"Katherine is right," Janine said with a slight shiver running down her body. "This topic is quite too depressing after dinner and cognac."

"Speaking of depressing," Vic said, "I have to be up early for work in the morning."

"Well, I enjoyed myself very much," Katherine said. "Thank you for inviting us this evening."

"It was our pleasure, *cherie*," Janine said as Vic helped into her coat. "We must do it again sometime."

As I stood, I held the back of Katherine's chair for her as Jean held her coat. Looking past Katherine to me, she said, "If you want to see the display, it opens tomorrow to the public, and there's no admission fee. It's hanging in the Asian Studies Department at Cal Berkeley."

"Thanks," I nodded as I turned to walk away, certain I would be seeing Jean Nagouri again soon.

Chapter
Twenty-six

Monday, November 22, 1971

THE FOLLOWING MONDAY, on a whim and not really wanting to return to my project, which had been occupying my time for over a month, I started my old truck and drove toward the ultra-liberal University of California campus at Berkeley. Asian Studies must have been a new department because I stopped and asked at least twenty students where it was located, and no one seemed to know. I was about to give up when I spotted an older man standing beside a vehicle in a parking lot, fumbling in his briefcase.

Thinking I had nothing to lose, I approached the man. "Excuse me, sir. I'm looking for the Asian Studies Department."

He looked at me blankly for a moment and then smiled as his hand pulled a set of keys from the briefcase. "I think it's over near Case Hall in some temporary buildings. Construction for a permanent site won't start for another year."

"And Case Hall would be where?" I smiled.

Pointing to a group of buildings in the distance, he said, "You see that tall building with the God-awful sculpture in front of it?" I nodded following his finger. "It's the smaller building just to the left of that. Houses the human sciences."

"Thank you, sir," I smiled again as I shook his hand.

By the time I pulled the truck into a slot behind what looked like a renovated Army barracks building, it was almost noon. I walked into the main doors of the wooden building and looked around for a minute. A glass-enclosed building directory told me that Asian Studies had its offices on the second floor. As I made my way down the second floor hallway, I looked at posters from Asian countries hanging along the walls, recognizing many of the places depicted. They had looked better in person.

Track lighting drew my attention to a large arrangement of photographs near the end of the hallway. An enormous, shadowed picture of a mushroom-shaped cloud served as the background for the exhibit. Its effect was both dramatic and foreboding. The bold title of the exhibit was made up of collaged newspaper headlines and articles and stood out elegantly against the dark wall. "And I am Become Death, the Shatterer of Worlds..." was a fascinating partial Hindu quote reportedly uttered by Robert Oppenheimer after he witnessed the first atomic test blast in New Mexico. If the pictures depicted God's work, then they forced the viewer to consider the consequences of that work. The display was divided into two parts, giving equal space to each devastated city. Stark black and white photographs, mounted in specially constructed frames that stood away from the wall at varying distances, were accompanied by simple captions explaining what each depicted.

The centerpiece of the Nagasaki exhibit was an excellent photograph of a Buddhist shrine I had visited at Nagasaki a few years earlier, surrounded by a series of smaller black and whites of the city before and after its destruction. As I gazed carefully at each picture, a familiar voice behind me said, "A totally unnecessary travesty against a defenseless population in order to justify a technological advancement."

Without turning around, I said, "These pictures don't do it justice really. It's a monument to the human spirit that rebuilt the city. It's a lovely and serene place today." I turned to face the lavender-tinted glasses and continued, "They say the spirits of the dead watch over the city to keep it safe."

"Ah, yes, that's right. You were there, as a curious tourist who wanted to see what the awesome military power of the United States had wrought," she frowned, glancing briefly over the display.

"I have a friend whose parents died at Nagasaki. I wanted to find their names on the memorial for her."

"Doing penance and seeking absolution?" Jean asked, looking up at me.

"I didn't need forgiveness for something I wasn't responsible for any more than those people needed to die for something they weren't responsible for."

"But you supported the war effort, didn't you?"

"I was five years old when those decisions were made, and the only thing I supported back then was my overalls."

"Having been in the military, however, I assume that you support American interventionist policies in Asia today as well."

"Actually, I didn't come here to engage in a political discussion about American foreign policy, as fascinating as that may be. I came to see this beautiful exhibit and to invite you to join me for lunch."

"Really?" she laughed derisively. "And why the hell would I want to do that?"

"You owe me."

"I just met you a few nights ago. I don't even know you," she huffed.

"We met briefly several weeks ago on our way to the police station."

A confused look crossed her face as she studied my face intently, followed by a smile as her memory came into focus.

"You kicked me," she smiled. "I'm sorry, but there was a lot going on that day. I'm afraid I didn't recognize you the other night."

"No reason you should," I said quietly. "But I remembered you."

Raising her arm, she checked her wristwatch. "I only have an hour before I have a class."

"No problem. We can go to the cafeteria in your Student Union."

Looking up at me, she frowned slightly. "You're not going to graciously take 'no' for an answer, are you?"

"No, ma'am. But if you're too busy today, perhaps we can arrange lunch for another day."

"No, I might as well do it, and get it over with. Just a minute." Walking a few steps to an open door, she said, "Linda, I'll be out of the building for a little while, but I'll be back in time for my class."

We had almost reached the stairs leading to the first floor when a young woman came quickly toward us. "Dr. Nagouri, I almost forgot. Dr. Phipps wanted me to remind you about the grants meeting later this afternoon."

"It's on my calendar, Linda. Thanks."

We didn't speak until we had our food and were seated at a small booth near the rear of the Student Union cafeteria.

"So you're a doctor," I said, duly impressed.

"I finished my Ph.D. last spring."

"That's great."

"What do you do, Ms. Owen, besides spend time in the back of police vans and invite total strangers to lunch?"

"That was a mistake. The van part anyway. I wasn't part of the protest. I was in the park working on a project and sort of got swept up with everyone else in the chaos of the moment."

"You must have extremely bad timing."

"What was the protest about anyway? I'm sure it was something life altering."

"Are you opposed to citizens exercising their constitutionally guaranteed right to vocalize their grievances against unjustifiable governmental incursions into the affairs of sovereign nations?"

I laughed out loud. "Did you read that somewhere in a propaganda pamphlet?"

She smiled despite an attempt to stifle it. She was already a beautiful woman, but her smile made her even more so.

"Back to your original question," I said, "I'm a student at San Francisco State."

"You're a little past the prime age for the freshman class, I'd guess."

"Just finished a twelve-year hitch with the Navy and decided to get out and carry on with my education."

"What are you studying?"

"It's called environmental design, but it's really glorified land-scaping."

"You're a gardener? No wonder my people can't get decent jobs with white people like you moving into their perceived area of exper-tise."

"I suppose I could take that as an insult, but I don't think I'll let you goad me into an argument right now. I enjoy being outdoors, and designing gardens lets me do that along with providing something that is functional as well as beautiful."

"Well, good luck. Personally, I have been known to kill plastic plants."

We only had a little time to get through our meal before I had to drive her back to the renovated barracks building for her class. As I opened the passenger door of the truck and offered her my hand to help her out of the vehicle, I smiled. She was a head shorter than me and absolutely American despite her distinctive Japanese features, but I liked her direct approach to everything. There wouldn't be any games with this woman.

"Would you care to join me for dinner this evening, Dr. Nagouri? I can promise you something a little better than cafeteria food."

"I have a meeting at four, and I'm not sure how long it will last."

"Tomorrow evening?"

Looking up at me, she took a deep breath before answering. "Are you asking me out on a date, Ms. Owen?"

With a slight smile I said, "Yeah, I suppose I am."

"And what makes you think that I would be even remotely inter-ested in going out with you? Or have you forgotten that I already have a girlfriend who might object?"

As my eyes looked into hers, I said, "Somehow, she just didn't seem like your type."

"And you think you are? You don't know a damned thing about me, Ms. Owen."

"I know you're a beautiful woman as well as extremely intelli-gent, although slightly arrogant and condescending. Am I wrong so far?"

"Well, no, but..."

"Do you live with your girlfriend?"

Her eyebrows moved together into a frown. "No, I don't."

"What time should I pick you up?"

"Eight."

A few minutes later, I drove away with an address stuffed in my jeans pocket, grinning like a total idiot. Other than an occasional one night stand overseas, I hadn't been seriously attracted to another woman since I had left Frost Valley. Jean Nagouri was condescending and arrogant, but there was something intriguing about her that had attracted me immediately. I laughed out loud trying to imagine a conversation between the quiet and serene Reiko Sanders and the abrasive, young Berkeley professor.

A LITTLE BEFORE eight the following evening, I pulled my truck to the curb in front of a modest low-slung one-story house in a lower middle-class neighborhood known by the locals as Little Tokyo. My slacks were pressed, and I checked my shirt to make sure it was neatly tucked in before walking to the front door and pushing the bell. A few moments later, Jean opened the front door and stepped onto the porch.

"I made a reservation at the Bird of Paradise," I said as I turned the key in the ignition. "I hope that was all right."

"It's a wonderful, traditional restaurant," Jean nodded.

When we entered, an older woman in a beautiful red silk kimono opened a sliding panel and bowed toward me with a hint of a smile.

"We have been expecting you, Ms. Owen," the woman said as she motioned us through the panel. Following our hostess through a series of narrow hallways before we stopped in front of another panel, we slipped our shoes off as she quietly slid the panel open, revealing large floor pillows surrounding a low, black-lacquered table. Taking Jean's hand, I helped her down onto a pillow before adjusting myself at the table.

While the older woman and several others served us a multi-course meal that was both delicious and relaxing, I was beginning to feel more at ease as Jean spoke briefly of herself, and her work at the university. I felt comfortable as we chatted our way through a number of courses, none very large, but which together added up to a very large meal. I was impressed with how quiet and demure Jean seemed during the meal. She was nothing like the loud, obnoxious woman in the police van, or the confrontational woman I had taken to lunch the afternoon before.

"You seem very reserved tonight," I commented near the end of our meal as I poured *sake* into a small porcelain cup.

"I'm trying to put together a thought, and it isn't coming to me very easily," she frowned.

"Are you trying to find a polite way to thank me for a lovely evening but wouldn't care to have another one...at least not with me?"

"I haven't decided yet," she smiled. "You're a very unusual woman, Callie."

"How so?"

"I don't know exactly. Tell me about your family."

Resting my elbows on the short lacquered table, I thought for a moment.

"I have two sisters, both younger than I, and three brothers, one older and two younger. My parents died by the time I was twelve, and

I was brought up by an aunt and uncle until I was eighteen and left home."

"Where is home?"

"Appalachia, back east, but I haven't been back in years. Not much there for me anymore, except one friend."

"You don't get along with your siblings?"

"After our folks died, we were separated and just sort of drifted apart over the years."

"Have you ever been in love?" she smiled, changing the direction of our conversation.

"Thought I was once," I laughed.

"And was your heart broken?"

"Among other things."

"Does your family know you're a lesbian?"

"I have no idea. Is it my turn to quiz you now?" I smiled.

"Fair's fair. Give it your best shot," she said crossing her arms in front of her as if ready to ward off a physical assault and taking a deep breath.

"Same questions, I guess. What about your family?"

"Not much to tell, really. I have an older sister, Cathy, and an older brother, James. Both my parents are still alive and live just north of San Francisco. My father is Japanese, but my mother is white." Frowning for a moment, Jean said, "And I suppose I should tell you that I was born in a prison."

"A born criminal?"

"During the war, my father was interned at the concentration camp at Tule Lake in northern California because he refused to sign a loyalty oath to the American government. My mother didn't have to go but refused to leave him."

"She must have loved him very much," I said softly.

"He's an extraordinary person, as is my mother."

"I don't know much about the internment camps."

"After Pearl Harbor, the government rounded up all Americans of Japanese descent on the west coast and moved them inland to what they euphemistically called internment camps for their own protection. My parents lost everything they had worked for when my father was ordered to Tule Lake in 1942. I was born there in 1944, a few months before we were released. It's not something you'll find depicted in many American history books. Just another act by white authorities against a minority group."

"I'm sorry your family had to go through that, Jean."

"We're very adaptable people. We adjusted."

"But you're still bitter about it."

"Wouldn't you be?" I saw a spark of hurt and anger in her eyes. "Japanese immigrants came to this country. They worked hard and were hated when they were successful because of that hard work. It was blatant legalized discrimination that enabled the white majority to steal everything they had built up."

"I hope you won't hold it against all of us."

"Ethnic prejudice isn't something you're likely to worry about since you're part of the majority."

"So is your mother, but she suffered as well. Discrimination and prejudice touch everyone. If you've ever looked at a beautiful blonde woman and thought she might be stupid, you'd be as guilty as anyone else. Despite what your parents endured, you hold what I'm assuming is a respectable position at a prestigious university that would have been unthinkable a few years ago."

"And some day I will be the chairman of my department, but probably only because I am part Japanese."

"Reverse discrimination," I smiled.

"I can live with that."

"Have you ever been in love?" I asked, changing the subject.

"No," she answered flatly. "There were always problems in the relationships I've had. Career problems, family problems, financial problems."

"Theirs or yours?"

"Mostly mine, I suppose. I set a goal for where I want my life to go, and what I want to achieve. I'm just taking the first steps in my career and won't allow anything, or anyone, to derail my plans."

"Everyone should have a goal, but it doesn't mean two people can't have diverse goals and still be one in their private lives. Do your parents know you're a lesbian?"

"They prefer to ignore it. I suppose they believe that it's only an experimental phase in my life."

"Is it?"

Her black eyes flashed as she answered in a firm voice. "No. What's your goal, Callie?"

I shrugged. "To be good at what I do, have a loving family, be comfortable."

"You want children?"

"I could be happy without them, but I believe that children make a family complete."

"And how are you planning to acquire these fictional children?"

"Well, where I come from, if I were a gypsy, I would kidnap them," I smiled. "But since that would probably mean another ride in a police van, I might have to consider adopting."

"No one would allow a single woman to adopt children."

"While I was stationed in Japan, I visited a couple of orphanages that cared for Amer-Asian children. Even though the Japanese culture is beautiful, within their society those kids don't fit in well and are regarded as outcasts. Even the Japanese inflict discrimination on others. Just a human tendency, I guess."

Jean rested her forearms on the table and looked at me. "You're an interesting woman, Callie. I can't quite figure out what you want or expect."

Leaning forward, I reached out and covered her small hand with mine. "I don't want or expect anything, Jean. You're a beautiful woman, and I'd like to know you better, but I don't want to play games with you. I could put on a show to try to lure you into my bed, but I wouldn't feel good about it later, and we wouldn't know each other any better other than physically."

"It's relatively presumptuous of you to believe I would consider allowing myself to be seduced into your bed."

"Is that a defense mechanism that works for you?"

"What?"

"It's just that I've noticed whenever you seem nervous or uncomfortable, you have a tendency to use very large words or extremely complicated sentences, syntax-wise, that is," I smiled. "I don't mean to make you uncomfortable. It's just harmless conversation anyway."

"Somehow, I don't think there's anything harmless about you, Callie Owen."

I poured a small cup of *sake* from the slender necked pottery container and handed it to her before pouring another for myself. Capturing my eyes with hers as she picked up the drink in a salute, she placed her hand over mine. The rice drink was almost as strong as the moonshine Reiko had forced me to drink before Doc Ayers had sewn up the wounds on my back and created the same hot burn as it slid down my throat. As she continued to cover my hand with hers, running a fingertip up and down the side of my index finger, I felt a different kind of burn spread through my body.

I picked up a small bell and rang it lightly. Immediately, the panel slid open and the hostess in red entered the room. "Was everything to your satisfaction, Ms. Owen?"

"Yes, it was wonderful as usual, Michiko," I smiled as I stood up and offered Jean my hand, pulling her up beside me. Stopping to slip into our shoes, she looked at me again.

"I know a small club near here if you'd be interested in a nightcap," she said.

"Just as long as it's something weaker than *sake*. It wouldn't take many of those to put me under the table," I chuckled.

"As intriguing as that sounds," she smiled beguilingly, "I think we can find something more familiar and less toxic."

Leaving the truck parked, we elected to walk to the club Jean promised was only a few blocks away. The entrance to the Blue Parrot Lounge was located more than halfway down a narrow alleyway that was noticeably lacking in lighting.

"You've been here before?" I asked hesitantly.

"Once or twice," she smiled. "Don't worry. It's perfectly safe."

When we entered through the bright blue door, I had to strain to see anything as I stopped to pay the cover charge. There was familiar rock music pumping loudly through a decent speaker system. As my eyes adjusted and I could finally make out shapes better, it became obvious that the Blue Parrot was exclusively a women's lounge. I had never known how anyone found places like this. Must be a secret passed around by word of mouth.

"Beer?" I asked, leaning close enough for Jean to hear me.

"Sure."

"Find us a table. I'll be right back," I said as I disappeared into the darkness.

I had always been a people watcher, and there were some fascinating people to watch in the back alley lounge as I waited for the bartender to fill my order. The women were an interesting blend, although many of them looked like people I wouldn't have cared to know other than as a casual observer. It was hard to imagine a woman like Jean Nagouri frequenting bars like this one. A few minutes later, I slid into a chair on Jean's left and set a mug of beer in front of her. It tasted good, and I finally felt like I was losing the taste of the *sake*.

"What do you think?" Jean asked.

"About what?"

"This place."

"It's different."

"Would you like to dance?"

The music was a hard driving rock tune that I wasn't familiar with.

"Think I'll pass. There's no way in hell I could dance to that."

There wasn't much conversation as several songs went by.

"We can leave if you're uncomfortable here," Jean finally said.

As I heard a slower tune that I did know begin, I stood up. "I can handle this one."

Her smile lit up our small area of the lounge. Taking her hand, I led her onto the dance floor. Without even thinking about it, I took her in my arms, pulling her close against me and stepped off into the dance. If she was surprised, she didn't say anything. Jennie had taught me years before how to at least slow dance, but I hadn't had much practice since then. Even though I was nearly a head taller than Jean, we seemed to fit together well. Other than an occasional pick-up, I hadn't been with anyone in years, and it felt good to be holding her in my arms. Jean rested her head against my chest as she slid an arm across my shoulders and stroked the short hair along the base of my neck as we danced, once again bringing back memories of Jennie. I was actually enjoying myself while at the same time silently questioning the wisdom of what I was doing. I wasn't sure what I really wanted or expected. I already knew I could easily fall in love with Jean Nagouri, but the fear of rejection, which I had always held deep inside, was beginning to creep coldly into my mind.

"You're an extremely handsome woman, Callie," Jean breathed against my neck.

"Thank you," I managed to get out as I let my leg move between hers so that it brushed against her inner thighs. It only took a moment for me to feel her hand tighten on my neck.

"That's very sensual," she said, her voice dropping into a huskier tone.

Without replying, I moved my hand to the small of her back and pulled her hips closer to mine so that my thigh pressed into her with every step. Even through my slacks, I could feel her heat against my upper thigh and her heart beating rapidly against me as the music finally faded away. We spent the next two hours dancing and getting better acquainted. Occasionally, another woman would ask her to dance, and I found myself becoming irrationally jealous of the time she was away from me and in someone else's arms. I was beginning to have what the Reverend Patterson would have considered inappropriate thoughts. Apparently, he had been unsuccessful in ridding me of the evil within my soul. It was well after midnight before we left the Blue Parrot.

"I've enjoyed myself this evening, Callie," Jean said quietly as we walked back to my truck.

"My pleasure."

We walked silently along the still busy streets, and suddenly there was nothing else to talk about. She was a delightfully enchanting woman, and I wouldn't mind spending more time with her. I didn't have many friends, and at least she would give me someone interesting to talk to.

When we reached her house again, I walked her to the front door. "Thank you again for a lovely evening," she said as she pulled her house key from her jacket pocket.

I didn't know what to say as I watched her turn the key in the lock and open the door.

"May I see you again, Jean?"

"I've enjoyed this evening more than I thought I would, Callie, but I'm not sure right now," she said as she stepped inside. After a short pause, she looked at me and closed the door. I didn't know whether she expected me to kiss her goodnight or not, but I didn't.

I drove halfway to my apartment before I pulled over and stopped. I wasn't sure what Jean had thought of me, but I knew I had never enjoyed being with another woman as much. There was no way I could deny that I had only been fooling myself about not knowing what I wanted. Against my better judgment, I turned the truck around. I had never done anything that foolhardy before and had to admit that I was a little nervous as I stood in front of her door for the third time that night. I could still just walk away, and she would never know that I had been there. But something inside me felt compelled to continue. I quickly raised my hand and knocked at the door before I could talk myself out of it. When there was no answer, I knocked again a little more firmly. Maybe she had seen me through the front window and decided that it wouldn't be worth it after all.

I started to chuck the whole idea and made a move to return to my truck when I heard the door lock click. A moment later, the door opened and the corners of Jean's mouth turned up slightly. She had already changed out of her clothes and was wearing a blue silk robe that ended halfway down her thighs.

"Did you forget something, Callie?"

"Yes, I did. May I come in?"

"Of course," she said as she stepped aside to allow me inside.

I turned toward her as soon as I heard the door click shut, stepping to close the distance between us, surveying her body appreciatively. We were only a few inches apart as I pulled open the tie on her robe and let it fall open. She lifted her eyes to mine and smiled. I leaned toward her, stopping my anxious lips close to hers as my hands drifted inside her robe and slowly along her sides and over her hips before continuing into her soft pubic hair. I felt her quick intake of breath as my fingers lingered along the inside of her thigh.

"Kiss me, Callie," she breathed, her eyes ignited by desire.

"Is that an order, Dr. Nagouri?" I smiled.

"You bet your sweet ass it is," she grinned.

Meeting her lips forcefully, demanding her kiss, I brought my left hand up her body and into the thickness of her sleek black hair while my right hand found the soft fullness of her breast, the dark nipple already hard beneath my palm. Breaking our kiss, I trailed my mouth along her neck and down the hollow of her throat, savoring the taste of her skin. I wanted her more than I had ever wanted anyone in my life. Her body felt warm beneath my hands, and her skin began to flush. Turning my head slightly, my tongue teased her dark, hardened nipple, and a low moan escaped from deep inside her throat. Her hands grasped my hair, pressing my head closer, as her hips began moving in rhythm with my mouth taking in her breasts. Slowly working my way down her abdomen, I knelt in front of her, my arms running along her thighs, and my hands covering her ass, pulling her into me as I deeply inhaled the scent of her arousal.

Reaching out to steady herself on the doorframe, she brought her leg over my shoulder, and I knew that she was close to losing herself. Running my tongue quickly over her clit and along her swollen lips, I savored every inch of her as she pressed herself against my mouth.

"I...can't stop it...Callie," she gasped as her body began to arch, her stomach muscles visibly tightening.

"Don't try to," I said as my fingers drove deeply into her hot wetness. "Let it go. I've got you."

A cry escaped her lips as my mouth and hand demanded everything she had to give. Her body was beautiful, glistening with sweat as she rode insistently against my hand. I needed to take her hard and fast in preparation for the slower lovemaking I knew would follow. I felt her tighten around my fingers and stopped the movement of my hand.

"No, don't stop, please God, don't stop," she begged.

I brought my thumb up and rubbed her swollen nerves as my hand resumed stroking into her, harder and more demanding with each stroke. I wanted all of her as my mouth joined my hand to drive her over the edge. Her body stiffened and was followed by the flood of heat running over my fingers and into my waiting mouth. I held her tightly as her body shuddered repeatedly, finally falling into a relaxed calmness. Standing, I swept an arm under her legs and carried her toward the bedroom, kissing her deeply, teasing her tongue and lips with gentle bites.

I laid her on the bed and leaned over her. "You're magnificent, Jean," I said softly as my lips found the still rapidly beating pulse on her neck.

Breathing heavily, she began pulling my shirt out of my slacks. Her eyes were moist and sparkled when she looked at me. "Let me just...catch my breath. Then you're mine," she smiled.

"I haven't finished with you yet," I said softly, catching her hands and pulling them away from my body, raging desire still pulsing through me, wanting to possess her again.

"I don't know if I could stand any more."

"Oh, I think you can," I smiled as my hand slid between her thighs again. "You're still wet." Her thighs parted as if they had a mind of their own at my touch. The thought that just my touch could draw such a reaction was still as overwhelmingly erotic to me as it had been the first time I had touched Jennie.

An hour later, we were both exhausted. I pulled her into my arms and held her as she rested her head on my chest.

"You haven't given me a chance to make love to you yet. I promise I will after we've rested a little."

"Not necessary," I said pulling her up to me and kissing her lightly.

"Why should you have all the fun?" she laughed. "No one's ever taken me quite that way before. God, what a feeling."

"I didn't hurt you, did I?"

"It was overwhelmingly, indescribably wonderful."

I reached over her and covered her body with the sheet as I felt her skin begin to cool. A few minutes later, I recognized the rhythm of sleep and allowed myself to doze off as well. As the sun was just beginning to come up, I was awakened as a hand moved gently between my thighs, and a breathy whisper entered my ear. "My turn. I can't believe you're still dressed," she purred as her fingers began unbuttoning my shirt while her mouth sought mine. As I opened my mouth to take in her tongue, I was startled by the touch of her hand on my skin, sliding along my sides toward my back. Grabbing her wrists, I stopped the movement of her hands and broke off the kiss.

"No," I said firmly. "I can't."

"Can't what?" she asked, surprised as I sat up.

"I can't...you can't touch me," I said, sliding away from her.

"I have to touch you, Callie," she laughed. "Otherwise, it would be very difficult for me to please you."

"Were you pleased?"

"You know I was. You have incredible hands," she said as she moved closer to me and wrapped her arms around my waist.

Placing my hands over hers, I moved them away and stood up. "Then that's all that matters. I have to go."

"What?" she said as her eyes widened. "But I haven't made love to you yet, and I want to."

"It's not necessary, Jean. I'm satisfied if you are."

Pulling her robe on and tying it firmly, she frowned, "That's absolute bullshit. Is that why you came back last night? Just to fuck me and then leave?"

I was hurt by her rebuke and didn't know what to say.

"Answer me, Callie!" she demanded.

"No. I wanted to make love to you, but..."

"But what?" she challenged.

"I thought it was what you wanted," I answered shakily, feeling tears beginning to form in my eyes as I looked at her.

I flinched and blinked hard when I saw her begin to raise her hand. She stopped when she noticed my reaction, dropping her hand back down to her side.

"Please leave, Callie," she said quietly as she turned away from me. "You got what you wanted."

"Jean, please, I didn't mean..."

"Just go."

I hadn't planned for any of it to happen, at least not that way, but once again I had let my desires and needs overwhelm my judgment. And once again, I had been hurt and hurt someone else in the process. We had both suffered because I hadn't been strong enough to control my wants. I didn't much like the woman I had become.

Chapter
Twenty-seven

Tuesday, November 30, 1971

I RETURNED TO my apartment from the environmental lab a week later, tired and wondering whether I had made the right decision by enrolling in college. I could have served eight more years in the Navy and retired with a guaranteed income until I figured out what I wanted to do. Everything had started out fine until I met Jean Nagouri and made a total ass out of myself. I had never been afraid of anything before, but I was scared to death of the way I felt about her. That was a lie. I was scared to death of how she would feel about me if I ever revealed the secrets of my past to her. I would rather face a life of loneliness than risk seeing the look on Jean's face if she ever saw my scarred body.

As I shuffled through my mail, I punched the play button on my answering machine and was surprised to hear Jean's voice. She wanted to see me and asked that I drop by her office at the university at my earliest convenience. There was a formality in her voice that indicated she must have been nervous or uncomfortable when she called, I thought with a smile. It was five-thirty as I dialed the number to Jean's office and was surprised when her secretary, Linda, answered the phone. Jean had already left for the day, but Linda had stayed late to complete some paperwork. I could hear the pages to a book flipping as Linda told me she had penciled me in for an appointment the next afternoon at three-thirty.

As I hung up my phone, I wasn't sure why Jean wanted to see me. I would be happy to see her again, remembering how her eyes had changed into a dreamy haziness as passion overwhelmed her. I hadn't been able to erase her face from my mind. I would keep the appointment, but knew it would be better for both of us to walk away. I would never be able to make her happy.

I was nervous as I trudged up the two flights of stairs to the Asian Studies Department the next afternoon. The hallway was empty as I walked quietly toward Jean's office and stepped into the reception area.

"She's expecting you, Ms. Owen," Linda smiled when she saw

me. "Please just go on in, and I'll let Dr. Nagouri know you're here."

I entered the office and looked around uncomfortably. There were pictures of people I assumed must be members of Jean's family. The older couple looked contented, but there was something about their eyes that revealed a sense of sadness. A few minutes later I heard voices in the hallway behind me. I was anxious to get this over with and get back to my studies.

"Hold my calls for the next hour, Linda," Jean's voice said before I heard the office door close.

"Please, have a seat," Jean said as she sat down behind her semi-cluttered desk.

"Thanks, but I don't think I'll be here very long."

"Do you know why I asked you to come here, Callie?"

"No."

"Me either," she smiled. "I just wanted to see you again."

Rising from her seat, Jean looked at me and came around the desk to stand in front of me. Folding her arms across her chest, she looked down at the floor between us as she leaned against her desk.

"I've been thinking about you quite a bit over the last week or so. I thought I might hear from you again, but when you didn't call I decided to take a chance that you'd respond to my message."

"I...I wasn't exactly at my best the last time I saw you. I didn't think you'd want to talk to me again. I didn't mean to upset you."

"If that wasn't your best, then I don't know if I could survive anything more intense, and you didn't upset me." Smiling to herself slightly, she looked at me. "That's a lie, and we both know it. I was upset. I need to know what happened that night, Callie."

"It was a personal matter that I don't care to discuss," I said stiffly.

"You gave me every indication that you were interested in pursuing a relationship of some type with me, and then it became more than a little lop-sided," she said matter-of-factly. "Is that what you're interested in, Callie? A one way relationship with you in control?"

"Of course not," I said as I shot her an involuntary angry glance.

"Then explain what you want from me."

Swallowing hard, I stared out her office window. "I don't want anything from you, Jean. I made a mistake and I apologize. If there is nothing else..."

Reaching out slowly, she cupped her hand on the side of my face, a concerned and gentle look in her eyes. "Who hurt you, Callie?"

I shook my head, but couldn't make myself look at her. It was too humiliating, too personal.

"Please," she whispered softly, bringing her lips closer to mine, "help me to understand."

"I can't, Jean."

She kissed me gently and held me in her arms. "I would never hurt you."

I knew that if I let her continue to hold me I would weaken, and we would both regret it more than I already did. It would be less cruel to end the hope of anything more between us now. Taking her arms firmly in my hands, I pulled them away, hoping my words would sound convincing.

"I made a mistake," I said coldly, "that's all."

Shaking her head, Jean said sadly, "That's not what I see in your eyes, Callie. If you won't let me touch you, I hope you will let some-one, someday."

My hands were shaking so hard by the time I left Jean's office and got into my truck that I could barely hold a match steady enough to light a cigarette to calm my nerves. What a fucking coward I had become. For the first time in years, I longed to have Reiko wrap her arms around the small child inside me and tell me everything would be all right. The butterflies would still come to the valley each year, the snows would always fall in winter, and the wildflowers would bloom each spring, making the air smell fresh and sweet. I wished my own life could be as constant and reliable as nature.

Chapter
Twenty-eight

NEARLY A MONTH went by as I learned and studied and prepared proposals for renovations in various city parks. Because I had
decided not to return to Tennessee for Christmas and didn't have
much else to keep me busy over the long Christmas break, I had vol-
unteered for extra shifts with the parks department, in addition to getting a jump on my spring studies. It was something I could
concentrate on for hours without tiring. The physical labor involved
was calming, and I would go home at night feeling like I had done
good work and sleep well. I had been working on a miniature model
for a large proposal, and it was after eight before I left the environmental lab to go home for the evening. I ran my hand through my hair
and ruffled it as I walked to my truck, not paying very much attention
to anything around me. My jeans and t-shirt were dirty, and I decided
that I might need to make a trip to the Laundromat over the weekend.
A nice long soak in the tub would feel wonderful I thought as I pulled
the truck into my assigned parking slot in the carport and entered
through the back door. Almost as soon as I turned on the kitchen light
to find something to heat up for dinner, I was interrupted by a knock
on the front door of the apartment. I didn't know what to say when I
saw Jean standing on my small concrete-slab porch.

"May I come in?" she asked, shivering slightly.

"Of course. I'm sorry. I just got home," I said as I pushed the
screen open for her.

"I know. I followed you," she said, looking around. "Nice apartment."

"It's small, but there's more than enough room for me. Can I get
you something to drink?"

"What do you have?"

I walked into the kitchen and opened the small refrigerator.
"Looks like water, milk, or I could make some hot tea."

"Tea would be wonderful," she said as she took her jacket off and
laid it over the back of one of the rockers.

I handed her a cup of tea a few minutes later and stretched my legs out in front of me as I leaned back on the couch and took a sip of my own drink. "It's good to see you again, Jean. How have you been?"

"Fine, just doing a lot of thinking." Smiling wistfully as she blushed slightly, she said, "I know it sounds pathetic, but I can't seem to get the feel of your hands out of my mind."

"You're a beautiful woman. You'll find someone else."

"I don't want someone else!" she said, standing quickly. "Please don't make me beg and humiliate myself, Callie. It's bad enough that I came here tonight to find out what I did that made you want to reject me."

Pushing myself up from the couch, I placed my hands on her shoulders, forcing her to look at me. "You've done nothing wrong, Jean. This is just about me. I lost control of myself when I should have known better. I'm sorry."

She brought a hand up and rested it lightly against my chest. "Since that night, it's been about me, too," she said softly. "I don't know what's wrong with me, but I've never felt like this about anyone before, Callie."

Taking her hand, I pushed her away. "Go home, Jean."

"I can't, damn it. Can't you understand that?" she said as she began pacing in front of me, her voice rising. "This contradicts everything I thought I believed. The idea that I would find myself groveling like this is ludicrous. I'm an intelligent, well-educated woman, for Christ's sake."

Stopping abruptly in front of me, her eyes flashing, her hand flew up, slapping my face hard. "That's for making me humiliate myself!"

My cheek stung as I turned my head toward her and grabbed her wrist. Glaring down at her, I released her arm and began to tear at the buttons on my shirt. There was no way she was going to let me escape without forcing me into doing the one thing that terrified me most. I couldn't bear to look at her as I jerked the shirt off my shoulders and turned quickly to reveal the hideous raised scars that crisscrossed my back.

"Are you happy now?" I demanded, my anger rising. "You've seen what you were so fucking curious about. Now get out and leave me the hell alone!"

"Sweet Jesus," she breathed as I shrugged my shirt back on and turned toward her, fighting back the tears I had never allowed myself to shed. She wrapped her arms around me and pulled me against her protectively. "What happened to you, baby?"

I wanted to push her away. I wanted to be left alone. I had been telling myself that for so long. Now with Jean's arms holding me tightly as she whispered softly to me, I felt the sorrow for everything I had given up or lost overwhelm me. I wrapped my arms around her, clinging to her like a child as tears finally began to leak out and I was crying uncontrollably. I struggled between sobs as I told her about

Jennie and our discovery by her father twelve years earlier. By the time I reached the end of the story, I was emotionally drained and physically exhausted from reliving every tortuous, painful moment that was supposed to save my soul. I had never told anyone, not even Reiko, and even the Navy doctors had believed my scarring was due to an accidental mishap with barbed wire. The tracks of her own tears stained Jean's face as I finally moved away from her and began buttoning my shirt.

"No," she said, stopping my hands with hers. Reaching up, she pushed the shirt back over my shoulders and turned my back to her, pulling the shirt off my body. As it fell away, the warmth of her lips kissed each scar across my back.

"Don't, please. I...I can't take any more of this," I begged as I felt tears slide down my face again.

"You're a beautiful woman, Callie."

I spun around, years of fury that had built up inside me finally exploding. "I'm a freak! And I don't need your fucking pity! I asked you to drop it, but you wouldn't. I don't need you, and I don't want you here. So leave and take your highly educated mind with you! I've gotten along fine up to now," I spat.

"By never letting anyone get close enough to touch you?" she asked quietly.

"I don't need to be touched! I need to be left alone!"

"Tell me why you're so angry, Callie. You're letting it destroy you. How can you ever be happy with all that anger inside you?"

As I closed my eyes, I could hear Reiko's gentle voice saying the same words. Let go and forgive to find happiness in the future. That had been twelve years ago, and I still had never been able to let go of my anger and conquer my emotions.

"Everyone needs to be touched, Callie," Jean's voice continued, trying to reach me. "You asked me out. You made the first move. To me, that means you want to be touched and loved as much as anyone else. Those scars don't show the person you are inside, where it matters the most."

She held my eyes, watching me try to bring myself back under control. She was right. While I had once enjoyed making love, it had become nothing more than an occasional necessary evil to relieve the stress in my life. I didn't make love to women; I fucked them, devoid of true emotion; merely desire or lust without the passion that would make it real or meaningful. I engaged in sex and nothing more tangible. No matter where I went, there had been women willing to let me fuck them for a few dollars without ever seeing my body.

I reached out to run my fingertips along her strong jaw line and let her pull me to her. She buried her face against me and tenderly ran her hands over my back. Feeling my body stiffen as her hands slipped into the back of my slacks and caressed the scars she hadn't yet seen, she looked up at me with the hint of a smile. "I won't hurt you," she promised again, drawing her hands slowly up my back to unfasten my bra and slip it down my arms, revealing my small breasts.

"Beautiful," she sighed, bringing her mouth to my breast.

I closed my eyes as my hands sought to hold her mouth firmly against me. God! It had been so long, so very long since anyone had touched me so intimately, so tenderly. Moving her hands and mouth commandingly over my upper body, she held me as I felt my defenses crumble. Even the slightest movement of her lips and tongue against my nipples sent powerful ripples down my body that made me gasp. My body thrummed with the promise of pleasure she was offering me. She had been shocked by what she saw on my body but hadn't pushed me away in disgust. A smile crossed her face as she ended her exquisite torture and picked up my shirt, slipping it up over my arms and shoulders.

"I'm going to my parents' home for the Christmas holidays tomorrow. I'd like it very much if you went with me, unless you already have plans."

"What would your parents say?" I asked as I re-buttoned my shirt, my fingers trembling.

"My father is very traditional, and my mother submits to him most of the time, but not always. They're both aware of the problems a non-traditional relationship can cause. I've already told them I might be bringing someone special home, hoping I could convince you to go with me. I guess the rest depends on whether you're brave enough to face them. My family is extremely important to me, Callie."

I looked down at her, seeing the hopeful expression on her face, the tingling feeling of her mouth covering my breasts still alive on my skin.

"What time should I pick you up tomorrow?"

"If we leave after lunch, we should be there in plenty of time," she said as she picked up her jacket. "I have to finish up a few things at my office before I leave. Can you pick me up there?"

"Of course," I answered as I walked her to the door and held it open while she adjusted her jacket.

Looking up at me, she grinned. "Are you going to kiss me good-night?"

"Are you sure you want me to?"

"Why are you so reticent, Callie? For a woman who makes love with the passion that you do, why would you be so reluctant to kiss me?"

"Maybe I'm scared," I shrugged.

"Of what?"

"That if I kiss you once I might not be able to stop." My hand cradled the side of her face as I looked at her. "You're so beautiful, Jean. You take my breath away."

"Let me make you feel as beautiful as you are, Callie," she breathed as her hand brushed against my breast.

My hands rested lightly on her hips as I leaned down and kissed her forehead, her eyelids, and the tip of her nose, pausing as my lips came within centimeters of hers. As my hands slipped up her sides and around to her back, I drew her closer to me and teasingly kissed her wonderfully full mouth. She stroked the back of my neck and brought us together in a slow, deep, probing kiss that began to fill me with genuine desire for the first time. Wrapping my arms securely around her, I lifted her up and held her as I kissed along her neck and across her collarbone. Every time I tried to release her, she pulled me into an ever-deeper kiss.

Although she had been shocked by what my body told her about my past, Jean couldn't have been more gentle and compassionate. That night she took my body to heights of ecstasy I had never imagined possible and brought me gently back to earth, in a way that would never cease to astound me with its passion and desire. I felt free for the first time in longer than I could remember. Jean didn't make it in to her office the next morning.

Chapter
Twenty-nine

Thursday, December 23, 1971

JEAN'S PARENTS LIVED about a hundred miles north of the Bay area in Cloverdale. Traffic going away from the city moved at a decent pace, and after we crossed the Bay Bridge, it thinned out considerably. Even though we chatted easily during the trip, I had to admit that I was nervous about meeting Jean's family. I didn't really know what kind of greeting I would receive, and I didn't want to ruin their holiday. I had already decided that if things didn't look like they were going well, I would take a room at a local motel and visit at the Nagouri's home for short periods of time.

Two hours later, with Jean sitting close to me, giving directions, I turned onto Ferndale Avenue.

"It's the last house on the right," Jean said as she began stuffing a small stack of papers she had been grading back into her briefcase.

"Looks like a party," I said, nodding to cars parked along the curb in front of the split-level ranch style house.

"We must be the last ones to arrive."

"Who else is supposed to be here?" I asked, surprised.

"Well, my brother and sister and their families always come home for Christmas."

"You didn't tell me that," I frowned.

"At least we can get all the introductions over with in one fell swoop. Don't worry about Cathy and James. It's Mama and Papa who might seem a little distant."

"Maybe this wasn't such a good idea, Jean," I said. "I don't want to cause a problem for your family over the holiday. I can get a motel room."

Turning to face me, Jean took my hand. "I want you to be here with me, Callie. I promised I would never hurt you. I won't let them hurt you either. Just be yourself, and I'm sure they'll love you as much as I do."

"You love me?"

With a smile that made my heart skip a beat, she said softly, "Did I forget to mention that?"

Jean laughed at the look on my face as she took my face in her hands and kissed me deeply. "How could I not love you?"

I didn't know how she could love me, but I steeled myself to meet her family as we carried our suitcases and packages up the front steps of the Nagouri home. Jean managed to free a finger to ring the doorbell. The front door swung open a few seconds later, and we were greeted by a stocky man with a shock of black hair that fell slightly onto his forehead. A broad smile crossed his face when he saw Jean standing there, laden down with brightly wrapped packages.

"Well, don't just stand there, you idiot," she laughed. "Take some of these before I drop them."

The man took the entire stack of packages and backed away, allowing us to enter the house.

"It took you long enough to get here, Jeannie. Mama's having a heart attack worrying about you," he said. "You know how she is about the baby of the family."

"I had some things to finish up at the university before we could leave," Jean said as she shed her jacket. It sounded more acceptable than what we had really been doing a few hours earlier. "James, this is Callie Owen. Callie, my brother, James Nagouri."

James shifted the packages onto his left arm while I set down a suitcase to shake his hand.

"Well, at least she looks normal," he said as he winked at his sister.

"Don't go there, James," she admonished.

Looking back at me, James laughed. "Jeannie usually brings home the most bizarre looking people she can find, so you'll have to excuse me."

"No problem," I said. "Where can I put these suitcases?"

"Top of the stairs, first room on the left," James instructed over his shoulder as he and Jean carried the packages into another room.

As I went toward the staircase, I glanced into a room near the front door and saw a beautifully shaped six-foot blue spruce, decorated with a combination of traditional American and Japanese ornaments. The lights on the tree reminded me of the small boats Reiko and I had set sail down the back valley stream to honor the spirits of my father and her husband. I was sure that his marriage to an American woman had caused Mr. Nagouri to adapt to a blending of their two cultures, and I smiled to myself knowing that that had created a new culture within their home to accommodate both.

When I found the room James had given directions to, I set our suitcases on a settee at the foot of the bed. My eyes were drawn to some framed drawings hanging on the wall over the headboard of the double bed. They were simple black and white, pen and ink drawings of ocean waves beating against and rising over stone monoliths protruding from the water. There was a simple elegance to the lines of the drawings that brought back memories of similar artwork I had seen in a few art galleries in Japan. I looked at the lower right hand corners of the pictures for the artist's signature but only saw a small series of Japanese pictographs. Although I had learned to speak passable Japanese, I had never been able to conquer the written language.

"Do you like them?" a strong voice asked.

Turning, I saw an older woman with dark, graying hair and a strong square jaw line standing in the doorway. She was wearing a plaid flannel shirt with the sleeves rolled up to her elbows over faded jeans and penny loafers. She was slightly taller than Jean and appeared to be a graceful looking woman. I bowed slightly toward her before answering.

"They're very beautiful, ma'am."

Taking a step into the bedroom, she offered me her hand. "I'm Jean's mother, Patricia Nagouri."

Her grasp was soft yet firm when I shook her hand. "Callie Owen, ma'am. You have a beautiful home. Thank you for allowing me to share it."

One side of her mouth formed a half smile as she released my hand. "My daughter tells me you have been to Japan."

"Yes, ma'am. I was stationed outside of Osaka for three years."

Walking past me, she moved closer to the bed and looked at the framed drawings.

"My husband drew these many years ago," she said without looking at me.

"They're very elegant, yet simple. I can understand now where Jean got her artistic talent."

Finally facing me, Mrs. Nagouri asked, "You've seen her paintings?"

"Yes, ma'am. I found them to be extremely thought provoking."

Laughing softly, almost to herself, she said, "That's an interesting response, Ms. Owen. You should join us downstairs, and let my daughter introduce you to the other members of our family."

While Patricia Nagouri hadn't been overly friendly toward me, she hadn't been standoffish either. At this point she appeared to be simply noncommittal. I wondered if Jean had brought many former lovers before me home to meet the family. Following Mrs. Nagouri out of the room and down the stairs, I heard laughter floating out of the room off the main hallway. When we reached the bottom of the stairs, Mrs. Nagouri did her best to smile politely.

"It sounds as if my children are in the living room, Ms. Owen. Please join them. I have to check on how my dinner is coming along."

"Do you need any help, ma'am?"

"No. Thank you for asking though."

Shoving my hands into the pockets of my slacks, I watched the reserved woman walk down the hallway before entering the living room. When Jean saw me, she stood up and joined me, wrapping an arm around my waist and pulling me farther into the room. The laughter stopped as seven pairs of eyes shifted toward us.

"Callie, these are my brother and sister and their families," she began. "You've already met James. Next to him are his wife, Louise, and their children, Terry and Lisa."

I shook hands with each of them as Jean continued around the room. "This is my sister Catherine and her husband Michael Logan. And the little one is their daughter, Chelsea." Looking up at me, she said, "And this is my friend, Callie Owen."

They were an interesting group. Apparently neither of Jean's siblings had married Japanese spouses. In fact, her sister, Catherine, seemed not to have inherited any Japanese features whatsoever and looked like a carbon copy of their mother.

"Where's Papa?" Jean asked.

"Same place he always is," James laughed. "Hiding out, seeking peace and quiet."

Jean took my hand, shaking her head slightly. "We might as well get it over with," she sighed. "I assume you've already met my mother."

"Yes, she came upstairs while I was putting our bags in the bedroom."

"I suppose she was civil, as usual."

"She was very polite."

"That bad, huh?"

"It'll be all right," I smiled. "Where are we going?"

"Outside. Papa is in his greenhouse."

The idea of a greenhouse interested me, and I figured I could make small talk about plants if I had to. The gardens in the backyard of the house had a distinctive Asian flair to them and I stopped once or twice to examine the decking and rockwork surrounding tiered gardens.

"Did your father build these?" I asked. "They're beautiful."

"Yes. Papa?" Jean called as she opened the door to a plastic-covered greenhouse. Glass-covered hotbeds filled an area along one side of the structure, catching the late afternoon sunlight. A slender man in his fifties, wearing chinos and a denim work shirt smiled as he turned toward us. Holding a small set of pruning scissors, he came toward us and swept Jean into his arms, hugging her tightly before releasing her.

"Papa, this is my friend, Callie Owen," Jean smiled. "This is my father, Ito Nagouri."

Doing the best I could to remember the Japanese etiquette I had learned, I bowed deeply toward Mr. Nagouri, looking directly at him. "It is an honor to meet you, Mr. Nagouri," I said in my best formal Japanese.

I remained bowed with my hands at my sides as he returned my bow and spoke to me in Japanese.

"What are you working on now, Papa?" Jean asked.

"I'm trying to save this poor Bonsai tree, but I'm afraid I'll have to clip away too much to help it," Mr. Nagouri said with a shrug. Turning to me, he said, "It has been a long time since I have seen a formal Japanese greeting, Ms. Owen. Where did you learn it?"

"In Japan, sir."

"I'll have to go there sometime. I was born in the United States, a Nissei, but my parents were Issei."

"What's wrong with the tree?" I asked, wishing Jean had told me about her father.

"It belongs to a neighbor who purchased it from a roadside vendor. Probably has some kind of parasite at the root level," he said, returning to his workbench.

"May I?" I asked as I looked at the spindly plant.

"Callie is studying landscaping," Jean explained.

"Be my guest," Mr. Nagouri said, motioning toward the plant.

I examined the anemic looking plant for a few minutes, but couldn't readily determine what might be killing it. I wished I could have Reiko look at it. It was probably some type of soil imbalance, but anything I tried might only make the problem worse.

"Have you replaced the soil and examined the root system yet?" I asked.

"Yes, but nothing has helped. Some things are just not meant to survive," Jean's father shrugged.

Standing away from the workbench, I glanced around the greenhouse.

"If we were closer to my lab, I could take some samples and look at them under a microscope, but you might want to separate this tree from your others just in case some type of bacterial blight is killing it. It could spread to healthy plants," I suggested.

"An excellent idea," he smiled easily.

"I think dinner is almost ready, Papa," Jean said. "You should get cleaned up before Mama has to come out after you."

Mr. Nagouri led the way out of his greenhouse and headed for the back door to his home. Halfway to the house, Jean stopped. "We'll be right there, Papa. I want to show Callie your exotic plants."

With nothing more than a wave of his hand, Mr. Nagouri stepped into the house. Taking my hand, Jean led me to the far side of the greenhouse. As soon as we had turned the corner, she pulled me closer. Leaning down, I smiled. "Are you the exotic plant I'm supposed to be looking at?"

"I don't think I would be very satisfied if all you did was look," she teased.

"Maybe I should have taken a motel room after all. Do your parents know you're a screamer?"

"Well, whose fault is that?" Jean asked, feigning anger.

"Mine, I hope," I said as my mouth covered hers.

By the time we left to return to San Francisco three days later, I wasn't sure I would be able to stand it until I could be alone with Jean again. She had teased me mercilessly during our visit with her family. Her parents had been civil to me, and I had been determined to do nothing to antagonize them needlessly, leaving both Jean and me frustrated.

Chapter
Thirty

Tuesday, July 10, 1973

IT TOOK ME nearly a year to convince Jean's parents that I was a decent human being. Although I knew they would probably never accept the fact that their younger daughter loved another woman, I wasn't planning to spend the rest of my life living with them. The few days a year we spent with Jean's parents seemed like a small sacrifice on my part, no matter how frustrating it might have been. At least they had finally begun calling me by my first name and stopped referring to me simply as "Jean's friend."

Although I was impossibly in love with Jean, I began to reach a point where I wondered about the future of our relationship. Despite her outspokenness, there was a shyness about her that only I saw. I had moved in with Jean just after New Year's the previous year and had suggested several times since then that we find a larger house and set up a home together, but she resisted the idea saying she wasn't ready.

"I thought we might go look at a few houses next weekend," I said one evening after dinner.

"Why are you in such a hurry, Callie? We're doing fine right here and taking on a bigger mortgage might not be a great idea right now. We're both still young and have plenty of time for that later," she said as she got up and cleared our plates from the table.

"Look, if you're worried about your parents, Jean, I think we're mostly past that now."

"This doesn't have anything to do with you, Callie."

"Of course it does. I know they don't like the idea of you being with me."

"No, they don't."

"So why are you?" I asked as I took her arm and pulled her onto my lap.

"Because I can't help it. I'm in love with you, damn it."

"And I'm in love with you, baby. I want to be with you forever."

"It's just that so much is going on right now. You have one more year left at State, and I'm in the middle of trying to expand my department at the university."

"If you're worried about our finances, I can buy a house using my military benefits, honey."

"I'm not worried about money, Callie. We hardly spend any at all."

"We need to make time for just us, Jean. Forget about school and work for just a couple of weeks and relax."

Kissing my forehead, she sighed, "That does sound heavenly."

"Let's take a trip," I beamed.

"Where?"

"I've been thinking that I'd like to take you back to where I grew up. I want you to meet the other important woman in my life. It only seems fair since I've already endured...um...met your family."

Poking me in the shoulder, she said, "My turn to do the in-law thing, huh?"

"I believe in equality, sweetie. No reason I should be the only one to suffer. But I know Reiko will love you. Maybe not as much as I do, but..."

She cut me off by kissing me soundly as she moved to straddle my legs.

"Mmm. I like that," I smiled as we finally brought our kiss to an end.

"Well, since we probably won't have much time alone while we're visiting your home, I thought I better stock up before we leave," she breathed into my ear as she nibbled along my face and neck.

I HAD PUSHED myself by attending summer classes and doing some extension work to complete my degree in three years. I hadn't been back to Frost Valley in eight years. It was a long drive from California to east Tennessee, and I doubted my truck would survive such a trip and borrowed Vic's car. It took me four long days to drive from San Francisco to Frost Valley, and it was nearly dark by the time I turned into the drive of the Sanders farm.

"Are we there?" Jean asked as she stretched.

"Yeah," I said. A few yards down the drive, I stopped and put the car in park.

"I hope you'll like Reiko, but she's pretty quiet. Give her a day or two. She doesn't have any friends out here that I know of. So if she seems a little reserved, well, it's just her way."

"Right now, I'm so tired of being in this damn car, I don't care if we're staying at Count Dracula's castle."

I touched her face and said, "I love you, Jean."

Shifting the car into drive, I drove to the house and parked near the front porch. Honking the horn, I got out and ran around to open the door for Jean. As I helped her out, I heard someone call my name.

When I turned around, I saw Tad jump off the porch and run toward me. He had grown into a man in my absence and nearly knocked me down as he wrapped his arms around me. He was tall and slender and had obviously been working out.

"What took you so long, Callie?" he asked, his voice much deeper than I remembered. "Mom's been keeping dinner warm for hours. Wouldn't even let me have a nibble until you got here."

"Sorry, but it took a little longer than I figured to come over the mountains," I said. Turning to Jean, I said, "Jean Nagouri, this is Tad Sanders, practically my baby brother."

Tad smiled and shook Jean's hand. I opened the trunk of the car, and Tad grabbed our bags.

"Let's go, Callie. I'm starving," he said.

I put my arm around Jean, and we walked up the steps into the living room. Tad was already galloping down the stairs and heading for the dining room.

"I put your stuff in your old room at the top of the stairs. Now let's eat."

As we followed him toward the dining room, Jean stopped me. "Is he Japanese?"

"Half. The other half is white. Like you."

"Where's your mother?" I asked.

He jerked a thumb toward the kitchen. Taking Jean's hand, I quietly opened the kitchen door. Reiko was standing with her back to me, pouring something into a large bowl. She looked smaller than I remembered, but was still slender. I cleared my throat and she turned around, a broad smile crossing her face when she saw me. Wiping her hands on her apron, she came across the kitchen toward me and reached up to take my face in her hands.

"You grow so big!" she said with a smile that brightened the whole room.

I hugged her and picked her up off the floor.

"It's good to be home again," I said as I set her down. "Reiko, this is Jean Nagouri. I told you about her on the phone."

"Ah, yes. It is pleasure finally to meet you," she said with a slight bow toward Jean.

"Jean, honey, this is Reiko Sanders."

Jean bowed slightly to Reiko and smiled.

Over dinner, I caught up with everything that had happened. The best news had been that Tad would complete his studies at UT-Knoxville during the next semester. Every now and then he had experienced a problem, but nothing as serious as what his mother had gone through. The influx of foreign students to major American universities had helped. Unfortunately, Reiko was still looked upon as an outsider and was unwelcome most of the places she went in Frost Valley or Boone, the closest town.

"You're driving now?" I asked.

"She can, but I take her where she needs to go. Sort of a chauffeur-body guard type of arrangement," Tad said between mouthfuls of food.

"How long have you lived here, Mrs. Sanders?" Jean asked.

"Since 1949," Reiko said quietly.

"And the people here still don't accept you? That's outrageous!"

"That's Frost Valley," Tad shrugged.

"But they've accepted you, haven't they?" Jean asked as she looked at Tad.

"Pretty much. But it's mostly because I'm Thomas Sanders, Jr., and they remember my dad."

"Tad play football," Reiko added with pride in her voice.

"What position?" I asked as I buttered another melt-in-your-mouth, homemade roll.

"Wide receiver."

"You weren't a very fast runner the last time I saw you."

"After you left, I had to run home every day to keep from gettin' beat up. I guess it paid off."

"I told Willie to keep an eye on you," I said.

"He did, but mostly from the backside. Not everyone was as anxious to get beat up for protecting me as you were," Tad laughed.

"I don't know how you can be so cheerful about it," Jean fumed. "How can you stand living in a place where everyone hates you?"

"This is husband's home," Reiko said quietly, her voice as resolute as ever.

"And she ain't givin' it up," Tad and I laughed in unison.

I was exhausted from the trip, and although I tried to be sociable, I could barely stay awake. I must have dozed off because I was startled by the touch of a hand on my shoulder.

"Go to bed now. We talk tomorrow," Reiko said, looking down at me.

Getting up, I took Jean's hand and led her upstairs. In a matter of seconds, I was stripped down to my underwear and under the sheet, sinking into a deep feather mattress. Sometime during the night I woke up and rolled toward Jean, but she wasn't there.

"Jean?" I said, adjusting my eyes to the darkness. I had no idea what time it was, and even though she had slept some in the car, I couldn't imagine why Jean wasn't sound asleep, too. My eyes finally located her sitting in an overstuffed chair near the bedroom window. I crawled out of bed and crossed the room toward her.

"Couldn't you sleep, honey?" I asked. "Sorry that I conked out on you."

"The least you could have done was tell me how Mrs. Sanders was being treated here because she's Japanese," she said. "It wasn't fair of you to bring me here without some warning." There was coldness in her voice that I hadn't heard in a while.

"I know and I'm sorry," I said as I knelt down next to the chair. "But what difference does it make?"

"Are you going to explain exactly why you wanted to come back here?"

"Now?"

"It's as good a time as any since we're both awake."

I rubbed my face and tried to gather my thoughts. I wasn't sure why I had wanted her to meet Reiko.

"Reiko's a special person in my life. She's the closest thing I have to a family, and I wanted you to meet her."

"Bullshit, Callie!" she said in as loud a whisper as she could without waking everyone else up. "It was her family that was killed at Nagasaki, wasn't it?"

"Yes, it was."

"And she chooses to live in the shadow of the place that created the weapon that destroyed everything she knew, surrounded by ignorant Gomers who can't, after thirty years, accept her as a human being? It's like a slap in the face every day. I think she'd have to be incredibly stupid to stay in a place where she's so obviously disliked."

"Don't you *ever* call her stupid again," I said heatedly as I stood up. "You're the one who's always running off at the mouth about discrimination, Jean, and you haven't suffered an iota of the discrimination Reiko or your parents have. She handles it her own way. With grace and dignity by enduring, not by trying to ram it down the throats of her neighbors."

Jumping up quickly, Jean faced me. "She's let herself be treated like a doormat. Is that what you expect me to be? A docile little Japanese woman waiting for you to come back to hearth and home each night and think nothing of it?"

I had to laugh. "A doormat! Have you ever had to shoot at your neighbors to protect yourself and your home? She's a tougher woman than you'll ever be!" I said through clenched teeth as I pointed my finger in her face. "She loved her husband and honored him by going where he went, but that sure as hell doesn't make her a fucking doormat. You can't change shit without staying around long enough to fight it. She lives within twenty miles of the place that helped to destroy everything and everyone she knew and loved, but she's winning in her own way, by persevering and forgiving. At least she didn't run away because of her fears like I did!"

Before she could open her mouth to spout any more of her Berkeley bullshit, I walked away from her. I don't know how, but I managed to find my jeans and shirt and pulled them on. I was still buttoning my shirt as I left the bedroom and went barefoot down the stairs. I needed to inhale fresh, smog-free air for a change.

The kitchen clock read four-thirty as I opened the back door and stepped outside. In another hour, everyone in the valley would be up, ready to work in their fields or milk cows. Digging a cigarette from my shirt pocket, I lit it and leaned against one of the ancient chestnut trees in Reiko's front yard. Maybe, I thought, this trip hadn't been such a great idea after all.

A few minutes later I heard someone coming toward me. Jean's face was partially illuminated by the setting moon.

"I'm sorry, Callie," she said as she reached me.

"Forget it," I said, not looking at her.

"Are you going to punish me now by not talking about it and making it worse?"

"No," I said pushing myself away from the tree trunk. "I'm sorry, I should have told you more about Reiko's situation before we got here."

I turned and looked at her. "I want our life together to be everything we both dream it can be. I guess I needed to come back to make some kind of peace with myself. I know that every place isn't as bad as this and not everyone thinks the way these people do, but I'm a product of this valley, Jean. It tried but couldn't teach me to hate people who are different. Hell, I'm different. I'm in love with and make love with another woman. I paid the price for that years ago and nothing that could happen to me because I love you could be any worse than that. I'd endure it again to convince you that I love you."

"Try not to get mad, Callie, but did you choose me because I'm Japanese and you expected me to be like Reiko?"

"I love Reiko for being the friend she was to me when I was alone and hurting and for the things she taught me when I was a child, but I don't expect you to be her. You and Reiko are both strong women in different ways. She stays here to honor her husband's memory, which is a pretty damn stubborn thing to do. I guess I thought if I brought you here you'd be able to understand why I'm the way I am."

"She made her choice about her life, Callie. And all I'll ever need to understand about you is that you love me."

"You'll never have a reason to doubt that," I said as I pulled Jean into my arms and held her tightly against me, feeling her warmth seep into my body. "Reiko's made a decent life here for Tad and herself. After the first few years, I think everyone just ignored her presence and went on about their own lives, but she had to get lonely once Tad left for college."

"Does she know you're a lesbian?"

"I'm sure she does now. I never told her about Jennie. I'm not really sure how well even she'll take that. Guess I'll find out soon enough if she's really as understanding as I've always thought she was."

I felt Jean shiver as I held her. "Cold?"

"No, just scared. I hope everything turns out the way you want it to."

I wrapped my arm around Jean's shoulders and kissed her lightly. "Let's go back to bed. I'm really bushed."

Chapter
Thirty-one

Wednesday, July 11, 1973

I WAS AWAKENED a few short hours later by a shaft of sunlight that had made its way through the bedroom window and fell directly across my face. Jean was still sound asleep, and I slipped out of bed and dressed as quietly as possible. I carried my shoes and waited until I was downstairs before putting them on and tying the laces. When I walked into the kitchen, Tad was seated at a small table near the back door, reading the newspaper.

"Morning," he smiled. "There's coffee on the stove."

"Where's Reiko?" I asked as I poured a cup full of strong black coffee.

"Off in the woods again, cataloguing the flora and fauna."

"She's still doing that?"

"I told her she needed to write a book or something, but she said it makes her happy to do it just for herself."

I looked out the kitchen window at the meadow behind the house and into the trees as I sipped my coffee, lost in my own thoughts.

"You want some breakfast? I can scramble up some eggs," Tad offered as he folded his paper.

"No, thanks, Tad," I smiled. "I'll wait until Jean gets up."

"Jean's your girlfriend, huh?"

I looked over my shoulder at the young man I had first seen as a toddler. "Yes, she is."

"How long have you been together?"

"About two years."

"I have a girlfriend, too. Mama doesn't know it yet, but I'm thinking about asking her to marry me."

"What's stopping you?"

"Carolyn's parents don't like me very much," he frowned.

"Jean's parents don't like me very much either," I laughed.

"Her parents are still clinging to that old anti-Japanese thing, I guess."

"At least you only have one strike against you. Mr. and Mrs. Nagouri tolerate me even though I'm not Japanese, and I'm not a man."

"We're a pretty screwed up little bunch, aren't we, Callie?" he said as he came to stand next to me and rest his arm around my shoulders.

"Yes, we are," I answered as I looked at him. "You're a good man, Tad, just like your father was."

Setting my coffee cup on the kitchen counter, I pushed open the back screen door and stepped out into the fresh air. I swear to God that it smelled exactly the same as it did when I was a kid. There was something earthy and dewy smelling about it that made me feel at peace with everything. I had tried to deny it for years, but I loved this valley. The valley didn't recognize differences in people and didn't care what they did as long as they took care of the land. It was only the people who inhabited the valley who had opinions.

I followed a small path that led past the barn, which looked as good as it had all those years ago when Reiko had ordered new paint for it, and found myself quickly swallowed up by the trees. It felt ten degrees cooler as the branches dispersed the sunlight. I was amazed at what Reiko had done in the forested area behind her house. Working alone, she had cleared most of the unnecessary underbrush, being careful to leave enough to keep the environmental balance intact. It took me a while, but I finally spotted her using a walking staff and carrying a large woven basket on her hip as she made her way down the ridge. She smiled when she saw me climbing toward her.

"Good morning," I smiled.

"Here, you take basket. Give old lady a rest," she said as she handed the basket to me.

"What do you have in here?" I asked as I glanced at the collection of dirt and green leaves. "Doesn't look edible."

"It is plant I find on other side of ridge. Have never seen it on this side."

"Maybe it's not supposed to grow on this side."

"Plant grow anywhere, but must adapt like people who move," she squinted up at me. "You sleep good?"

"Best rest I've had in years."

"Tell me what you doing now in California," she said as she continued down the hill.

"I have one more year of school left, and I'm still working for the parks department."

"You mow grass?"

"Sometimes," I laughed. "But I've been working on a design to renovate some of the parks, and make them more accessible to people."

"People always damage plants and trees," she frowned again. "No respect for hard work nature does. What Jean do?"

I was a little taken aback by the change in questions, but I knew that sooner or later Jean would become a topic of conversation. "Jean's a teacher," I said, deciding that it wouldn't matter to Reiko whether Jean taught first graders or college students.

"What she teach?"

"She teaches classes about Japan and the other Asian countries mostly."

"People pay money for this?"

"Yes."

Reiko stopped occasionally to squat down and examine a plant as if she had never seen it before and periodically added one to the increasingly heavy basket.

"Where are we taking this, Reiko?"

"To garden," she said as she walked on. "Jean very pretty girl."

"Thanks, I'll tell her you said so."

"In Japan, girls like Jean not acceptable."

The statement stopped me dead in my tracks. "What do you mean not acceptable?"

"Woman who love other woman not acceptable," she said as she stopped and turned to look at me.

"Then I guess I'm not acceptable either, Reiko, because I love Jean."

"It never work, Callie. You both get hurt. Better you not together. Bring great shame and dishonor to her family."

I couldn't believe what I was hearing. I would never have expected Reiko, who had suffered so much because she loved an American, to ever say such things to me. I could have accepted disappointment or misgivings, but she was just flat telling me to give Jean up and to live a conventional lifestyle. I was furious. I had driven across the country to the one person I had hoped would understand, and she had slapped me in the face and was no better than the people who had shunned her. Using the wooden walking stick, she made her way back to where I was standing.

"Her family suffer because of what she do. She become outcast, and it your fault. You poison her mind and turn her against her traditions, her family. Family everything, and you make her dishonor them and memory of her ancestors. Family will be punished because of this love you say you have. If you love her, then you must give her up, for sake of family," Reiko said in a firm voice.

Tears were filling my eyes as I listened to words I never thought I would hear from this woman I had respected so much. "I can't, Reiko. I won't give her up. I thought you, more than anyone else, would understand. You and Tad are my family, and I love you, but I wouldn't give Jean up even for you." I set the basket down and looked at her, "I'm sorry that I've disappointed you," I said as I turned to walk back to the house.

"Callie," she said as I turned away from her. Stopping, I looked back at her as a tear slipped down my cheek. I waited as she walked toward me again. Looking up at me, she reached her hand up and brushed away my tears.

"This is same as I hear when I fall in love with Thomas," she said, smiling slightly. "My heart broken, but I love him too much, and we make new family, new home. Now you and Jean must do same thing. You must teach your heart and not let heart become teacher. Only you know what you have taught it. Same as me."

It took a moment for relief to flood through my body, and I laughed through my tears as I leaned down to embrace that wise woman who never stopped changing my life.

Pushing me away slightly, Reiko said, "Get basket before plants die. Then I fix breakfast."

It wasn't until a couple of days later that I finally told Jean about my conversation with Reiko that morning. If I had told her earlier, she would have been as furious as I was. The relief over Reiko's acceptance was so strong that we could only hold each other and laugh through our tears.

I HAD SPENT some time studying Reiko's gardens behind the old barn and was fascinated by the variety of plants she had gathered. A few times, either I, alone, or both Jean and I would accompany Reiko on her excursions through the ridges and valleys in search of new plants or an occasional mutated version of a more common variety. Occasionally, I would watch Jean and Reiko talking quietly but never inquired about their conversations. I figured if Jean wanted to share what was said to me, she would.

I had noticed but not really investigated what seemed to be a rather unusual blend of small animals around Reiko's home. She and Thomas had planned to start raising livestock but hadn't gotten to it when he was killed. Now it seemed that every time I stepped out the back door of her house, some new creature greeted me. Usually ducks or geese and once, a peacock.

Late one afternoon, we were enjoying a glass of fresh lemonade under a canopy in the backyard when I spotted movement out of the corner of my eye.

Smiling, I asked, "What the hell is that, Reiko?"

Looking around, she pushed her ever-present straw hat back off her head and glanced in the direction I was pointing to.

"Duck," she stated.

"I know that," I said. "What's wrong with it?"

"Horse step on. Back broken. Very tough duck," she explained as she casually continued to sip her lemonade.

Jean and I looked at each other and broke out in laughter. The little yellow duck was leaving a small dust cloud in its path as it waddled along the dirt drive, and I couldn't resist getting a closer look. I couldn't believe how quickly the little guy darted around as he tried to avoid capture. Jean was almost hysterical with laughter, and even Reiko was forced to giggle as I was outmaneuvered by a disabled duck for several minutes before finally managing to grab it. Returning to my chair, sweating profusely in the summer heat, I examined the duck more closely.

"What is this?" I asked as I turned the irate bird over in my hand.

"Back broken. Duck can no walk right. Leather help protect beneath," Reiko said as she looked carefully at the small bird. "Must replace soon."

With its broken back, the duck was forced to drag its rear end along the ground when it walked. I imagined that continual rubbing had worn off any feathers that would have protected it. Reiko had made an almost diaper-like contraption of leather that she had fitted to the bird with a small harness.

"It looks like a skid plate," I smiled as I set the duck gently down on the grass and watched it skitter merrily on its way. "I didn't know you had any animals here."

"No animals. Too much for woman alone. Children bring hurt duck here."

It finally dawned on me that Reiko had found some measure of acceptance by caring for the injured duck. Perhaps the new generation was less influenced by old habits.

"Do you have other animals here now?" Jean asked.

"Just bird. A few chicken and duck. Chicken good for eggs. Have problem with black duck."

"What kind of problem?"

"Duck is confused. In love with chicken," she shrugged. "Cannot catch chicken because of duck. Very protective. Every day must go to barn and find eggs. Chicken not stay in coop."

I smiled, "Maybe you should just get rid of the duck."

"Duck just confused. Maybe you and Jean catch duck for me. Sneaky fellow, though."

I knew a challenge when I heard one and took a deep breath. An hour later while Reiko disappeared into the house to prepare dinner, Jean and I walked into the barn. Reiko had told us that the chicken in question laid eggs all over the barn, and we would have to search for them. If we were lucky, we would find the chicken alone and be able to return her to the hen house. We managed to collect about a dozen eggs from the first floor of the barn before we climbed the wooden ladder into the second story loft. I went up the ladder first with the basket of eggs, setting it down to help Jean up when she reached the top rung of the ladder.

We were poking around a few old hay bales for more eggs when I heard a loud hissing noise from behind me. It was one of the strangest sights I had ever seen. A tan and white hen sat calmly in the corner of the loft, her black eyes darting around, while a rather large, and obviously pissed off, black duck paced back and forth in an arc a few feet in front of her. The hen clucked periodically, apparently working up another egg, as the duck hissed at us and lowered its head.

"Do ducks bite?" Jean asked as she grabbed my forearm.

"Sort of," I answered quietly as the duck and I eyed one another. "Do you know how to tell if it's a male or female?"

"How the hell would I know that?"

"I dunno. I read somewhere that the Japanese are the only people who can tell the sex of a chicken when it's still a chick. Thought maybe it would work for ducks, too."

"Since I'm only half-Japanese I might not have inherited the chicken sexing gene," Jean chuckled. "Besides, it's not likely I would have spent much time gazing at chicken crotches."

I wasn't worried about being bitten by the angry duck, but figured I'd have a real fight on my hands if I tried to separate him from his oddball mate.

"Let's separate," I said. "One of us can try to distract it while the other one grabs the hen."

"You better do the grabbing, honey. I have no idea how to even pick up a chicken unless it's wrapped in plastic and on the meat aisle at Safeway."

"Okay," I nodded. "Ready?"

"I really feel stupid doing this, Callie," Jean mumbled as we separated.

"Yeah, life on the farm is a real education."

It seemed that no matter how far we got from one another, the duck could watch us both and increased the speed of its paces in front of the hen. I tried to step closer and was met with an outrageous fit of duck tenacity each time. I had to hand it to that damn duck, though. If Jean was ever in danger, I knew I would act the same way to protect her. Glancing around the loft, I finally came up with an idea.

"I'm going to climb out the window over here and work my way around on the roof to the window on your side," I told Jean. "When you see me, try to get the duck's attention while I reach through the window and grab the hen."

"Whatever you say, Old MacDonald," Jean smiled.

What a smart ass, I thought as I climbed out the loft window. But at least she was a cute smart ass. The angle of the roofline over the first story of the barn was steeper than I remembered, and I had to inch my way along the side with my back to the wall. A few minutes later I reached the window on the other side and peeked in. When Jean saw me, she nodded and began sidestepping across the loft floor with the duck pivoting to watch her. A minute later, I looked in the window to see where they were. The duck's back was to me as I repositioned my feet so that I could reach inside. Barely breathing, I leaned over the sill of the open window and reached over for the hen. I almost had her when the duck suddenly spun around and saw me. For a split second our eyes met before it launched itself toward me, smacking squarely against my arms, its beak grabbing and pinching down hard on my forearm.

"Grab the hen!" I yelled to Jean as I tried to get the duck away from me, feeling the soles of my sneakers slipping on the barn shingles. Glancing around, I knew I was going to fall off the roof as I slapped the duck away from me. I didn't want to hurt it, but I had more important things flashing through my mind at that moment. I couldn't remember what was on the ground below the barn, but I hoped it was nothing as my feet went out from under me, and I rolled toward the edge of the roof. In what seemed like an eternity later, I heard a loud snapping sound as I hit the ground. Pain shot up my leg, and I gasped to regain some of the air that had been driven from my lungs by my impact with the ground. Dazed and glancing around for the duck, I heard Jean's voice. A moment later, she came running around the side of the barn with Reiko right behind her. When I picked my head up and squinted at them, I dropped my head back down to the ground laughing.

"Callie, are you all right?" Jean asked as she knelt down beside me, the hen tucked securely under her arm.

"I think I broke my leg," I continued laughing. "But at least you got the damn chicken."

I winced as Reiko gently felt up and down my leg. Nodding at me, she said, "Leg broken."

"Sorry about the vacation, sweetie," I exhaled as I took Jean's hand.

"I guess you'll have to do what I say for a while now," she smiled down at me.

"Bummer," I laughed as the hen clucked contentedly in Jean's arms.

By the time we returned to the valley again, we had started our own family and Jean's family, no matter how dishonored they might have felt, had learned to accept me as a permanent part of their lives.

Chapter
Thirty-two

IT WAS STILL slightly overcast, but the temperature had risen a few degrees by the following morning. I found an old pair of snow boots that must have belonged to Tad and trudged my way through still deep snow toward the big red barn behind the house. I managed to kick aside enough snow to pull a door open. It smelled musty inside, and it didn't look like it had been used much. Reiko's old car was parked inside and covered with a tarp. It probably didn't have more than a few thousand miles on it. Parked next to it was Thomas's old truck, and it looked like Reiko had had it restored. I wandered around the barn for a few minutes and finally found what I was looking for. Reiko's selection of tools wasn't very large, but I managed to cut eight squares of walnut about five by eight inches. I sanded them down and located an old can of lacquer on a shelf. When the first side was well coated, I left the barn and returned to the house. As I stomped snow from the boots, I heard Jean and Carolyn talking and laughing in the kitchen. I pulled off my coat and hung it on the coat rack just inside the kitchen door.

Jean smiled when she saw me, "And where did you get off to?"

"Just working on a little project in the barn," I shrugged with a smile as I walked over to her and kissed her lightly. "Smells good," I said as I peered into the large pot she was stirring.

"I could tell you I was soaking your socks, but it's actually a recipe Carolyn has for stew. Might have to get a copy to take home."

"If we ever get home," I said looking at the snow that still buried our car.

"Wouldn't bother me to stay for a while. It's so peaceful, and no matter what I think about the people here, it is beautiful."

"Where is everybody?"

"Tad and Monica are doing something on the computer," Carolyn said. "And I think Lauren and Nolan are building a snowman."

"You might want to go talk to Rachel, honey," Jean said softly.

"Is something wrong?"

"She's just acting a little weirder than usual."

"Okay," I said as I poured two cups of coffee.

I found my daughter sitting on the couch in the parlor, watching Nolan and Lauren attempting to create an artistically pleasing snowman. Lauren seemed to be directing Nolan in the fine art of making snow stick together.

"I thought you might like a cup of coffee," I said. "Still pretty chilly today."

"Thanks, MC," Rachel smiled up at me.

"May I join you, or would you rather be left alone?"

"It's okay, I was just watching Nolan make a total fool of himself," she said as she took a tentative sip from her cup.

"You think he's smitten?" I chuckled.

"I think he's absolutely around the bend over that girl. Better keep an eye on him, or you and MJ might find yourselves grandparents again."

"That serious, huh?"

"Could be," she shrugged as she returned to watching her brother and Lauren.

"He told me he was just interested in her brush stroke technique," I said as I sipped my coffee.

"He might be interested in her strokes, but I don't think it has anything to do with brushes," Rachel smirked.

"God, Rachel! What a thing to say," I blushed at her outspokenness.

"I'll bet you and MJ thought Nolan was gay, didn't you?" Rachel asked as she returned her attention to me.

I didn't know what to say, although his apparent disinterest in girls had come up between Jean and me once or twice. "It wouldn't matter to us either way, Rachel. We just want you and Nolan to be happy."

"Very PC response," she smiled. "But he's definitely not gay."

"How the hell would you know that?"

"Because, believe it or not, Nolan and I have actually been known to converse from time to time when neither of you were around. Trust me, he's interested in more than her artwork."

We sat quietly for a few minutes, and I smiled as I watched my usually quiet and reserved son frolic in the snow like a child again. I couldn't remember him even seeing snow more than three or four times in his life, and that had been mostly from a distance. Turning her head to look at me, Rachel said, "Can I ask you a question, MC?"

"You know you can ask me anything, sweetheart." I just hoped she was willing to accept my answer.

"What do you honestly think about Ron?"

I had to think about that for a moment. Rachel had married Ron Kirk against our wishes eight years earlier. He was a handsome man and well educated and had a good job when they married. But there was always something about him that bothered me in particular. Jean had finally decided that Rachel's personal life wasn't any of our business. I was the one with the lingering doubts about our son-in-law. He had worked to support their family as an accountant until Rachel had graduated from veterinary school and then inexplicably quit his job, saying he wanted to find something different. It had now been three years, and he still hadn't found it. Rachel sat patiently waiting for my answer. Jean had taught her that, and I sometimes found the silence aggravating.

"Does he make you happy?" I finally asked.

"Very," Rachel smiled.

"Then it shouldn't matter what I think, Rachel. You have to live your own life just like Momma Jean and I did. A very wise woman told me that a long time ago."

"Ron and I have been talking a lot lately about how we want our lives to be. We want the girls to be happy and not feel pressured."

"That makes sense," I shrugged.

"He's afraid of you, you know," she said, looking back out the window. "But he respects you very much."

I had to laugh despite the seriousness of our conversation. "Why the hell would he be afraid of an old woman like me? He should be scared of Jean."

"I know, but he considers you to be the head of our household," she shrugged. "I know you and MJ share everything equally, but Ron doesn't see that."

"Well, hell! Now he sounds like your Uncle Edwin who pretends I'm a man, so he can feel more comfortable."

"Well," Rachel grinned, "you do sort of wear the pants in our family."

"That's a clothing preference, not a sexual statement," I frowned.

Taking a deep breath, Rachel looked at me. "Ron wants to stay home with the girls, and I don't want to give up my practice. I love the girls, but I don't want to stay with them twenty-four seven. Ron doesn't want to turn their care over to a total stranger."

"So he wants to stay home and cook and clean and take care of the girls," I summarized.

"That's pretty much it, MC. And recently, he's begun a hobby that he loves and has even made a little money from it."

"What would that be?"

"Stained glass. I never knew he was so sensitive and artistic until he took a couple of lessons. Then he just took off like a bat out of hell."

"I didn't know that. Where does he work on it?"

"We converted a part of our garage, but we're talking about having a workshop built out back. He's afraid the girls will get into the glass and cut themselves, Momma Callie."

It was the first time in more than ten years since she had last called me that, but it made me feel good. I reached over and played with a loose strand of Rachel's beautiful black hair for a moment before I let my fingertips trace her delicate jaw line.

"I think," I started, "that you and Ron are making a good decision, Rachel. I know I've been a little hard on Ron the last few years, but I know he loves you and the girls. He makes you happy, but he needs to be happy as well. I promise that I will apologize to him when we get home."

"Oh, Momma Callie," Rachel said as she flung her arms around me and hugged me tightly, "Thank you. He's been scared to death about your reaction to all of this, but he's really a brilliant designer. He's working on a piece for your house right now."

"I haven't commissioned any glass for the house," I said.

"It's supposed to be a surprise for your anniversary. So act surprised when we bring it over for him to install."

Laughing, I said, "I'll do my best, honey."

Leaving Rachel to call her husband on her cell phone, I wandered into the study where Tad and Monica were involved in a spirited game on the computer.

"Who's winning?"

"We are," Tad smiled. "Monica challenged some guy and his friend to a match."

"Guys think they're so smart," Monica grinned. "Wait until this moron sees our next move."

"You're on the Internet?" I asked.

"Yeah," Tad said. "I convinced Mom to get it out here a couple of years ago. That way she could use it as a tool for looking up her plants and ask questions of an expert somewhere else."

"Good idea," I said as I finished my coffee. "After you finish what you're doing, and if you don't mind, could I use it for a few minutes to look something up?"

"No problem. Monica's right. Shouldn't take too much longer to finish these gentlemen off."

I eventually found myself going through the desk and closet in a small room off the main hallway that Reiko had apparently made into a workroom. I needed some small dowels and paper and felt sure she would have them around someplace. I had stopped my search for a few minutes and was looking at framed photo collages she had mounted on the walls. Almost all of the pictures were old black and whites. I couldn't believe that all those years had passed. God, I was a gangly child. I was smiling to myself when I felt familiar arms slide around my waist.

"You were a pretty cute kid, you know it?" Jean chuckled as she looked at the pictures.

"I looked like a malnourished giraffe."

"But a cute giraffe. And you grew into such a handsome woman," she smiled up at me.

"You're prejudiced," I said softly as I hugged her to me. "Still don't know what you ever saw in me."

"Prejudice isn't always a bad thing."

Tilting her chin up toward me, I said, "Thank you for being prejudiced then." I kissed her gently and felt the warmth I always felt spread through me.

"You'll have to do better than that later," she said in a low, seductive voice.

"I'll do my damnedest, but just remember we're getting older," I smiled.

"You're only as old as you feel," she grinned as she squeezed my upper arms, "and right now I'd say you feel about forty."

I wrapped my arms around her and held her close to me. I would never stop wanting her.

"What are you looking for in here besides memories?" she asked when I finally reluctantly released her.

"Reiko used to have some paper in here that I could use for that little project I'm working on."

"You and your projects," she sighed.

I pulled open a drawer on an old chest of drawers near the door and looked inside.

"Ta-da!" I said. "I knew she would still have some."

"It's beautiful," Jean said as I handed her a roll of colorful thin paper. "Tissue paper?"

"Sort of, but a little thicker. More like a vellum."

After lunch, I was back to the barn. I drilled four small holes in each piece of walnut I had cut and varnished that morning and glued small dowels about four inches long into each hole. While I waited for the glue to dry, I set off through the trees to check the stream that ran along through the back of the Sanders property, about a third of the way up the side of the valley's western ridge. The snow that had made it through the tree branches wasn't nearly as deep as the snow in the yard and field, and it was easy to make my way up the ridge. About halfway up, I could hear the sound of water moving. I had been afraid that the little stream would have frozen over, but the trees had protected it well enough to continue flowing out of the ground and make its way along the upper shelf of the ridge.

By the time I got back to the barn, the glue had set. I cut the vellum-like paper into strips and attached them to the dowels. I had completed four of the little boats when I heard the door to the barn open. Turning, I smiled when I saw Tad squeeze through the door.

"What are you up to out here, Callie? Carolyn and Jean are curious as hell," he said as he walked to the workbench. When he saw the completed boats, he smiled. "What a great idea!"

"Want to finish a couple?" I asked.

Taking a piece of walnut, he picked up a strip of paper and began placing it around the dowels. "What are you going to write on the lantern paper?"

"I've been trying to think of something profound, but haven't come up with anything yet. What did Reiko write on the ones she made?"

"I was little back then, so I'm not really sure. She just said it was something about lighting the spirit's way on its journey. Wasn't that it?"

"We're pathetic, Tad," I laughed. "Might have to break down and ask Jean and then hope our combined Japanese is good enough to write it. I wanted these to be a secret, but looks like that isn't going to work."

"The three of us can keep it a secret from the others," Tad smiled. "Mom would understand."

When we were alone that evening, I told Jean about the little boats and that I needed her help writing something on the sails. She thought about it for a long time before she came up with the perfect words. Tad showed us where Reiko had kept her ink and brushes and Jean practiced her Japanese calligraphy a little while before we returned to the barn to complete the project. By the time we went to bed, I was happy with the way they had turned out.

Chapter
Thirty-three

Saturday, April 3, 2004

THE SUN HAD finally been able to cut through the overcast skies by mid-morning the next day. Tad and I carried the little boats as we led our families through the woods to the stream. We handed a boat to everyone and explained its symbolism just the way Reiko had explained it to us more than fifty years before. Tad and I lit the candles inside the paper chimneys for our families and watched them flicker and take hold. Tad squatted down next to the stream and pushed his boat gently away and watched it bob around for a minute before it was caught by the main current and moved away. Each of us pushed our boats away a little behind the one in front of us until mine was the last to float downstream to join the others. When they were all out of sight, I took Jean's hand and squeezed it as we walked back toward the house. It was such a simple thing, and yet it made me feel at peace, which was what Jean had painted on the sails enclosing the candles. Reiko's spirit was at peace to rejoin her parents and her husband. If she had a problem, I hoped my dad's spirit would help her again, too.

As we walked Tad said, "I forgot to give you the present Mom left for you, Callie."

"What is it?" I asked.

"I have no clue. She wrapped it up not long before she passed away."

I was sure it was some little trinket that I had liked as a child, but no matter what it was I would cherish it. As soon as we entered the house, Tad left us to retrieve the gift Reiko had left for me. She couldn't have known I would return to the valley. Jean and I were looking out the front window at the snowman Lauren and Nolan had made the day before when Tad came back down the stairs carrying a long tube and a large envelope. The tube was wrapped in bright orange and yellow origami paper. Japanese writing followed by my name was on the front of the envelope. I didn't recognize the Japanese script and handed it to Jean as I unwrapped the tube, pulled the top off, and slid out two large rolled sheets of vellum. I carried them to the dining room table to roll them out.

I couldn't believe what I was looking at. The top sheet was a precise grid of the wooded area behind her house with each plant identified as to its name and location. It was basically the area on either side of the stream we had just visited and up the sloping ridge behind the barn. The second sheet was more drawings of what she had envisioned the same area would look like some day.

"It's a plan for a botanical garden," I said. "And a pretty ambitious looking one at that." Looking at Jean, I asked, "What does the envelope say?"

Jean looked at me for a moment. "It says 'For the future, my dream.'"

I took the envelope from her and opened it. Inside was a letter and what looked like a small bank passbook. I pulled a chair away from the dining room table and sat down as I read a neatly printed letter. Tears filled my eyes as I refolded the letter and slid it back into the envelope a few minutes later. I opened the passbook and let the tears roll down my face. Reiko had left over seven thousand dollars in an account in my name for her dream. I couldn't force myself to say anything even though I wanted to. Jean, who had been reading over my shoulder, enclosed me in her arms and held me as I tried to collect myself. Sensing that I needed to be alone, Tad and Carolyn left me with my thoughts. Reiko hadn't seen me in years, and yet she had entrusted me with her dream, a gift to a people and a place that had hated her. Suddenly, I couldn't stand it any longer, and I stood up and walked away, leaving Jean alone.

I made my way back up to the stream and sat down on a flat stone that partially extended over the stream. I sat there thinking for what seemed like a long time but may have only been a few minutes. I looked at the work Reiko had done already. She had spent half a century creating what Tad had called her Noah's Ark for plants and had tended them with such care that none of the environment around them had been disturbed. As I contemplated the drawings she had left along with the letter, I saw what she had wanted done. But without the physical resources to assist her, it would have been impossible for her to do alone.

"Callie?" Jean said as she made her way to where I was sitting. "Are you all right, sweetheart?"

I smiled as I looked around at her. "Never better, my love. Just planning in my mind."

"You know exactly what she wants, don't you?" she smiled.

"Yep. I can see it. And so will everyone else in six months or so."

"It can be done that soon?"

"Maybe sooner. But none of the work can be done with machinery. It all has to be done by hand in order not to damage what's already here," I said taking Jean's hand. "You know that means I'll have to be here when the work is being done?"

"Reiko didn't trust anyone else to do it, and I wouldn't either."

"There's one other thing, honey. It might cost a little more than she thought."

"We can afford whatever it is, Callie," Jean smiled as she shivered.

I pulled her closer to me and wrapped my arms around her to keep her warm. "Better get you back inside before you freeze out here," I said as I kissed her.

Two days later, the narrow roads over the ridges began to thaw out and we rescheduled our flight back to San Francisco. The day we left Reiko's farm I promised Tad that I would be back in a month to start the most important project of my life. Nolan spent the entire time we were loading the car talking to Lauren Sanders and looking longingly in her eyes. I had already figured he would be back with me in a month and hoped his phone bill wouldn't approach the national debt during that time.

Chapter
Thirty-four

Saturday, May 8, 2004

OVER THE NEXT month, I managed to convince six members of my work crew to leave home for the next four to six months to work on Reiko's dream. Of course, the extra separation pay I promised them was a powerful incentive. All I left behind was a skeleton staff to maintain the work we had already pledged to perform at home. Jean would fly back east and join us once the spring semester ended. I missed her almost as soon as our trucks pulled away. Nolan seemed particularly anxious to leave, and it wouldn't have surprised me if I returned home with a future daughter-in law. He had spent a considerable amount of time researching stone native to eastern Tennessee and contacting local quarries. And, of course, he had spent hours on the phone with Lauren and faxing information to her.

Most of my crew had never been out of California. The six men and women I took with me had been with my company for years, and we had always worked well together. They rarely argued over who had to do what work and never questioned my directions. I had to smile at what the impressions of the locals might be to these total strangers who were mostly Hispanic and Asian. Geraldo Montoya had been my crew supervisor for the last ten years and had decided to groom our youngest member, Oscar Santiago, to someday take his place. Jean had referred Hakiro Yamaguchi and his son, David, to me a few years earlier. She had never interfered with the way I ran my company, but when she learned that Hakiro had been born in an internment camp just as she had, she had strongly advocated their employment. The two women on the crew, Maya Parker and Heike Lindstrom, had been partners for several years. One of them was African-American and the other Caucasian. Frost Valley would be getting a lesson in multiculturalism it would never forget.

Four days later, the three trucks bearing the logo for Owen Environmental Design slowed and turned onto the gravel drive toward Reiko's home. I drove the lead truck and parked along a fence that separated Reiko's property from the meadow next to it. As I got out of the truck cab and stretched, I directed the other two trucks to a spot closer to the barn. It was late in the afternoon, and the sun was resting along the top of the ridge in front of us. I was surprised to see Reiko's car and Thomas's truck parked in front of the barn instead of inside. Before I could think much more about it, the back door of the house opened, and Tad and Carolyn came out to greet us, followed a few minutes later by Lauren and Monica.

I hugged Tad and his wife. I was glad to see them again, but the trip had been exhausting.

"Dinner will be ready in about half an hour," Carolyn announced. "I don't know anything about landscaping, but I sure as heck can cook."

"We wouldn't be able to exist without you," I laughed. "But I should warn you that this is going to be a pretty hungry group almost all the time."

"She's been stocking the freezer and refrigerator for a month," Tad smiled.

Nolan and two of the other workers began unloading duffle bags and suitcases from the covered bed of one of the trucks. I noticed he hadn't gotten very far before Lauren began pulling him toward the barn. When she saw the look on my face, Carolyn laughed. "Looks like Lauren can't wait to show Nolan what we've done to the barn."

"Come on," Tad beamed. "It was Carolyn's idea."

My workers followed us toward the big red building. I was amazed when I opened the door. They had renovated the majority of the interior into two bedrooms downstairs and two in the loft. Each floor had its own bathroom with showers and closets. The large work area where I had made the boats was still there and much better organized. They had installed a large television, telephones, and a small kitchenette with a refrigerator and microwave.

"Looks like you two have been busy," I smiled. "I'm sure my crew will appreciate it. Beats sleeping in tents."

"I've spoken to the county and state governments since you left, too," Tad said. "They and a couple of organizations in Oak Ridge provided most of the material and labor to make the barn livable."

"Tell her the other news, Tad," Carolyn said excitedly.

"When I told a few people about Mom's project, they pulled some strings and actually got the county and state to match her funds. And the best part is they don't want any credit for it. They have some kind of grant program that the funds will come from. The only catch is that the natural area has to be made available to the area schools."

"We can add some natural walkways through most of the area," I smiled. "Reiko would like to have children come here. The only hitch would be vehicular traffic. You don't need them around the house, and the exhaust fumes could eventually damage the forest growth over a long period of time. You might want to see if the county would be willing to foot at least part of the bill to cut another road onto the property with a parking area at least a quarter mile from the tree line," I suggested.

"Guess I can add that to my list of things to do," Tad sighed.

"Isn't this great, MC?" Nolan asked as he and Lauren joined us.

"Yes, it certainly is," I said as I looked around the barn. "I have a couple of ideas for this old barn once the natural portion is done."

"Project: Phase Two?" Nolan asked.

"It isn't my area of expertise, but this would make a great museum and information center," I said to Nolan.

"MJ will go wild!" Nolan laughed.

"Well, that's enough future planning for now," I said. "We still have phase one to do first." Turning to my crew I said loudly, "Dinner in twenty minutes! After dinner we'll go over the plans and get to bed early." Pulling Carolyn forward a little, I said, "This is your new best friend, Carolyn Sanders. She's the woman who's going to make sure you get fed and watered, so you might want to start kissing up to her now."

Carolyn blushed as my crew descended on her offering to do chores or anything she needed done in exchange for extra portions of food. The rest of us laughed as we left Carolyn surrounded by her newest fans.

The next two weeks were full of hard manual labor as we transplanted plants and moved foliage temporarily to build up a few areas with additional soil. The crew even waded into the cold water of Reiko's stream to examine what was growing along the stream banks and on the bottom. After discovering the small fish that inhabited the pool I had helped Reiko form years before, Maya and Heike came up with a plan to divert some of the water into additional stair-stepped pools to allow visitors to actually observe them before they swam on their merry way toward a larger body of water.

There was quite a bit of underbrush that would have to be removed or cut back to make room for the paths through the gardens, and the ground would have to be leveled and stabilized beneath them. Without using heavy machinery, much of the work became backbreaking drudgery, but I had to hand it to my crew. They never complained and most of them had never eaten so well. The one thing that I found surprising was that no one from the valley had been by the farm. News of our work had to have spread.

Near the end of May, as I was making my way along the ridge to inspect buried rebar for stabilizing the walkways, I saw a familiar vehicle pull up near the house and watched as Katie stepped from the driver's side. She stood staring into the trees for a few minutes before I decided I should find out what she wanted. I was still wiping my grimy hands when I reached her.

"Katie. How are you?" I asked.

"I was curious about what you were doing out here, Callie, and since you haven't come by, I thought I'd come to see you," Katie said.

"Well, we've been a little busy, but I was planning to come by when we're a little further along."

"What are you doing out here anyway?"

Pulling a cigarette out of my shirt pocket, I lit it before answering her. "We're working on a project that Reiko asked me to do before she died."

"What kind of project?"

"It's a garden and nature preserve for the community. A gift, so to speak," I said as I exhaled a cloud of smoke.

"Are the children here with you?" Katie asked.

"Only Nolan came back with me. Rachel had to get back to her practice and her children."

"And Jean?"

"She's flying in the end of next week for the summer."

"How long will this project take you?"

"A few months. It's moving along quicker than I thought it would."

"Callie? Can I donate something for the project?"

I looked at her and she must have seen the question on my face.

"It's just that a few years ago, Mrs. Sanders came to our house. We have a huge number of dogwoods in the woods behind the barn. I guess she saw them when they were in bloom and stopped to ask about digging some of them up. There are some here but not many, and she saw that some of ours were a different variety. Could you transplant some of them over here?"

"I don't know, Katie," I shrugged. "I'd have to take a soil sample, and see if the soil makes it more difficult for them to grow here. It might not be acidic enough."

"It was just a thought," she shrugged.

"How about if Nolan and I come over in a day or two and check them out?"

"Come and stay for supper. Bring everyone if you'd like," she smiled. "I know everyone thinks I'm a simple-minded fool, but I'm really not, you know. I just get along."

"Time is slow to pass here, Callie," Katie said quietly as she looked around the property. "And so are memories. You were right. I should have gotten to know Mrs. Sanders better, but I wasn't as brave as you were."

"It only matters what you do now," I said as I hugged her good-bye.

I had to admit that at that moment I began to regard Katie with a new respect. She didn't like the way I lived my life, but she had opened her home to Jean and our children, even though she still let an occasional stupid remark escape. And she had always kept in touch with me. In a way, that made her a better person than I was.

IT TURNED OUT that Katie knew more than I would have expected about what grew in Frost Valley. She was a little surprised and perplexed when I showed up two days later with my multi-racial crew, but I had to hand it to her; she was pleasant and generous to all of them. Even Edwin got in on the trek through his wooded property and seemed to have a fairly good day. We located and tagged a number of dogwood trees that looked young and healthy enough to survive a transplant. For some reason the soil on Edwin's farm was slightly more acidic than on Reiko's, but I thought that if the trees were young enough and had a little help from soil treatments, they would adapt to the change.

As we hiked through the woods, I occasionally noticed Nolan and Lauren walking hand-in-hand and felt a little annoyed. I would be glad when Jean arrived, so I wouldn't feel so lonely. I knew I would miss her; I just hadn't realized how much.

Chapter
Thirty-five

Friday, June 4, 2004

AS I STOOD in the lobby area of the Knoxville airport, I couldn't wait to see Jean. She would love seeing how Reiko's garden was coming along, and I couldn't wait to tell her the plans we were making for the museum. I had made some changes to Reiko's original sketches for the garden, and I hoped Jean would like it. When I saw the arrival board flashing, announcing that the flight from San Francisco by way of Atlanta had finally arrived about twenty minutes late, I felt my pulse increase and my heart pound nearly out of my chest with happiness. I watched passengers making their way down the long walkway toward the lobby. When I finally saw her, I couldn't suppress a smile. Our eyes met from a hundred yards away, and I knew I was home again. In what seemed like an eternity later, I met her as she came through the one-way door into the lobby, pulling her gently aside to greet her with a warm, sweet kiss that melted me the way they always had.

Taking her suitcase, and ignoring the looks of strangers passing by, I slipped my arm around her waist and walked with her to the baggage claim area.

"How was your flight?" I asked.

"Pretty calm," she smiled up at me. "I almost finished the book I brought with me."

"We'll buy you some more," I said, knowing that she couldn't live without something to read.

"How many bags?" I asked as the first of a planeload of luggage began making its way down the cargo conveyer ten minutes later.

"Just two. I decided to travel light this time."

"Well, there's a first," I laughed.

It was a little after four that afternoon when we finally pulled away from the airport. Jean sat in the middle as usual, her hand resting warmly on my thigh. She looked relaxed as she slid her sunglasses on and watched the city flow by.

"How's the project coming?" she asked. "I can't wait to see it."

"It's been amazing, sweetie. Reiko would be so proud. It's as if we're all possessed by something."

"Maybe Reiko is watching over you," she smiled

"Nolan and our future daughter-in-law spend all their time shaping that big piece of stone into something, but they're pretty secretive about it."

"Has he asked her to marry him yet?"

"Any day now. Probably waiting for you to get here before he has to face Tad."

"Tad wouldn't object, would he?"

"Are you kidding? He and Carolyn have spent hours telling Nolan everything there is to know about Lauren, including showing him her baby pictures."

"She must be mortified," Jean laughed.

A few miles outside of Knoxville, I changed lanes and exited the highway. Ahead on the access road we entered a small town that looked as if it hadn't changed in twenty-five years.

"Hungry?" I asked as I looked at her.

"Only for you," she grinned, squeezing my thigh.

"I was hoping you'd say that. I told Nolan we wouldn't be back until tomorrow."

I pulled the truck into a parking space and almost ran to the check-in counter of the Fairfield Inn. I got a room with a king-sized bed on the ground floor that came equipped with a small sunken patio not far from the pool. I grabbed the small duffle Jean used for short trips and locked her other suitcases in the truck. I pushed the key card into the door lock and waited for the flashing light to turn green. I swung the door open and held it for her as I set her bag on a chair. Taking my hand she backed toward the bed.

"Anxious?" I grinned as I closed the space between us and stood in front of her.

"I haven't felt your touch in a month," she smiled as she drew my lips closer to hers. "I've missed you so much."

I knew her body better than I knew my own, but she felt so damn good as we kissed deeply and let our fingers do the walking to refresh our memories. I found the place on the side of her neck that I knew would drive her crazy, and we were half undressed by the time we fell onto the bed laughing and getting reacquainted.

I COULDN'T REMEMBER when I had felt so happy as I let the truck drift down the ridge toward the Sanders farm. Off and on the night before, I had told Jean about the proposed museum, and I knew that mentally she was already working on it. We made it back in time for one of Carolyn's simple but more than filling lunches. As we came in the back door, everyone smiled and greeted Jean warmly through mouthfuls of food. Nolan got up and picked his mother off the floor in one of his patented bone-crushing hugs. Putting her down, he looked at me and grinned, "Good night's rest?"

Even though I was pretty sure I was blushing, I nodded. "Momma Jean was really tired after the trip, but we're both much more relaxed today. Anything new here?"

"A nursery from Oak Ridge will be here in a little while, so we can transfer the dogwoods from Aunt Katie's; the sites for them are already prepped," Nolan said as Jean made her way around the table hugging and talking to everyone.

Fishing the truck keys out of my jeans pocket, I handed them to him. "Get your mother's suitcases from the truck, please, and take them up to our room for me."

When he groaned remembering the amount of luggage she usually managed to haul along on our trips, I smiled. "It's only one duffel bag and two suitcases this trip."

"Hey, Oscar! Give me a hand with MJ's stuff, will you."

Oscar stood up as he finished a huge glass of iced tea and wiped his mouth before following Nolan outside. In less than an hour, we had all finished eating lunch. Maya and Heike insisted on cleaning up over Carolyn's protests.

"Show me this museum, Callie," Jean said as she slipped her arm around me.

I tried to explain some of the ideas everyone had come up with as we walked across the back yard, still sipping Carolyn's sweet tea, which I was finding highly addictive. Jean had some ideas of her own as she surveyed the barn that was temporarily serving as living quarters for my crew. Maya and Heike had set up a homemade drafting table in their spare time and done some preliminary drawings. Standing at the table and looking through the blueprints they had begun, Jean liked some of it and didn't like other parts.

I stood next to her and rested my hand on her shoulder. "Think we can get this museum open about the same time the garden and nature areas are ready?"

"We're going to need a carpenter for some of the displays, Callie. Some of the interior walls will have to be redone."

Clearing my throat, I said, "I think the museum and its displays should reflect the totality of the Japanese experience since Pearl Harbor."

"That's probably more than Reiko intended, honey. I think she was only interested in bringing the natural assets of this area to people's attention but not in making a statement about discrimination. That wasn't her way."

"She left this project for me to complete as I saw fit, Jean," I said stubbornly.

Looking over her shoulder at me, she said, "Why are you doing this, Callie?"

"Reiko's dream should be more than just this garden and preserve. It should be a statement about the human spirit and triumph over tragedy. Maybe what Reiko wanted me to do here can help make us all more understanding and accepting of one another."

"This is really getting to you, isn't it?"

"Yeah, it is."

Hugging Jean tightly, I rested my chin on the top of her head. "The laboratories near here destroyed the life Reiko knew, and yet she survived and found forgiveness."

"I know you'll do the right thing, sweetheart, for Reiko. Now you better haul your cute ass out there, and make sure they get everything exactly where you want it," Jean smiled.

Chapter
Thirty-six

FOR THE FIRST time, I actually enjoyed the evening that Jean and I spent with Katie and Edwin. After dinner, we traded stories about growing up in Frost Valley during a spirited game of pinochle. I had never spent the night in their home, but we were all tired by the time we decided to call it a night. Edwin had spent most of the day working with us on the nature project that we had all begun calling simply "Reiko's Garden." The work had been moving along at a steady pace and it had taken patience to make sure the plants that had been transplanted had been able to establish themselves and adjust to the slight chemical difference of the soil within the garden. The sculpture that Nolan and Lauren had been working on was beginning to finally take shape and look less like a shapeless chunk of rock. How they could envision something inside the rock amazed me. I knew it was something I could never do, but Nolan had a gift for working with the stone that Lauren was quickly picking up as well.

Jean and I discussed the plans for the museum often, and she had eventually convinced me, with a subtlety that was all her own, that I was straying too far away from what Reiko would have wanted. While there was nothing she would have loved more than creating an exhibit honoring Japanese-Americans and their experiences, she opted for large photographic displays showing the development of the region. She convinced students from small universities near Frost Valley to donate their time photographing plants indigenous to the area for a botanical display. She was the expert at setting up museum quality displays, and I left the planning for the museum to her while I returned to what I loved and knew best, getting my hands dirty.

The weather had been hot and dry nearly all of July, but the weatherman had promised a chance of rain soon. I could tell that even in the shade of the trees, the breezes had been much hotter than usual. Although it was against my nature to help things along, we had recently transplanted some saplings, and I didn't want them to die before their roots had a chance to take hold. I had ordered my crew to water them in the evenings to make sure they had enough moisture and felt sure that once the roots were established they would sink themselves deep enough to form solid taproots where they would find enough water to survive.

As Jean and I got ready for bed, I was feeling at ease for the first time since I had returned in May. As usual, Jean had to spend at least thirty minutes reading before she could go to sleep. It was another hot night, and after I pulled on my shorts and sleep bra, grateful that Katie and Edwin had installed air conditioning a few years earlier, I crawled under the sheet and rolled onto my side, resting my arm across Jean's abdomen. With her reading glasses perched halfway down her nose, she absently stroked my hair as she read.

"You're beautiful," I said contentedly, enjoying being close to her.

"I bet you say that to all the girls," she smiled as she turned a page.

"Only until I met you," I said as I looked up at her. "I didn't know what real beauty was until then."

Pulling her glasses off, Jean looked at me and smiled as she snapped her book closed and set it and her glasses on the nightstand next to the bed. She turned off the light and slipped down on her pillow to face me.

"You're happy, aren't you, Callie?"

"Delirious," I answered, leaning toward her and kissing her lightly.

"I meant about the project," she chuckled.

"It's going to be beautiful. I think Reiko would approve of what we're doing."

Jean snuggled her body against mine and held me in her arms. "Have I told you today how much I love you?"

"Every time you looked at me, but I can never hear it often enough."

We drifted off to sleep holding one another as we had so many times. I felt incredibly lucky.

I was awakened by a hand shaking my shoulder but tried to ignore it until the overhead light in our room came on. I frowned as I opened my eyes and squinted over my shoulder and saw Katie standing next to the bed, looking down at me. "What?" I asked, trying to make my brain wake up.

"Callie, get up. Tad called. There's a problem at his place," Katie said.

Pushing myself up, I ran my hand over my face. "It's the middle of the night. What kind of problem?"

"What is it, Callie?" Jean asked sleepily.

"My God! What happened to your back?" Katie asked, her eyes wide as she saw the scars she had never seen before.

"What's wrong at Tad's?" I asked again, ignoring her last question.

"They're in the middle of a static electrical storm at that end of the valley."

"Shit," I mumbled as I threw the covers off and found my socks and jeans and began pulling them on. "Any damage?"

"He said there was a fire. They've called the county fire department."

"Shit, shit, shit," I said, picking up a t-shirt and pulling it over my head as I slipped a foot into my work boot.

"What's wrong?" Jean asked as she got out of bed.

"Electrical storm," I answered over my shoulder. "I have to get over there."

"I'll go with you."

"I'm already dressed. Katie can bring you when you're ready. Is that okay, Kate?" I asked as I pulled on the second boot.

"Edwin is getting dressed, too," Katie nodded. "We'll be right behind you."

Grabbing my truck keys from the dresser, I ran down the hall and flew down the stairs, wishing I had a cup of coffee. A minute later, I was pulling out of Katie's drive and heading down the valley road. I could see flames across the fields at the Sanders farm from a quarter mile away. It was worse than I thought. I had seen electrical storms once or twice when I was a kid, and they had always been scary. The air was too dry and static electricity had built up in the dryness before launching itself into a dry electrical storm. It was like a rainstorm but without the rain. Once when I was little, I had seen a narrow bolt of lightning come straight through our front door and dance across our living room floor. It was still lightning, and it could still kill. The conditions in the upper valley had been so dry that it would have been easy for a fire to start.

I skidded the truck to a stop, and my heart sank. Despite its lightning rods, Reiko's old barn had been struck and flames were licking out the top floor windows. I looked around quickly and saw most of my crew running around with hoses and buckets, trying to douse the flames.

I grabbed David Yamaguchi as he ran by me. "Is everyone out?"

"Except Oscar," he said as he breathed heavily. "Nolan went inside..."

Before he could finish, I took off as fast as I could toward the burning building. As I looked up, black smoke was pouring from the loft windows. As I reached the door, a hand grabbed me. Tad's face was covered with black sooty smudges, and he was coughing as he tried to speak.

"Can't go in, Callie," he finally managed. "Too much smoke."

"My son is in there," I said as I jerked my arm away. Near the side door, Geraldo and Hakiro were using a garden hose to do what they could, but the water pressure wasn't enough to reach much effectively. Taking the hose from them, I doused my head and clothes with water and pulled a rag from Geraldo's back pocket. Wetting it thoroughly, I pulled open the door and ducked inside. We had oxygen masks somewhere among the equipment in our trucks, and I wished I had one of them, but I couldn't waste the time searching for it. The barn was old, and even with the renovations, I couldn't be sure how stable the wood still was after all the years since it had been built or doubted it had ever been treated with any type of fire retardant coating.

The wet rag helped, but the thick smoke inside the building burned my eyes. The air around me was hot, and I knew it wouldn't be long before the heat dried out my clothes. Squatting down, I took as deep a breath as I could before I pulled the rag away from my face.

"Nolan! Oscar!"

Staying half bent over, I put my arm out and moved forward a step at a time. The sound above me was roaring, and my eyes burned as I tried to see through the smoke. I heard a loud cracking sound near me and froze, not sure which way to go and afraid that the area above me might collapse. The heat building in the first story of the barn blew out a side window in an explosion of glass, sucking smoke out, clearing the air for a few seconds, allowing me to find the stairs leading to the loft bedrooms. There wasn't enough moisture left in the rag to do any good, and even though I stayed as low as I could as I started up the stairs, I knew I was inhaling some smoke.

"Nolan!" I screamed.

I heard a shuffling sound as I reached the top of the stairs. "MC!" a welcome voice called back. "Over here!"

Fighting my way toward the direction of Nolan's voice, I almost ran into him before I actually saw the hazy, diffused outline of his body. He had Oscar's arm around his shoulder and was dragging him toward the stairs. Taking Oscar's other arm and pulling it over my shoulders, I said loudly over the roar of the fire, "We have to hurry before the floor collapses!"

I knew that Nolan couldn't be far from becoming overcome by smoke inhalation. I was struggling to take in enough good air myself but tried to remain calm as we dragged Oscar to the stairs with Nolan leading the way down. I felt the heat from the floor through my work boots and mentally gave us less than a minute to get the hell off the staircase before it was so weakened that it collapsed. I still hadn't heard any sirens to signal the arrival of fire trucks and wondered what the hell was keeping them. Nolan and I both started coughing and gagging halfway down the steps, and it made our progress even slower. We were almost to the bottom when I felt a strange vibration through my boots.

"Go now!" I yelled urgently to Nolan as I released Oscar's arm. "Go! Go!"

I felt Nolan pull Oscar away at the same time that I heard the joints holding the staircase slip. I made one more step before the stairs collapsed, dropping me the remaining five or six feet. Covering my head to protect it from falling debris, pain shot up my right leg as I crumpled to the floor. The bottom wooden flooring was hot against my scars as I lay there a moment, biting back the pain. It was that damned duck's fault, I thought briefly. Same damn leg. I knew I couldn't stay there, and the memory of me dragging myself out of the woods after my beating flashed by me. One arm at a time was all I could think, but it hurt almost too much, and I wasn't eighteen any more. I buried my face in the crook of my arm and tried to gasp even a few molecules of good air before picking my head up and blinking against the smoke, praying that Nolan had found the door and gotten Oscar out safely. The walls of the lower floor had superheated to the point that they had combusted into flames. I blinked against the gathering smoke, taking shallower breaths, and then I saw her. Reiko was there, motioning to me to follow her. I pulled myself toward her, but the next time I blinked Jean had taken her place, ordering me to move my ass. *Come on, Callie, you can do it.*

I wanted to laugh, but I couldn't. I was going to die. I was having delusions, seeing people I couldn't possibly be seeing.

"Jean," I gasped. "I can't. I love you, baby." I was suddenly so tired that I couldn't keep my eyes open.

MY EYES FLEW open, and I was racked by the worst coughing fit I had ever had in my life. Rolling partially onto my side, I tried to take a deep breath and succeeded only in vomiting out thick black mucus. The effort to breathe hurt, which was only exceeded by the throbbing pain in my leg. My eyes moved around, and I didn't see anyone I recognized until I felt a familiar warm hand take mine and saw Jean's face lean over me, a worried look on her face. The sight of her brought tears to my eyes, and I broke down in hacking sobs as she whispered in my ear and stroked my filthy face and hair.

"You're going to be okay, baby," she whispered softly. "I love you. Don't you dare leave me."

My lips moved, but I couldn't speak for a moment. "N...No...lan," I said, uncertain I wanted to hear the answer.

"He's okay, honey, but Oscar was burned pretty badly."

"Stand back," a rough voice ordered. "We need to get to the hospital."

"I'm riding in the ambulance with her," Jean said, refusing to release my hand.

"Family only. Now move out of the way."

"No," I rasped. "Jean."

I felt a rough hand trying to separate us and wanted to get up and hit the son of a bitch. I could see the fury in Jean's eyes as her mouth opened to speak. But she was interrupted as I saw Nolan's face, contorted by anger. He grabbed the larger man arguing with Jean by a fistful of shirt and jerked him closer. Nolan seethed with a rage I would never have believed him capable of.

"These are my parents!" he said loudly. "If my mother wants to ride in the fucking ambulance with my other mother, then she will. But you *will not* separate them. Understand?"

"Take it easy, buddy," the man said.

"Don't fucking tell me to take it easy! It took you a goddamn hour to get your sorry asses out here! We could have all died before you showed up and gave a shit!"

"Nolan, sweetheart, let them go," Lauren said as she wrapped an arm around him and began leading him away. I heard the same gentle tone in her voice that Jean had when she tried to calm me down.

The gurney I was lying on bumped a little way before it slid into the back of the ambulance. Although Jean and I were separated for a moment until she climbed into the back of the ambulance, my hand didn't have time to cool before she grasped it again. My grip on her hand remained tight throughout the ride to the hospital in Oak Ridge, her eyes never leaving my face as the technician called in his report and administered an IV line. The longer the ride took, the more difficulty I had breathing. The oxygen mask covering my nose and mouth wasn't doing much to help and fear began to constrict my chest. I closed my eyes for a moment, suddenly exhausted, my heart pounding as I opened my mouth, struggling to breathe.

"How much longer?" I heard Jean ask the EMT as she continued to stroke the side of my face. The sound of her voice made me open my eyes. I did the best I could to smile for her as oxygen tried to push its way through my lungs. My mouth moved, but the mask obliterated my voice. I looked at the EMT and back at Jean. Reaching out, she lifted the mask away from my face.

"I...love...you," I breathed out. Just the energy it took to say those three words exhausted me. Jean leaned over and kissed me softly before replacing the mask.

WHEN MY EYES opened again, it was easier to breathe, but other than that I couldn't move. I felt paralyzed and as the panic rose, my heart beat faster. Somewhere I could hear a beeping sound that seemed to increase as my panic increased. I looked around trying to figure out where I was, making grunting sounds. Within a few minutes, Jean's face came into my line of sight, and I heard the beeping noise slow as she touched me.

"You're going to be okay, Callie. The doctors had to put a tube down your throat to help you breathe the night we came in," Jean said softly, stroking the side of my face.

I guess she could see the questions in my eyes as she smiled down at me.

"You broke your right leg, again, and have a couple of pretty bad burns, not to mention inhaling a barn-full of smoke, but the doctors say you'll be out of here in a few days. Do you understand me, sweetie?"

I nodded the best I could and jerked my arm trying to touch her.

Smiling, she said, "Let me get your nurse."

FIVE DAYS LATER, I was wheeled out of the hospital and into bright sunshine. For the most part, we had all been lucky. My leg would take a little time to heal, but the rest of my injuries had been relatively minor. Oscar would have to remain in the hospital a few more days before he would be stable enough to be flown back to California, so his family could take care of him. His burns had been more serious and would require more care than we could give him. When Nolan had come to visit me in the hospital, I was shocked to see his hands wrapped with heavy bandages. He had burned them getting to Oscar and, as I found out later, returning to find me. Despite the injuries to his hands, he had been in a good mood when he and Lauren visited. Katie and Carolyn somehow managed to bring the other crew members to visit me and Oscar, and everyone seemed to be in a better mood than I would have expected.

I pulled myself out of the wheelchair and balanced on crutches, as Jean and two nurses helped me into our truck. In a role reversal I was unaccustomed to, I managed to buckle myself into the seat next to Jean and rested my hand on her leg as she pulled away from the hospital entrance.

"Sure you can handle this truck," I smiled.

"I can handle you, can't I?"

"Any time you want," I laughed.

"It sounds like you're well on the way to recovery if you can still flirt," she smiled.

"You'll just have to run slower, considering my temporary handicap. How's it going with the project?"

"Well, we've had to rethink the museum since the barn was destroyed. I took everyone to town a couple of days ago, and we replaced most of the clothing they lost. Maya and Heike are staying in the main house. Katie and Edwin are putting up the rest of the guys."

"You're kidding?"

"Nope," she laughed. "They insisted that David, Hakiro, and Geraldo stay at their farm."

It secretly made me happy that at least one or two people were accepting the members of my crew. On the few trips we had made into town, they had never received anything more than curious, wary looks from the townspeople.

"I'm sorry about the museum, Jean."

"We hadn't done that much to it. Thank God, the displays hadn't been brought out from Knoxville yet. It could have been so much worse. I'd never heard of dry electrical storms before that night."

"They're pretty unusual, but I've never seen a good one. How long will Nolan be out of commission?"

"Probably a few weeks until the burns heal."

"How will his hands be afterward?"

"The doctor said there could be some scarring, but he should regain full use of them. He didn't lose any muscle, and there was minimal nerve damage."

"Well, we're just a family of scars, aren't we?" I smiled.

"Scars give you character."

"I don't recommend getting them as a character building experience." I frowned.

"Maya said there was some damage to a few trees in the garden, but nothing serious. She and Heike have already begun replacing anything that was too badly damaged to save. How much longer do you think it will take to complete that part of the project?"

Taking a deep breath and blowing it out, I shook my head. "Well, we're three crew members short now without Nolan, Oscar, and me. I know you have to go back to California in a few weeks, but I don't know if it will be done by then. That would be asking more from my crew than they can probably do."

Jean eased up on the gas pedal as she let the truck drift down the ridge into the valley. As we approached the turn off to the Sanders farm, I saw nearly two dozen cars and trucks parked along the sides of the gravel road, and the area near the main house was a beehive of activity.

"What the hell?" I said.

Jean brought the truck to a stop near the back of the house and got out as I scooted across the seat. When she opened the passenger door, I handed her my crutches and slowly slid out, bearing my weight on my left leg. I was still adjusting the crutches under my arms and had just taken my first step when I saw Tad coming toward us, sweat trickling down his charcoal-smudged face.

"What the hell's going on, Tad?" I asked. "Who are all these people?"

"You won't believe it, Callie," Tad said as he pulled a handkerchief from his back pocket and wiped his face. "I guess Mom had been spending some time over the last few years working with various local youth groups like 4-H. When they read about the fire in the paper this morning, a bunch of kids and their sponsors showed up bright and early volunteering to help clear out this debris. They're planning to

haul it away today and tomorrow and begin building a new barn over
the weekend."

"What about the gardens? They can't be tramping around up
there."

Tad laughed. "Don't worry, Maya and Heike are practically
guarding it with shotguns to make sure the plants don't get damaged."

Looking around, I saw Edwin leading a team of Belgian draft
horses away from the barn as the big animals pulled chains attached to
the blackened beams that still stood after the fire. He waved when he
saw us watching him and turned to speak briefly to a young man
wearing a green John Deere baseball cap, who took the reins from him.
Wiping his face, Edwin walked toward us, smiling.

"How does it feel to finally be out of the hospital, Callie?" he
asked.

Jean and I looked at each other. Damned if Edwin hadn't called
me by my whole name for the first time I could remember.

"Pretty damn good. What are you doing, Edwin?"

"I know you don't want heavy equipment up here, so when Tad
called I decided that Charles's Belgians would be just as good as a
tractor. We'll load up everything on tobacco sleds, and take it out of
here. We'll be careful. Besides, them little gals up in the woods are
watching us like hawks," he laughed.

"Who's paying for all this?" I asked.

"Well, labor's free. I got a bunch of wood that I had milled after I
cleared some land a few years back stored in my barn," Edwin
shrugged. "If that ain't enough, I can get more. Old man Adams's
grandson talked him into coming over, too. He used to be the best
barn builder in the valley before he retired."

"I don't know what to say Edwin," I said as I shook my head and
watched the activity around us. "The people here wouldn't give Reiko
the time of day for decades, and now they want to help?"

In a move I would never have expected, Edwin put his hand on
my shoulder and squeezed it. "You don't have to say nothing, Callie.
We owe it to Miz Sanders for the way she was treated all those years.
These kids just reminded us how unneighborly we'd been." Shifting
his weight uncomfortably, Edwin cleared his throat and looked back at
the men working to tear down the remains of the old barn. "And we
owe it to you, too. Your kin helped found this valley, and the people
here weren't very nice to you, either."

"It was no one's fault that my parents died, Edwin."

"Katie told me about your...your back...the scars," he squinted as
he looked at the ground. "I didn't know they went that far, Callie."

Mention of the scars on my back made my body stiffen. "What are
you talking about?"

"Maybe we should go somewhere, so you can sit down and get off that leg first."

I was getting tired of standing on one leg, and my arms were already aching from the pressure of the crutches under my arms. I could feel old anger rising in my stomach and moving up into my chest. All I had wanted to do was create the garden Reiko wanted, but somehow what should have been fulfilling work was now the catalyst for dredging up painful memories. It took us a few minutes to negotiate the steps into the back door of Reiko's house. As soon as I entered, Carolyn was hugging me, and I almost lost my balance. Edwin reached out and steadied me until I got the crutches back in the correct position to hold me up.

"How about some of that sweet tea you like so much?" Carolyn said cheerfully.

"I'm going to become a diabetic if I keep drinking that stuff," I smiled. "But I would love some."

"Why don't you and Edwin go into the front parlor," Jean said. "I'll bring the tea."

Nodding, I led Edwin slowly toward the front of the house. I decided that the couch was too low for me and went instead to a taller wingback chair near the fireplace and eased myself down. As soon as I was seated, Edwin picked up my leg carefully and pulled an ottoman under it.

"Broke my leg once, and I always liked proppin' it up someplace."

Jean appeared and handed Edwin a glass of tea before carrying a cold glass to me. I took a drink, hoping it would settle my stomach, as Jean sat on the arm of the chair and draped her arm around my shoulders. I couldn't bring myself to say anything and just looked at Edwin. He pushed back his hat and cleared his throat after taking a long drink of Carolyn's tea. Then he leaned forward and rested his elbows on his knees.

"Back then, I mean, I reckon most people knew about you and that Patterson gal. She was a real looker, I can say that, but she was trouble. Her daddy moved her from some place over in the Carolinas because she got in some trouble over there. Don't know exactly what, but I reckon it must have been about the same thing. I only know what I know because Reverend Patterson worked with my daddy over at Oak Ridge, and they were sort of friends, I guess."

"Her father was a minister?" Jean asked.

"Well, I don't think he was trained or nothin'," Edwin answered. "He was just some backwoods circuit rider who traveled around to little churches that didn't have nobody else regular. Plus I reckon he knew a lot about the Good Book. I never heard him, but I heard he was a real hell fire and damnation type. Anyway, one night he came by our place, and I overheard him talkin' to my daddy. I didn't know what they were talkin' about really. They were out on our front porch, and Reverend Patterson kept goin' on about Sodomites and how they were among us, and a bunch of stuff like that."

"He called me that...a Sodomite," I said quietly, my hand feeling the scar on my upper abdomen through my shirt.

"Hell, Callie, I didn't even know what that was. I was only about fifteen and hadn't even kissed a girl yet. I didn't start courtin' Katie until you were already gone."

I almost had to smile thinking back to how innocent we had all been fifty years earlier. "How do you know they were talking about me?"

"I didn't really, not until Katie told me about seein' your back. Then I reckon I just put it all together. You missed about a couple of weeks of school, Reverend Patterson quit his job, and then him and Jennie just up and disappeared. I didn't think much about it at the time. I should have known it was something bad, though. Reverend Patterson sounded kind of crazy when he was talkin' to my daddy that night. Went on about doin' the Lord's work. He said somebody was messin' with his girl and makin' her do all kinds of unnatural stuff." Edwin stopped and cleared his throat again, a red flush moving up his neck. "Then he said he had caught them red-handed and took the vengeance of the Lord out on whoever it was. If I'd have known before it happened I would have warned you, but I didn't know until it was too late."

I took a long drink of my tea and tried to force my feelings down. Jean squeezed my arm as she looked down at me. When I thought I was under control, I finally looked at Edwin. There were things about what happened that day that I hadn't even been able to tell Jean, preferring to give her a cleaned-up version.

"Jennie Patterson was indeed a very beautiful girl," I said calmly. "But she knew what she was doing, which is more than I can say for myself. I'd never had anyone show me that kind of attention before and I'm not ashamed to say that even at eighteen, I was more than a little naive. I guess I knew deep down that what we were doing wouldn't be considered right; otherwise we wouldn't have needed to hide what we were doing. But what I was feeling was all so new to me."

I could feel myself losing control of my emotions slightly but pushed on, holding Jean's hand tightly. "I like to think that no matter how or why Jennie picked me and seduced me that she actually might have cared for me. Anyway, that day, I met her like I had before, but we hadn't done much before her father and two other men showed up. I don't know if they ever did anything to Jennie, but they hadn't while I was still conscious. I didn't know the men with Patterson, but one of them held me while the other one beat me up pretty good. I had been beat up before for being friends with Reiko and helping her out, so I could have taken that and maybe even understood it eventually. But the other..." I said as my voice faltered. I tried to stop the tears, but I couldn't. Jean hugged me to her and held me until I could gather myself again.

Almost reflexively, I brought my hand up to my stomach, still able to feel the old scar beneath my shirt as I forced myself to continue. "But he was so enraged, that it was as if he couldn't stop, he didn't want to stop what was happening. One of the men held me while the other...the other one...carved an S on my stomach with his knife, so I would never forget what I was. Then they held me against a tree, cut the rest of my clothes off. I didn't last long past the first couple of times I was hit after that. Old Doc Ayers figured that I had been whipped with wild blackberry shoots because of the thorns he dug out of my back."

The look of horror on Edwin's face was followed by tears that he didn't try to hide.

"When I came to after dark sometime, it took me the rest of the night, stumbling around in the woods, to make my way here. When Doc Ayers arrived, Reiko loaded me up on moonshine for the pain, but it didn't matter. I passed out anyway. Doc Ayers had to dig the thorns out of my back, my butt, and the backs of my thighs. I can't remember how many thorns there were now, but Patterson must have used a dozen blackberry switches on me. You ever been stuck by one of those thorns picking wild blackberries, Edwin?"

He nodded. "Afraid so."

"How long you think those thorns are? Quarter to half an inch?"

"They're like razors. Even my cattle have gotten cut by them."

"If they'll cut through cowhide, then you can imagine what they could do to the soft skin on your back and ass," I said as I began to lose control, my voice rising steadily.

Jean moved to kneel in front of me, forcing me to look at her in order to calm my shaking body. Wiping my eyes, I let my eyes settle into hers.

"I'm sorry, Callie. For you to survive that and not bleed to death was a miracle. Why didn't you have him arrested?" Edwin asked.

"He was already gone by the time I could return to school, and no one around here would have blamed him for doing it, any more than they would've blamed him if I'd been a black man caught doing the same thing. And I didn't want any of that to spill over onto Katie and the others. I could go away, but they were still stuck here. Their lives were messed up enough as it was without me adding to their problems."

"Honestly, Callie, I don't think Katie knew about any of it until the other night."

"I don't blame Katie for anything, Edwin. I let my own anger project onto other people. You and Katie have always been decent to me and to my family."

"You're family, Callie, you and Jean and the kids. Frost Valley will always be your home. I wish it had been a little kinder to you. Those other people, like Patterson, just passed through."

"Edwin," I said as he rose to leave, "I'd appreciate it if you didn't tell anyone else about our conversation. I've always said that my injuries were from an accident with barbed wire, and I'd like to keep it that way. If you tell Katie that I was beaten up, that's fine, but the rest..."

"I'm not very good at keeping secrets, Callie, but there's no reason for anyone else to know everything."

Pushing myself up, I picked up my crutches and placed them under my arms.

"Thank you, Edwin. I'll be out in a little bit."

When Edwin was gone, Jean took my face in her hands and kissed me tenderly. I wanted to throw my crutches on the floor and hold her, but knew I would knock her down.

"Carolyn and I switched bedrooms early this morning, so you wouldn't have to go up and down the stairs," she said as I maneuvered around. "Why don't you go lie down for a while and rest? Lunch will be ready in about an hour, and I can get you up then."

"Yeah, that sounds like a good idea."

A few minutes later, Jean swung my legs onto the bed as I lie back on a pillow and felt my head sink into the feather filling. Jean perched on the edge of the bed for a minute, and I scooted over a little to make room for her.

"I'm tired, Jean," I said softly as I rested my arm across her lap.

"I'm very proud of you, Callie," she said, running her fingertips down my cheek.

Taking her hand in mine, I brought her fingers to my lips and kissed them. "Because I'm tired and admit it?"

"Because your whole life you've taken care of people. Reiko, your brothers and sisters, your father, me, our children, and you've never asked for anything in return. Now it's my turn to take care of you for a while."

"You've always taken care of me in every way that mattered, honey."

"And you've done what you admired Reiko for. You've survived and forgiven."

"I've tried to forget it, Jean, but sometimes it just sneaks up on me."

"I imagine Reiko never forgot either, sweetie."

I slipped away into a peaceful sleep as Jean brushed through my hair with her fingertips.

Chapter
Thirty-seven

Wednesday, June 22, 2005

TEN MONTHS HAD passed since Jean had convinced me to fly back to California with her near the end of August last year. There hadn't been much that I could do while my leg repaired itself other than sit around and supervise. Geraldo was as capable of doing that as I was, and I had begun to feel like more of a burden to the work than a help. Even at home, I was restless and spent hours on the phone talking to Nolan about the project. Before I left Tennessee, the barn had been rebuilt but still stood empty.

Now as Jean and I waited once again for luggage to be unloaded from our plane and sent down the baggage carousel, I couldn't wait to get back to the Sanders farm. The garden and preserve wouldn't be open to the public for a few more days, but Tad and Carolyn had planned a private showing for everyone who had worked so diligently on the project or contributed to it in some way. I spotted the first of our suitcases as it slid down the conveyer belt and onto the circular luggage carrier. A hand stopped me as I started toward it.

"I'll get it, Callie," Ron said.

Since returning to California, I had done what I promised Rachel I would do and had spent more time getting better acquainted with my son-in-law. The window he had designed and installed in our home had been beautiful, incorporating elements illustrating both my background and Jean's Japanese heritage. When the sun struck it in the late afternoon, I found it to be soothing to look at.

"Gramma Callie," a small voice said as I felt a hand pull lightly at my hand.

"What is it, sweetie?" I asked, bending down to look into my granddaughter Elizabeth's face.

"Can we go to the cemetery and visit Great-grandma while we're here?"

"Of course, we will. Tomorrow or the next day," I smiled. "I promise."

Rachel had surprised both Jean and me when she named her girls after my mother and Jean's mother. At seven, Elizabeth was a curious little girl who loved being outdoors and loved animals. Patricia, at

five, was much more shy. We loved them both the same, but they had
each apparently decided which grandmother they wanted to be with
most. Rachel had always been an outspoken independent child, and it
looked as if Lizzie was going to follow in her footsteps.

"You don't have to hold her all the time, MJ," Rachel said as she
watched Patricia snuggle against Jean's shoulder.

"I don't mind," Jean smiled.

"Momma Jean likes to snuggle," I said, grinning at her.

Twenty minutes later, Ron loaded our bags into the trunk of a
rental car, and we began another trip to Frost Valley. Since Ron and
the girls had never been to the valley, I drove slowly enough to point
out a few things along the way. By mid-afternoon, I reached the turn-
off leading to Reiko's house. Stopping just inside the gate, I looked
down at Lizzie, who had insisted on sitting in the front seat between
Jean and me.

"Do you want to drive us the rest of the way, Lizzie?"

I didn't have to ask her twice. She had unbuckled her seat belt and
was climbing into my lap in an instant, settling her hands on the steer-
ing wheel waiting for me to step on the accelerator. We had done this
many times at home when we had driven in the country. When I
braked near the house, she reached down and shifted the car into park
and turned off the ignition. Patricia had fallen asleep in the back seat,
and I would let her steer another day.

I opened the driver's side door and whispered into Lizzie's ear.
She nodded and slid off my lap, running around the car to open the
door for Jean. Even as I stepped away from the car, I spotted Nolan
and the others walking toward us. Handshakes, hugs, and collective
talking took up the next half hour before I helped Ron pull our luggage from the truck. It was going to be a long, event-filled week. I
hadn't realized a year before how much things would change; just as I
hadn't realized fifty years before how much meeting Reiko would
change my life.

When I returned to California, I would have to hire practically a
whole new crew. Maya and Heike had unexpectedly fallen in love
with Frost Valley. Tad and Carolyn had decided to remain in their
home in Oak Ridge and turned the farm over to an historical and environmental preservation group from Knoxville, which had then turned
around and offered the two women positions as directors and caretak-
ers for Reiko's Garden. They had been thrilled to accept the work and
were making plans to return to college to pick up more coursework. I
had no doubt that Reiko's dream would be in good hands. Even
though the barn had been rebuilt, the decision was made to convert
the house, already an historical landmark, into a visitor's center and
museum. The upstairs would be renovated into living quarters for
Maya and Heike. Geraldo had returned to California and would
remain my supervisor, and, after months of rehabilitation, Oscar had

returned to work as well. Hakiro and David had opened their own landscaping business with my blessing and were doing well.

As much as it broke my heart that I wouldn't see him as often, Nolan had also decided to stay in Tennessee. He and Lauren would be getting married in a couple of days in the place where they had met, with Reiko's Garden as their backdrop. Jean and I had discussed what we could give them as a wedding present, and I thought we had picked the perfect, albeit costly, gift. When Katie had called to tell me that our old home, built by my grandfather, had been vacated and was up for sale, I bought it and turned the repairs over to a contractor. Edwin and Katie had made sure that the work was done correctly, and I would give the keys to Nolan and Lauren the day they got married. An Owen should own the house, and it would serve as an excellent studio for their work.

I was anxious to see the finished gardens and wandered off, leaving the others to chat and make decisions about sleeping arrangements. Other than an occasional visit, I doubted very much that I would be returning to my childhood home. As appealing as I still found Frost Valley, I knew my home was in California, and my life was with Jean. Our children were grown and living their own lives, as it should be. As I walked along the completed paths of the garden and nature areas, I felt genuinely at peace for the first time. I was happy with my life, but there had always been something unidentifiable that it lacked. As I gazed at the beautiful statue of Reiko, complete with her walking staff, basket, and straw hat, that Nolan and Lauren had created as well as other smaller pieces of sculpture that blended seamlessly into the wooded areas around them, I realized that the real gift Reiko had given me had been the peace I now enjoyed.

She taught me how to use my own inner strength to face hardships and survive. Like water constantly flowing over stones in a stream, what Reiko taught me had finally smoothed my rough edges allowing me to find and accept love with Jean, joy in raising our children, and beauty in my work. As I stared at the statue, I saw the strength and determination in her eyes. She had carefully planted the seeds of how to have a life worth living, and I had been her garden, struggling through my own bitterness and anger until I blossomed into the person she knew I could be. No one could have asked or hoped for more than that. I was attempting to swallow back the lump that was forming in my throat when I felt a warm hand slip around my waist as Jean leaned against me.

"It's beautiful, isn't it," I said quietly.

"The whole place is. Reiko would be happy," Jean said.

"I hope so," I said, looking down at her.

"Katie called. She and Edwin are coming over in about an hour."

"Is the old house finished?"

"Yes. She said it had turned out better than she thought it would."

"There'll be something waiting for you when we get back home," I said. "Just a little something from me that I thought you should finally have."

Moving in front of me and placing her hands lightly on my hips, she pulled me toward her and looked up at me. "What did you do?"

"It's supposed to be a surprise, woman. You can't make me tell you," I teased. I knew I would tell her what the surprise was eventually, but we always played this affectionate game. During the renovations on the old Owen farmhouse, I had arranged for the contractor to remove one of the four original hand-carved mantles, and ship it to a contractor in California. Once there, the old mantle would be refinished and installed in our home, hopefully before we returned from this trip. The contractor in Tennessee had a reproduction of the mantle carved and installed in its place. I didn't think Nolan and Lauren would object to the loss.

"Oh, really? Is that a challenge?"

"I've been tortured by the best, you know," I grinned.

"You know you can't keep any secrets from me, Callie Owen."

"Well, it'll cost you this time."

"How many kisses will it cost me?" she said, running her hand up and down my arm.

"I'll have to think about that one, but you could make a down payment now, if you wanted to."

Leaning down, the smile on my lips was immediately covered by her mouth as we met in the sweetest, most tender kiss I could have imagined. As we broke the kiss, I held her in my arms and didn't want to let go. "You're going to be in some kind of trouble if we ever find a moment alone this week," I whispered.

"I hope that's a promise," she laughed as she squeezed me tightly. "But we'd better get back before they send a search party out for us."

An hour later, we had unpacked and changed into more comfortable clothing. I was standing in the kitchen in my jeans, t-shirt, and work boots, leaning against the counter, enjoying a glass of Carolyn's sweet tea, when I heard a car coming down the gravel drive toward the house. Jean, who was chopping carrots for the stew Carolyn was preparing, stood on her tiptoes and looked out the window.

"Must be Katie and Edwin."

"Looks like she's not alone," Carolyn said as she dried her hands and looked out the window next to Jean.

"Great," I said. "Just what we need. More people."

Grabbing my hand, Jean said, "Come on, grumpy. Let's go greet your sister. She promised to bring dessert for dinner."

Setting my glass on the counter, I reluctantly let Jean lead me out the back door. Letting go of my hand, Jean hugged Katie briefly and spoke to her a minute before taking a tray from her. As I stood with my hands in my pockets, people began getting out of the two cars that had followed Edwin's down the drive. I saw Jean motion me to Katie's car. As I approached, the back door of the vehicle opened, and I was surprised as my sister Annie got out and closed the door. When she saw me, she smiled and met me half way. Even though we both hesitated, we eventually reached out to one other like the strangers we were, as Annie drew me into a hug.

"It's good to see you again after all these years, Annie," I said as I hugged her back.

"I'm not alone, Callie. Look who else is here," she grinned as she released me and pointed at the other two vehicles. I shielded my eyes from the late afternoon sunlight that was streaming over the tops of the pines along the ridge. A man helped a woman out of the back car, and I watched as they joined a second couple waiting for them beside the vehicle behind Katie and Edwin's car. When I saw the two men smile, I knew instantly who they were, and tears began filling my eyes as I recognized Cleve and Mack coming toward me. They were much older than the last time we had seen each other, but in my mind they were still young. In two quick steps, I was swept into Cleve's still strong arms and clung to him fiercely. He had been my rock and my protector when we were just barely more than children. He kissed my cheek as I released him and pulled Mack closer. There was so much I wanted to say. How much I'd missed them being in my life. Within a few seconds, the five of us were all talking at once and touching one another to make sure we were real, crying and laughing. We hadn't been together in one place as a family in over fifty years. Somehow it seemed that even Willie was there in spirit. Reiko had once told me that it's only important that you begin a journey, not that you complete it. It would take the five of us longer than a few hours or a few days together to catch up with each other's lives, but it was a beginning.

When we had all regained control of ourselves and began making our way into the house, I saw Jean standing off to the side, watching us with a smile.

"You knew about this?" I asked as I went over to her.

"Katie told me what she was planning, and unlike you, I can keep a secret," she grinned.

Resting my forehead against hers, I said, "Now you're really going to pay."

"I should hope so," she laughed as she put her arm around my waist and walked with me into Reiko's house.

More Brenda Adcock titles:

Pipeline

What do you do when the mistakes you made in the past come back to slap you in the face with a vengeance? Joanna Carlisle, a fifty-seven year old photojournalist, has only begun to adjust to retirement on her small ranch outside Kerrville, Texas, when she finds herself unwillingly sucked into an investigation of illegal aliens being smuggled into the United States to fill the ranks of cheap labor needed to increase corporate profits.

Joanna is a woman who has always lived life her way and on her own terms, enjoying a career that had given her everything she thought she ever wanted or needed. An unexpected visit of her former lover, Cate Hammond, and the attempted murder of their son, forces Jo to finally face what she had given up. Although she hasn't seen Cate or their son for fifteen years, she finds that the feelings she had for her Cate had only been dormant, but had never died. No matter how much she fights her attraction to Cate, Jo cannot help but wonder whether she had made the right decision when she chose career and independence over love.

Jo comes to understand the true meaning of friendship and love only when her investigation endangers not only her life, but also the lives of the people around her.

ISBN 1-932300-64-3

978-1-932300-64-2

Available at booksellers everywhere.

Redress of Grievances

In the first of a series of psychological thrillers, Harriett Markham is a defense attorney in Austin, Texas, who lost everything eleven years earlier. She had been an associate with a Dallas firm and involved in an affair with a senior partner, Alexis Dunne. Harriett represented a rape/murder client named Jared Wilkes and got the charges dismissed on a technicality. When Wilkes committed a rape and murder after his release, Harriett was devastated. She resigned and moved to Austin, leaving everything behind, including her lover.

Despite lingering feelings for Alexis, Harriet becomes involved with a sex-offense investigator, Jessie Rains, a woman struggling with secrets of her own. Harriet thinks she might finally be happy, but then Alexis re-enters her life. She refers a case of multiple homicide allegedly committed by Sharon Taggart, a woman with no motive for the crimes. Harriett is creeped out by the brutal murders, but reluctantly agrees to handle the defense.

As Harriett's team prepares for trial, disturbing information comes to light. Sharon denies any involvement in the crimes, but the evidence against her seems overwhelming. Harriett is plunged into a case rife with twisty psychological motives, questionable sanity, and a client with a complex and disturbing life. Is she guilty or not? And will Harriet's legal defense bring about justice – or another Wilkes case?

Available July 2007

FORTHCOMING TITLES

published by
Regal Crest

Come This Way
by Victor Banis

This collection is unique in that it spans nearly a half century of the author's prodigious literary outpouring-nearly 150 published books and numerous shorter works.

Come This Way, a collection of nearly two dozen stories, edited by Lori Lake and with an introduction by eminent gay scholar, Drewey Wayne Gunn, is in a sense a retrospective of a unique career that has seen more than 140 novels and numerous shorter pieces in print.

What is even more astonishing, however, than the author's prodigious output, is the breadth, the sheer variety, of his writing. These stories look at life from myriad points of view.

The Story of God as History's First Trannie is a satirical look at pre-Christian goddess worship: "...only a little while earlier...men got together in the shade of the hawthorn fig tree...sacred to the Goddess, and ate the fruit of the tree...now, a bunch of Hebrew scribes were telling a story about this wicked, wicked woman who conned an innocent man (oh, right!) into eating this fruit off a tree and causing the good times to stop rolling..."

Jesus Days moves one hundred years into the future, to a U.S.A. ruled by fundamentalist fanatics.

Jackie Returns offers a glimpse into the life of the super-rich. The characters in Neighbors live in a trailer park.

Queer Titles pokes fun at the fine art of jacket copy. Tell them Katy-Did is chilling, An Apple a Day whimsical. Spiro Does a Day's Work captures the innocent eroticism of puppy love, while in If Love Were All, two damaged souls struggle to make a connection.

Indeed, love-getting, losing, the defining of it-is a common thread through most of these stories, and the author's love for the people of whom he writes shines through in all of them.

And in The Emerald Mountain, which begins, "We are all hearts in exile, stumbling alone in the dark...the author has perhaps created a new literary genre all his own: the erotic metaphysical mystery story.

There are surely few writers more prolific, and it is difficult to imagine any more versatile, or who could spin a yarn any better.

Available May 2007

Close Enough
by Jane Vollbrecht

A historical romance in three parts, *Close Enough* demonstrates the ineffaceable bonds of the heart. Part I, set in 1941, tells the story of Hilda Stenkiewicz, an eighteen-year-old girl who gives her illegitimate baby away to virtual strangers. To try to put her life back together, Hilda moves away from her hometown and finds herself falling in love with the landlady at her boarding house. Part II recounts the life of the child Hilda surrendered. Frannie Brewster, like the birth mother she never knew, finds herself drawn to love women. Unlike her mother, however, heartbreak seems to be her constant fate. Part III picks up Hilda Stenkiewicz's story more than forty years after she gave her baby away. Hilda has never abandoned her dream of one day finding her child. With almost no clues to guide them, Hilda's niece and nephew go in search of their cousin. They draw ever closer to finding Hilda's offspring, but can they get close enough?

Available July 2007

OTHER REGAL CREST PUBLICATIONS

Brenda Adcock	Reiko's Garden	978-1-932300-77-2
Lori L. Lake	Different Dress	978-1-932300-08-6
Lori L. Lake	Snow Moon Rising	978-1-932300-50-5
Lori L. Lake	Stepping Out: Short Stories	978-1-932300-16-1
Lori L. Lake	The Milk of Human Kindness	978-1-932300-28-4
Greg Lilly	Fingering the Family Jewels	978-1-932300-22-2
Greg Lilly	Devil's Bridge	978-1-932300-78-9
Cate Swannell	Heart's Passage	978-1-932300-09-3
Jane Vollbrecht	Heart Trouble	978-1-932300-58-1
Jane Vollbrecht	In Broad Daylight	978-1-932300-76-5

About the Author:

A product of the Appalachian region of Eastern Tennessee, Brenda now lives in Central Texas, near Austin. She began writing in junior high school where she wrote an admittedly hokey western serial to entertain her friends. Completing her graduate studies in Eastern European history in 1971, she worked as a graphic artist, a public relations specialist for the military and a display advertising specialist until she finally had to admit that her mother might have been right and earned her teaching certification. For the last twenty-plus years she has taught world history and political science. Brenda and her partner of ten years, Cheryl, are the parents of three grown children and one still in high school, as well as two grandchildren. Rounding out their home are four temperamental cats. When she is not writing Brenda creates stained glass and shoots pool at her favorite bar. She may be contacted at adcockb10@yahoo.com and welcomes all comments, good or bad.

www.ingramcontent.com/pod-product-compliance
Lightning Source LLC
Chambersburg PA
CBHW050530260626
47157CB00004B/1548